SONIC THE HEDGEHOG™
ARCHIVES VOLUME 19

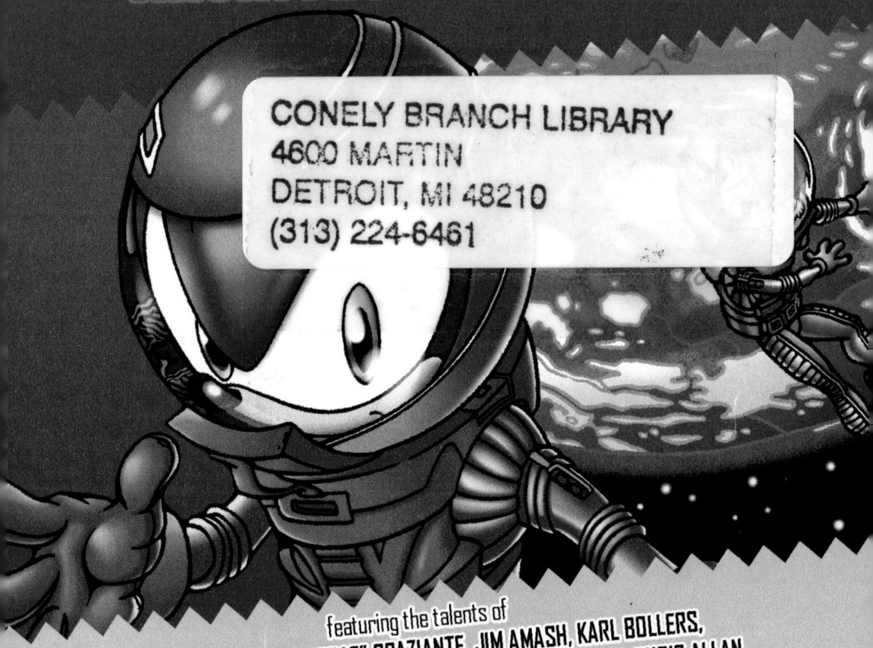

featuring the talents of

IAN FLYNN, PATRICK "SPAZ" SPAZIANTE, JIM AMASH, KARL BOLLERS, ART MAWHINNEY, HARVEY MERCADOOCASIO, JOSH & AIMEE RAY, CHRIS ALLAN, FRANK GAGLIARDO, KEN PENDERS, BARRY GROSSMAN, DICK AYERS, SUZANNE PADDOCK, PAM EKLUND, JEFF POWELL, & STEVEN BUTLER

cover by
PATRICK "SPAZ" SPAZIANTE

SPECIAL THANKS TO ANTHONY GACCIONE & CINDY CHAU @ SEGA LICENSING

ARCHIE COMIC PUBLICATIONS, INC.
JONATHAN GOLDWATER, publisher/co-ceo
NANCY SILBERKLEIT, co-ceo
MIKE PELLERITO, president
VICTOR GORELICK, co-president/e-i-c
JIM SOKOLOWSKI, senior vice president sales/business development
HAROLD BUCHHOLZ, senior vice president publishing/operations
PAUL KAMINSKI, executive director of editorial/compilation editor
ADAM TRACEY, director of publicity and marketing
VINCENT LOVALLO, assistant editor
STEPHEN OSWALD, production manager
ROSARIO PEÑA & DIGIKORE STUDIOS interior cover colors
IAN FLYNN, compilation consultant
JAMIE LEE ROTANTE, proofreader/editorial assistant
ELIZABETH BORGATTI, design intern

ISBN: 978-1-936975-19-8

TABLE OF CONTENTS

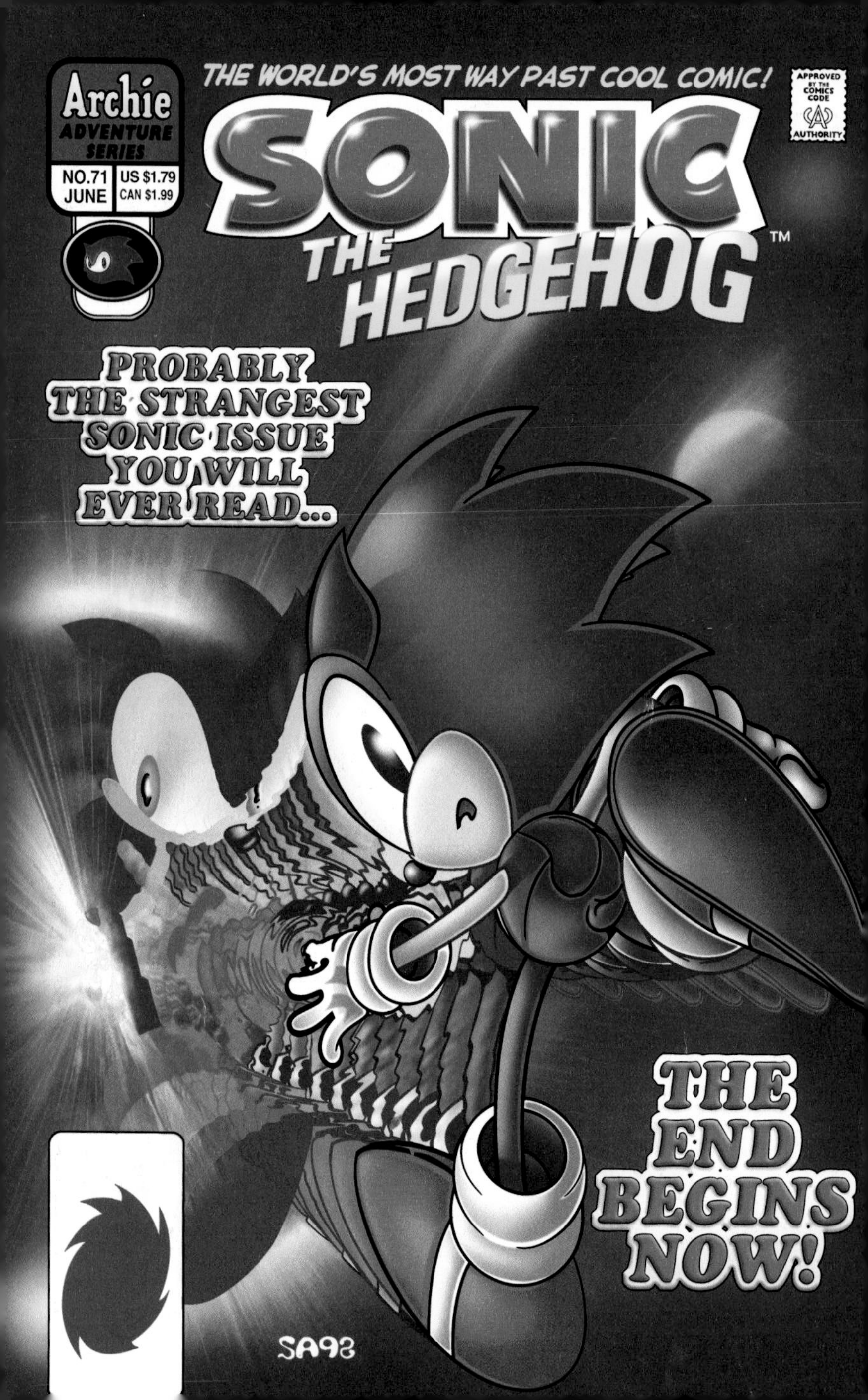
Archie
ADVENTURE SERIES
NO.71
JUNE
US $1.79
CAN $1.99
THE WORLD'S MOST WAY PAST COOL COMIC!
APPROVED BY THE COMICS CODE AUTHORITY
SONIC THE HEDGEHOG™
PROBABLY THE STRANGEST SONIC ISSUE YOU WILL EVER READ...
THE END BEGINS NOW!
SA98

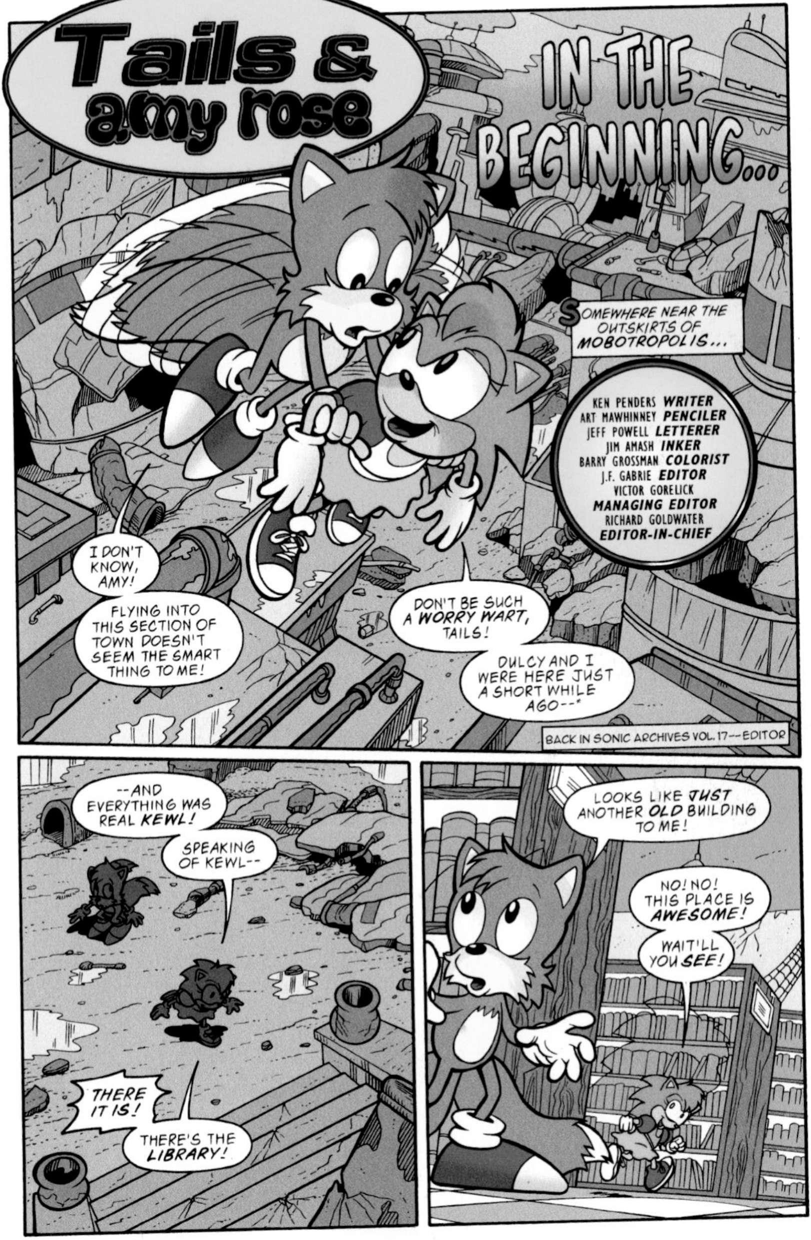
Tails & amy rose
IN THE BEGINNING...
SOMEWHERE NEAR THE OUTSKIRTS OF MOBOTROPOLIS...
KEN PENDERS WRITER
ART MAWHINNEY PENCILER
JEFF POWELL LETTERER
JIM AMASH INKER
BARRY GROSSMAN COLORIST
J.F. GABRIE EDITOR
VICTOR GORELICK MANAGING EDITOR
RICHARD GOLDWATER EDITOR-IN-CHIEF
I DON'T KNOW, AMY!
FLYING INTO THIS SECTION OF TOWN DOESN'T SEEM THE SMART THING TO ME!
DON'T BE SUCH A WORRY WART, TAILS!
DULCY AND I WERE HERE JUST A SHORT WHILE AGO--*
*BACK IN SONIC ARCHIVES VOL. 17--EDITOR
--AND EVERYTHING WAS REAL KEWL!
SPEAKING OF KEWL--
THERE IT IS!
THERE'S THE LIBRARY!
LOOKS LIKE JUST ANOTHER OLD BUILDING TO ME!
NO! NO! THIS PLACE IS AWESOME!
WAIT'LL YOU SEE!

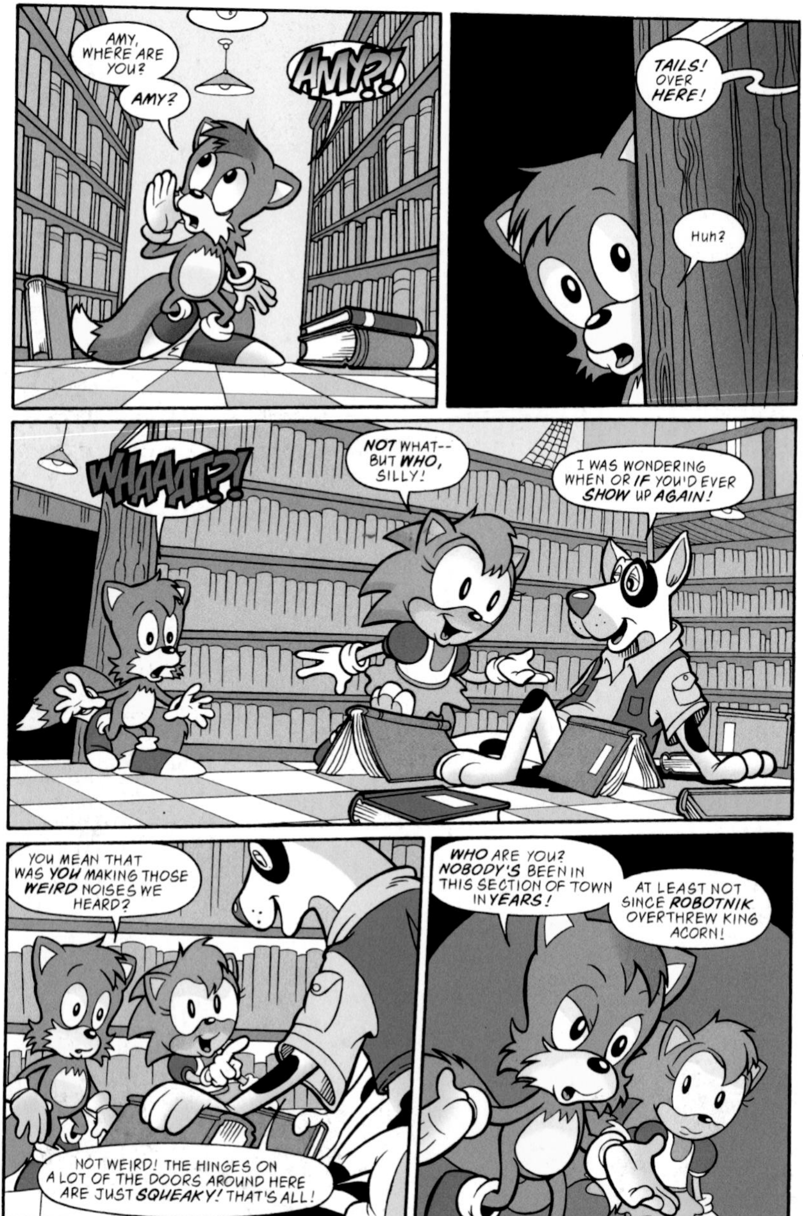
AMY, WHERE ARE YOU?
AMY?
AMY?!
TAILS! OVER HERE!
Huh?
WHAAAT?!
NOT WHAT-- BUT WHO, SILLY!
I WAS WONDERING WHEN OR IF YOU'D EVER SHOW UP AGAIN!
YOU MEAN THAT WAS YOU MAKING THOSE WEIRD NOISES WE HEARD?
NOT WEIRD! THE HINGES ON A LOT OF THE DOORS AROUND HERE ARE JUST SQUEAKY! THAT'S ALL!
WHO ARE YOU? NOBODY'S BEEN IN THIS SECTION OF TOWN IN YEARS!
AT LEAST NOT SINCE ROBOTNIK OVERTHREW KING ACORN!

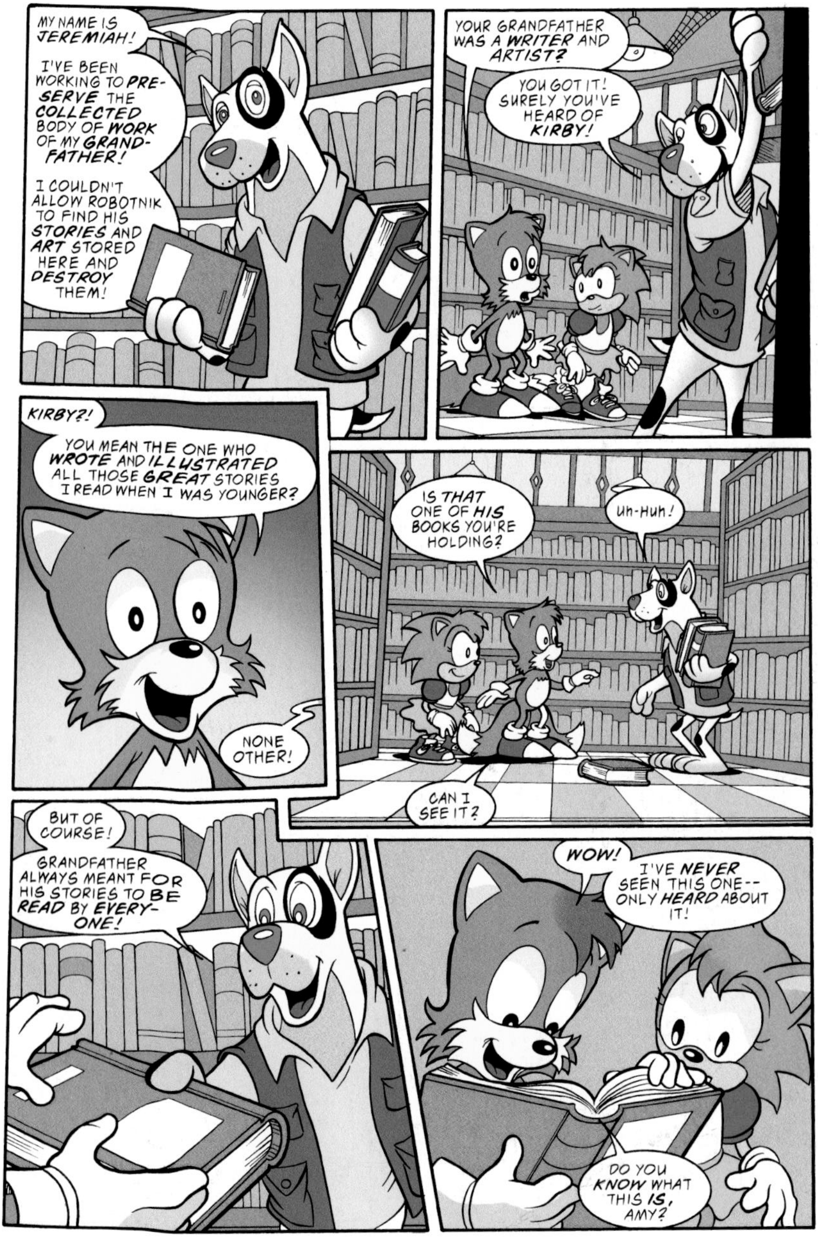
MY NAME IS JEREMIAH!
I'VE BEEN WORKING TO PRE-SERVE THE COLLECTED BODY OF WORK OF MY GRAND-FATHER!
I COULDN'T ALLOW ROBOTNIK TO FIND HIS STORIES AND ART STORED HERE AND DESTROY THEM!
YOUR GRANDFATHER WAS A WRITER AND ARTIST?
YOU GOT IT! SURELY YOU'VE HEARD OF KIRBY!
KIRBY?!
YOU MEAN THE ONE WHO WROTE AND ILLUSTRATED ALL THOSE GREAT STORIES I READ WHEN I WAS YOUNGER?
NONE OTHER!
IS THAT ONE OF HIS BOOKS YOU'RE HOLDING?
Uh-Huh!
CAN I SEE IT?
BUT OF COURSE!
GRANDFATHER ALWAYS MEANT FOR HIS STORIES TO BE READ BY EVERY-ONE!
WOW!
I'VE NEVER SEEN THIS ONE-- ONLY HEARD ABOUT IT!
DO YOU KNOW WHAT THIS IS, AMY?

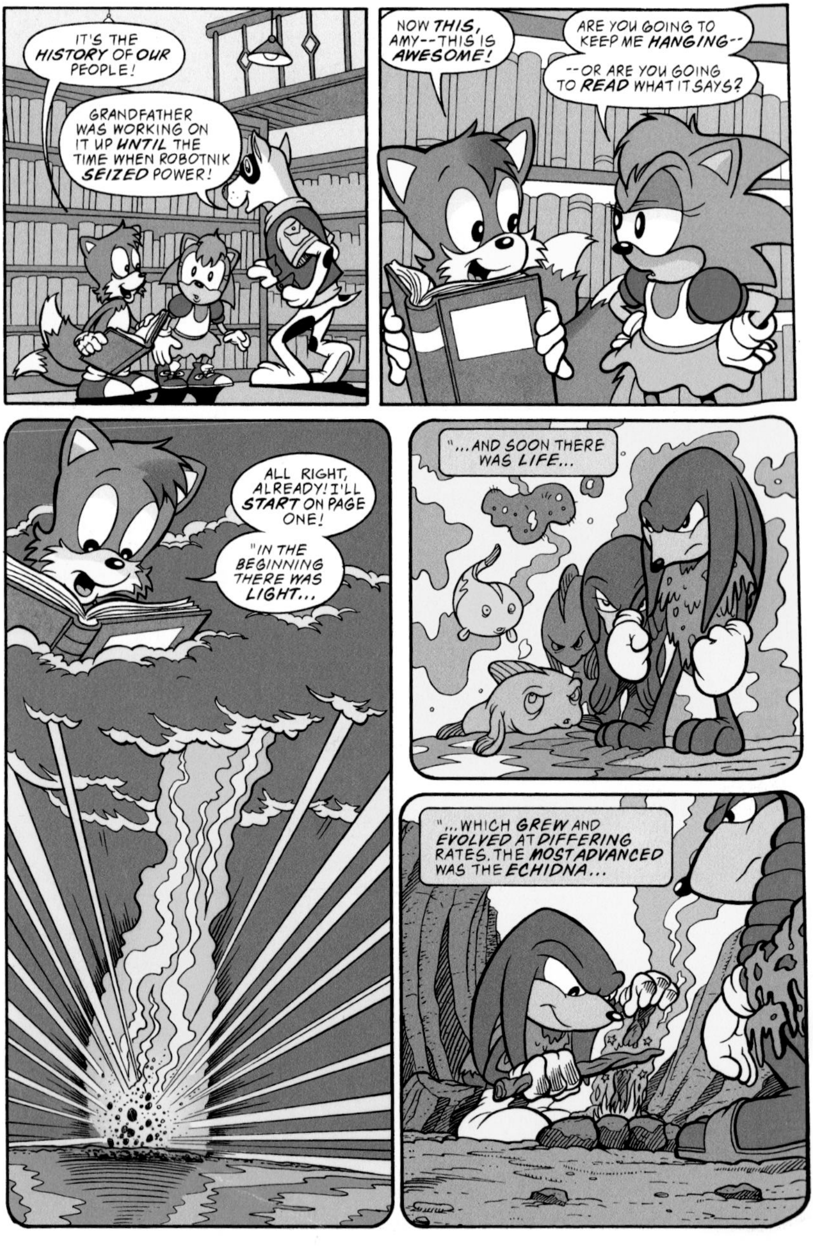
IT'S THE HISTORY OF OUR PEOPLE!
GRANDFATHER WAS WORKING ON IT UP UNTIL THE TIME WHEN ROBOTNIK SEIZED POWER!
NOW THIS, AMY--THIS IS AWESOME!
ARE YOU GOING TO KEEP ME HANGING--
--OR ARE YOU GOING TO READ WHAT IT SAYS?
ALL RIGHT, ALREADY! I'LL START ON PAGE ONE!
"IN THE BEGINNING THERE WAS LIGHT...
"...AND SOON THERE WAS LIFE...
"...WHICH GREW AND EVOLVED AT DIFFERING RATES. THE MOST ADVANCED WAS THE ECHIDNA...

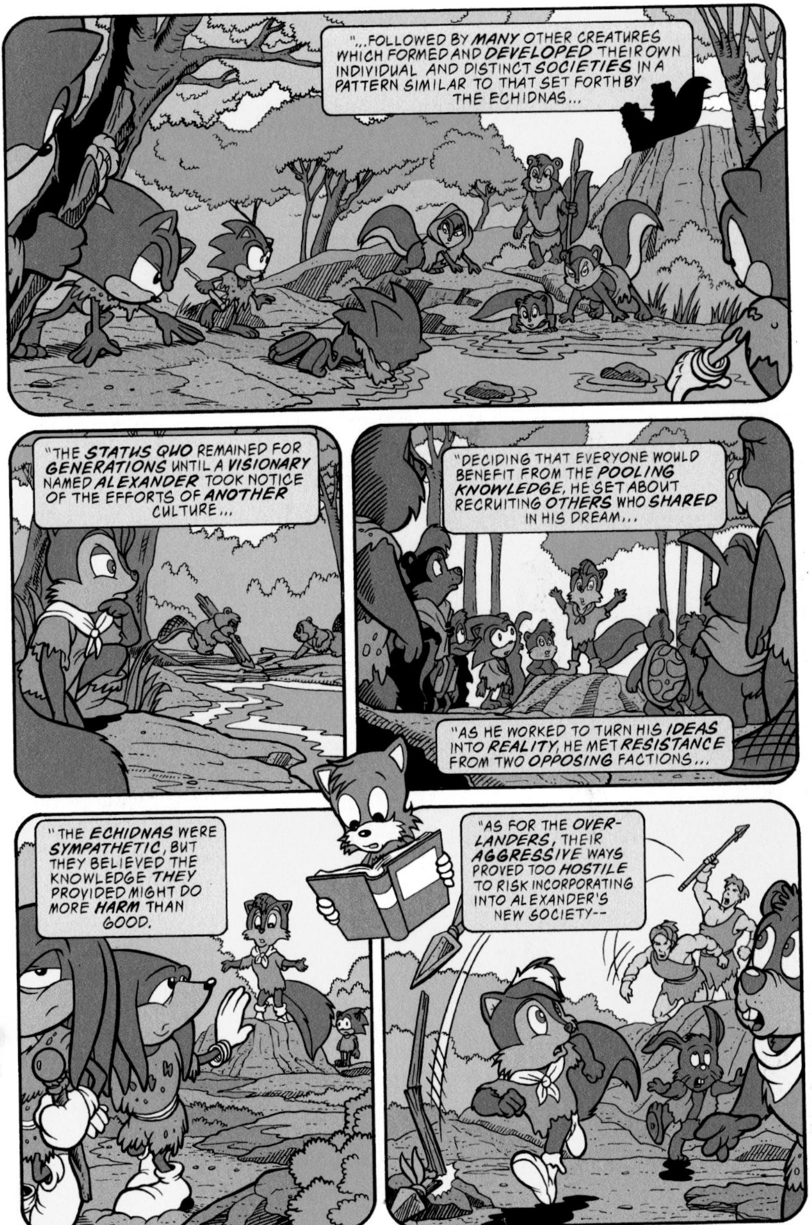
"...FOLLOWED BY MANY OTHER CREATURES WHICH FORMED AND DEVELOPED THEIR OWN INDIVIDUAL AND DISTINCT SOCIETIES IN A PATTERN SIMILAR TO THAT SET FORTH BY THE ECHIDNAS...
"THE STATUS QUO REMAINED FOR GENERATIONS UNTIL A VISIONARY NAMED ALEXANDER TOOK NOTICE OF THE EFFORTS OF ANOTHER CULTURE...
"DECIDING THAT EVERYONE WOULD BENEFIT FROM THE POOLING KNOWLEDGE, HE SET ABOUT RECRUITING OTHERS WHO SHARED IN HIS DREAM...
"AS HE WORKED TO TURN HIS IDEAS INTO REALITY, HE MET RESISTANCE FROM TWO OPPOSING FACTIONS...
"THE ECHIDNAS WERE SYMPATHETIC, BUT THEY BELIEVED THE KNOWLEDGE THEY PROVIDED MIGHT DO MORE HARM THAN GOOD.
"AS FOR THE OVER-LANDERS, THEIR AGGRESSIVE WAYS PROVED TOO HOSTILE TO RISK INCORPORATING INTO ALEXANDER'S NEW SOCIETY--

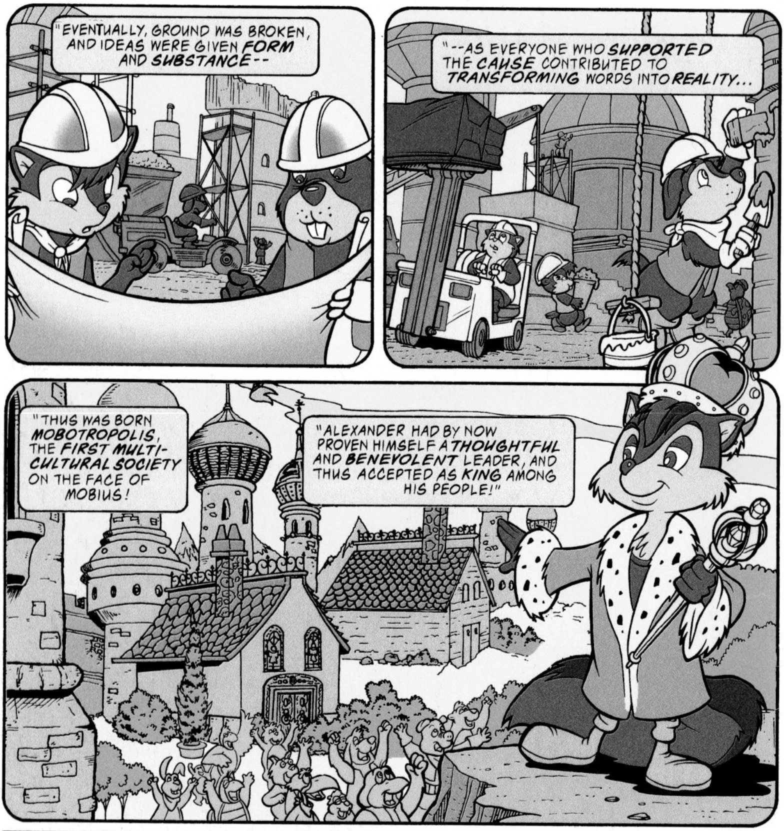
"EVENTUALLY, GROUND WAS BROKEN, AND IDEAS WERE GIVEN FORM AND SUBSTANCE--
"--AS EVERYONE WHO SUPPORTED THE CAUSE CONTRIBUTED TO TRANSFORMING WORDS INTO REALITY...
"THUS WAS BORN MOBOTROPOLIS, THE FIRST MULTI-CULTURAL SOCIETY ON THE FACE OF MOBIUS!
"ALEXANDER HAD BY NOW PROVEN HIMSELF A THOUGHTFUL AND BENEVOLENT LEADER, AND THUS ACCEPTED AS KING AMONG HIS PEOPLE!"

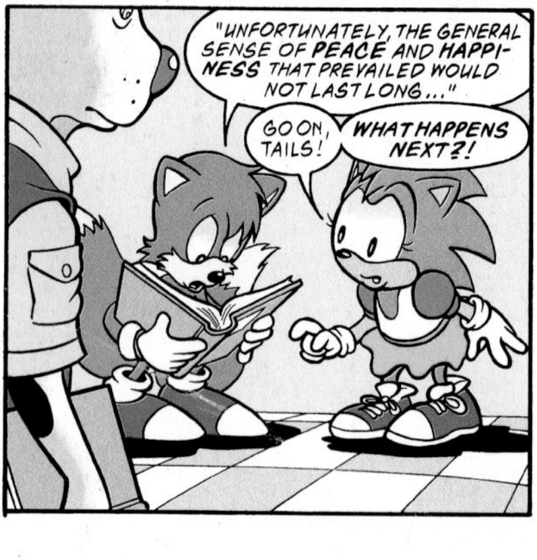
"UNFORTUNATELY, THE GENERAL SENSE OF PEACE AND HAPPINESS THAT PREVAILED WOULD NOT LAST LONG..."
GO ON, TAILS!
WHAT HAPPENS NEXT?!

WHAT DOES, INDEED, DEAR READERS?!

AT LONG LAST, YOU'RE GOING TO FIND OUT THE HIDDEN SECRETS TO THE **GREAT WAR**!!

READ ON AND DISCOVER THE ANSWER TO THE BURNING QUESTION

WHATEVER STARTED THE GREAT WAR IN THE FIRST PLACE ANYHOW?!

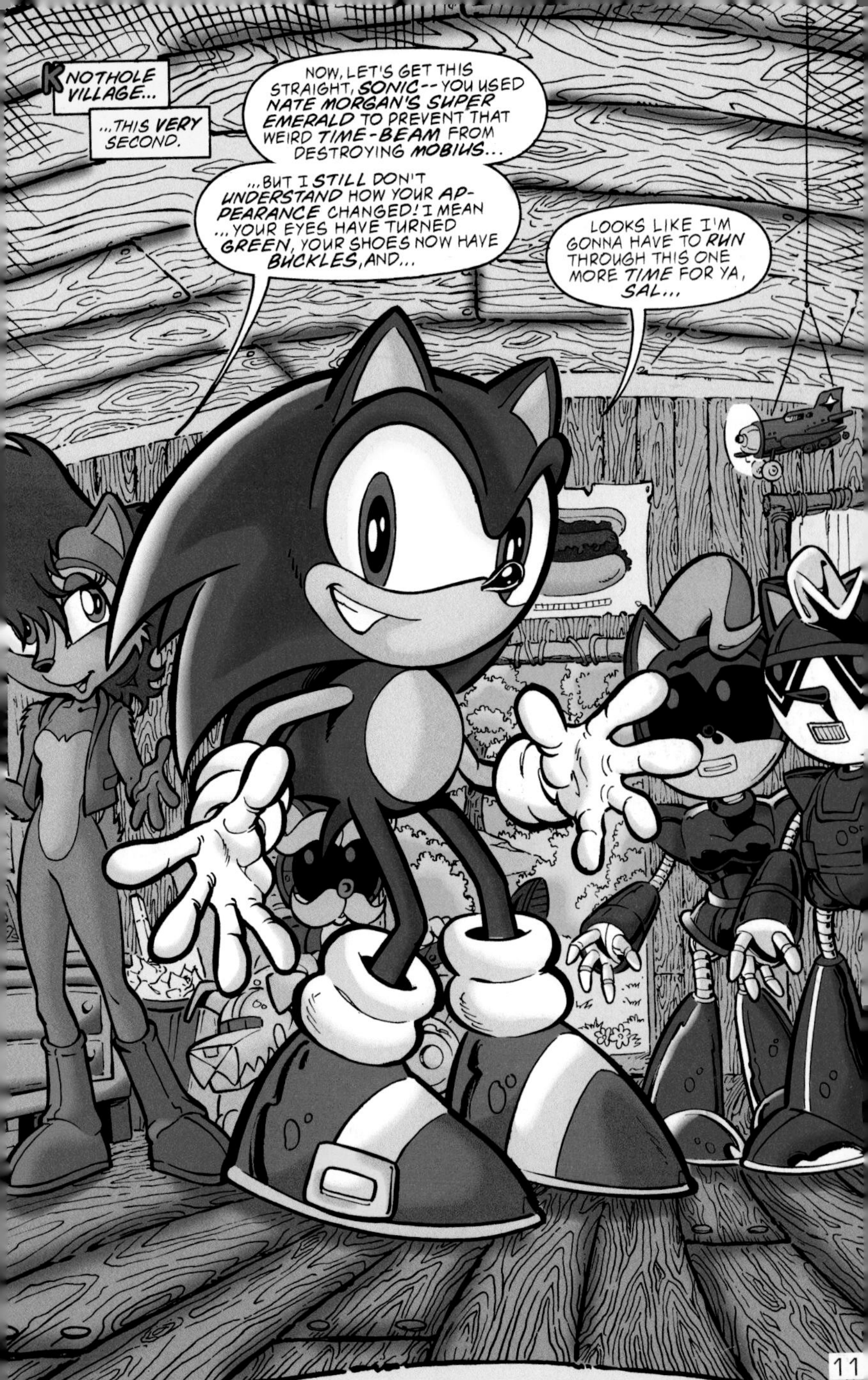

KNOTHOLE VILLAGE...
...THIS VERY SECOND.
NOW, LET'S GET THIS STRAIGHT, SONIC--YOU USED NATE MORGAN'S SUPER EMERALD TO PREVENT THAT WEIRD TIME-BEAM FROM DESTROYING MOBIUS...
...BUT I STILL DON'T UNDERSTAND HOW YOUR APPEARANCE CHANGED! I MEAN ...YOUR EYES HAVE TURNED GREEN, YOUR SHOES NOW HAVE BUCKLES, AND...
LOOKS LIKE I'M GONNA HAVE TO RUN THROUGH THIS ONE MORE TIME FOR YA, SAL...

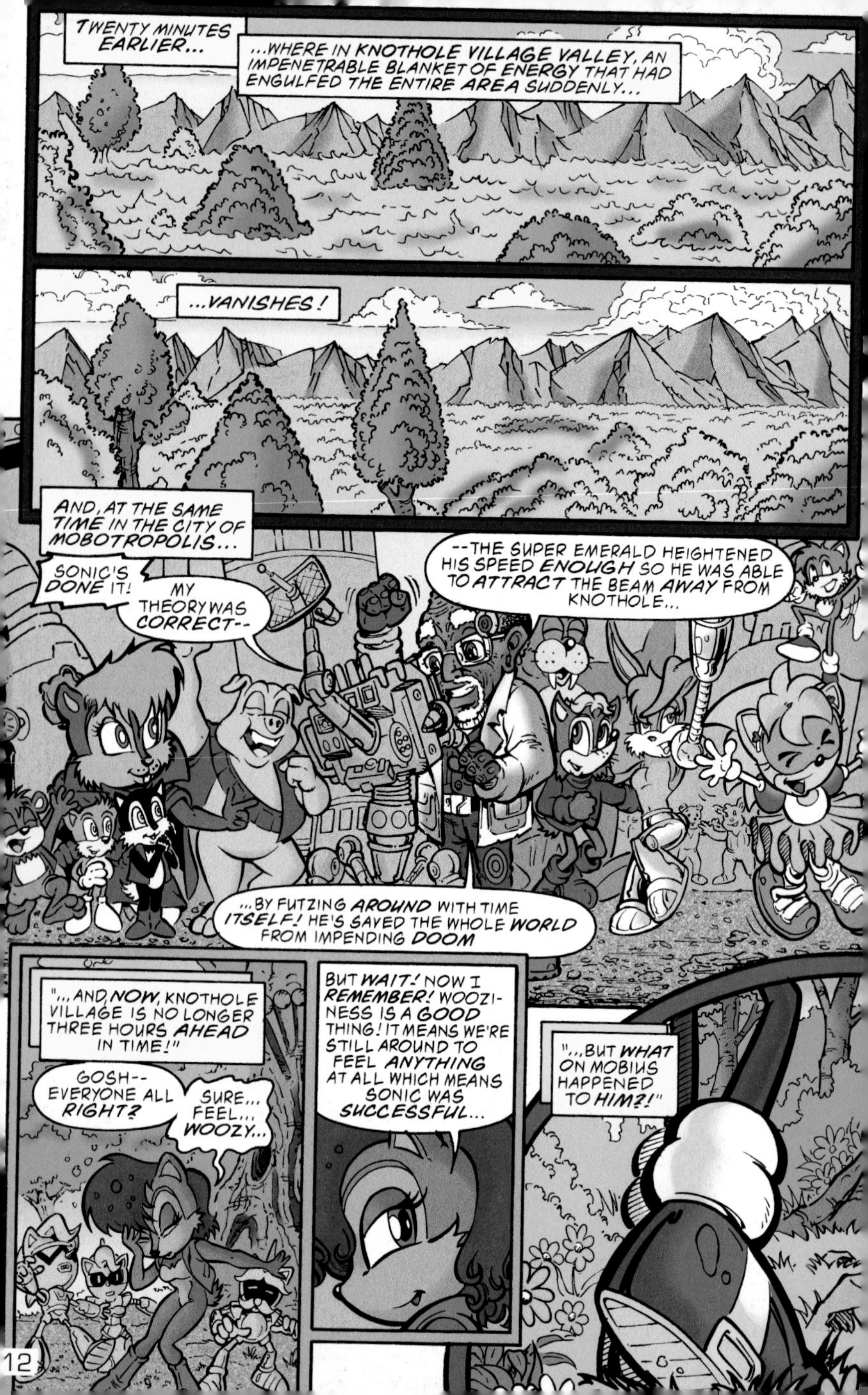
TWENTY MINUTES EARLIER...
...WHERE IN KNOTHOLE VILLAGE VALLEY, AN IMPENETRABLE BLANKET OF ENERGY THAT HAD ENGULFED THE ENTIRE AREA SUDDENLY...
...VANISHES!
AND, AT THE SAME TIME IN THE CITY OF MOBOTROPOLIS...
SONIC'S DONE IT!
MY THEORY WAS CORRECT--
--THE SUPER EMERALD HEIGHTENED HIS SPEED ENOUGH SO HE WAS ABLE TO ATTRACT THE BEAM AWAY FROM KNOTHOLE...
...BY FUTZING AROUND WITH TIME ITSELF! HE'S SAVED THE WHOLE WORLD FROM IMPENDING DOOM
"...AND, NOW, KNOTHOLE VILLAGE IS NO LONGER THREE HOURS AHEAD IN TIME!"
GOSH-- EVERYONE ALL RIGHT?
SURE... FEEL... WOOZY...
BUT WAIT! NOW I REMEMBER! WOOZINESS IS A GOOD THING! IT MEANS WE'RE STILL AROUND TO FEEL ANYTHING AT ALL WHICH MEANS SONIC WAS SUCCESSFUL...
"...BUT WHAT ON MOBIUS HAPPENED TO HIM?!"

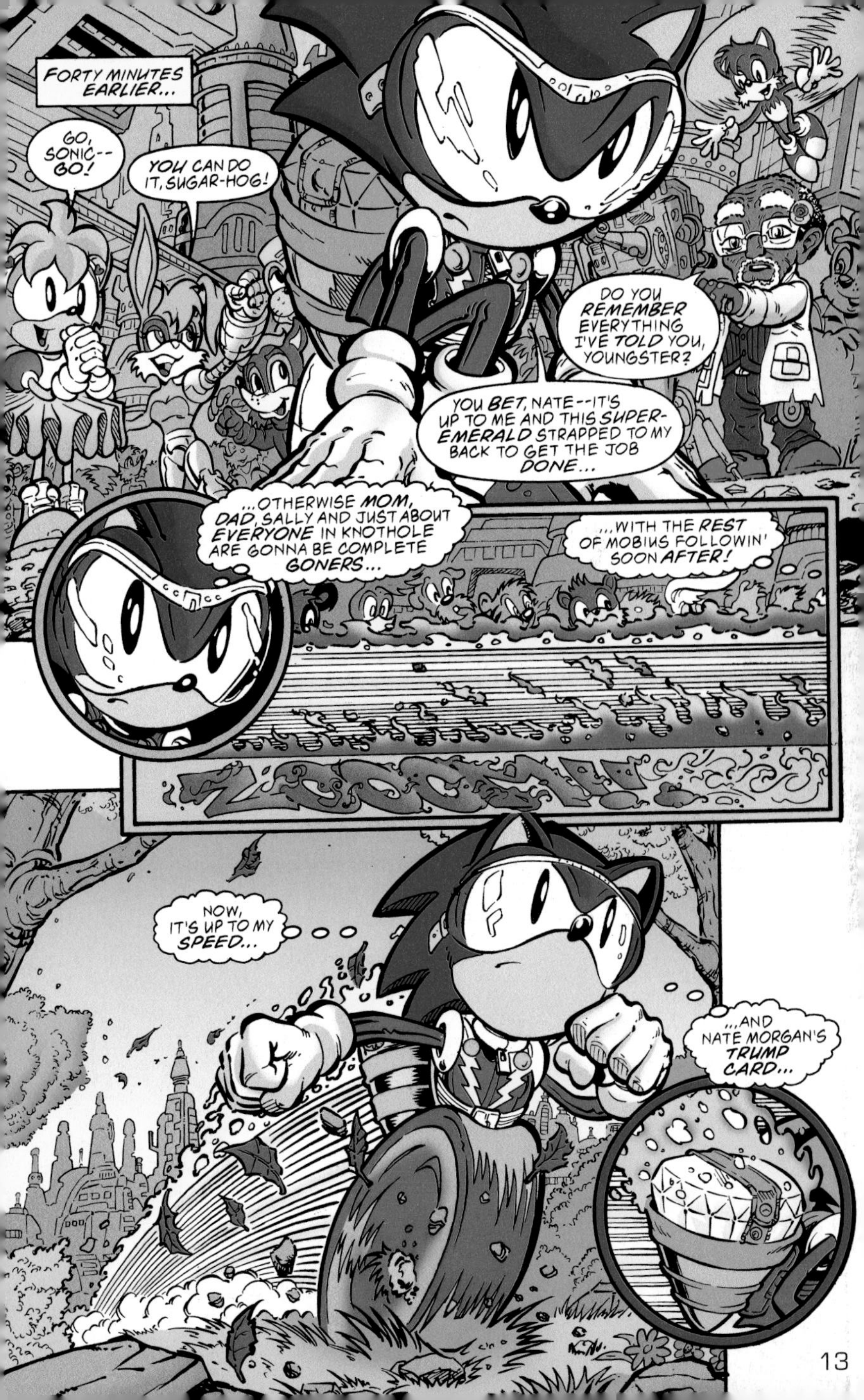
FORTY MINUTES EARLIER...
GO, SONIC-- GO!
YOU CAN DO IT, SUGAR-HOG!
DO YOU REMEMBER EVERYTHING I'VE TOLD YOU, YOUNGSTER?
YOU BET, NATE--IT'S UP TO ME AND THIS SUPER-EMERALD STRAPPED TO MY BACK TO GET THE JOB DONE...
...OTHERWISE MOM, DAD, SALLY AND JUST ABOUT EVERYONE IN KNOTHOLE ARE GONNA BE COMPLETE GONERS...
...WITH THE REST OF MOBIUS FOLLOWIN' SOON AFTER!
ZOOOM!
NOW, IT'S UP TO MY SPEED...
...AND NATE MORGAN'S TRUMP CARD...

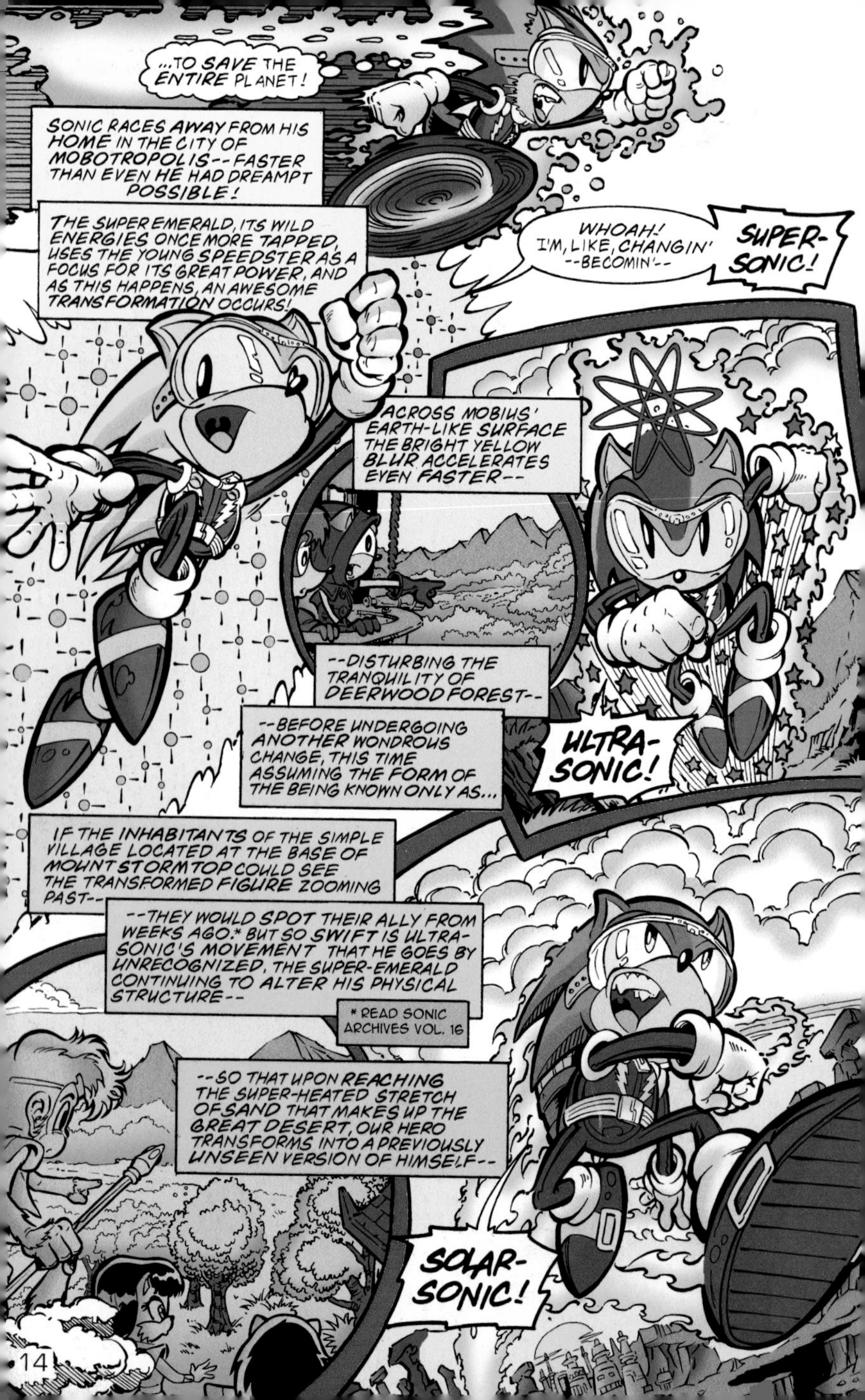
...TO SAVE THE ENTIRE PLANET!
SONIC RACES AWAY FROM HIS HOME IN THE CITY OF MOBOTROPOLIS--FASTER THAN EVEN HE HAD DREAMPT POSSIBLE!
THE SUPER EMERALD, ITS WILD ENERGIES ONCE MORE TAPPED, USES THE YOUNG SPEEDSTER AS A FOCUS FOR ITS GREAT POWER, AND AS THIS HAPPENS, AN AWESOME TRANSFORMATION OCCURS!
WHOAH! I'M, LIKE, CHANGIN' --BECOMIN'--
SUPER-SONIC!
ACROSS MOBIUS' EARTH-LIKE SURFACE THE BRIGHT YELLOW BLUR ACCELERATES EVEN FASTER--
--DISTURBING THE TRANQUILITY OF DEERWOOD FOREST--
--BEFORE UNDERGOING ANOTHER WONDROUS CHANGE, THIS TIME ASSUMING THE FORM OF THE BEING KNOWN ONLY AS...
ULTRA-SONIC!
IF THE INHABITANTS OF THE SIMPLE VILLAGE LOCATED AT THE BASE OF MOUNT STORMTOP COULD SEE THE TRANSFORMED FIGURE ZOOMING PAST--
--THEY WOULD SPOT THEIR ALLY FROM WEEKS AGO.* BUT SO SWIFT IS ULTRA-SONIC'S MOVEMENT THAT HE GOES BY UNRECOGNIZED, THE SUPER-EMERALD CONTINUING TO ALTER HIS PHYSICAL STRUCTURE--
* READ SONIC ARCHIVES VOL. 16
--SO THAT UPON REACHING THE SUPER-HEATED STRETCH OF SAND THAT MAKES UP THE GREAT DESERT, OUR HERO TRANSFORMS INTO A PREVIOUSLY UNSEEN VERSION OF HIMSELF--
SOLAR-SONIC!

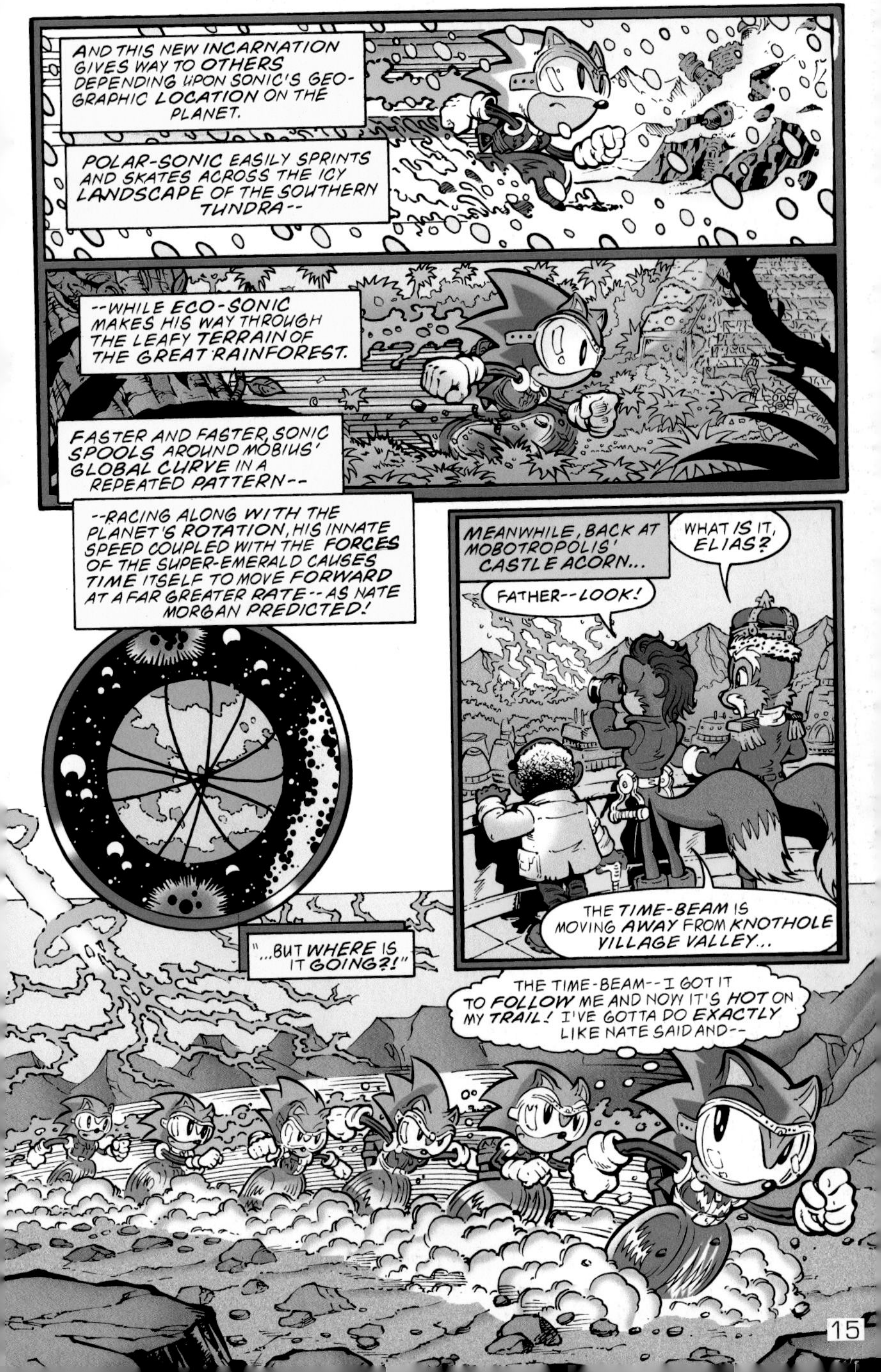
AND THIS NEW INCARNATION GIVES WAY TO OTHERS DEPENDING UPON SONIC'S GEOGRAPHIC LOCATION ON THE PLANET.
POLAR-SONIC EASILY SPRINTS AND SKATES ACROSS THE ICY LANDSCAPE OF THE SOUTHERN TUNDRA--
--WHILE ECO-SONIC MAKES HIS WAY THROUGH THE LEAFY TERRAIN OF THE GREAT RAINFOREST.
FASTER AND FASTER, SONIC SPOOLS AROUND MOBIUS' GLOBAL CURVE IN A REPEATED PATTERN--
--RACING ALONG WITH THE PLANET'S ROTATION, HIS INNATE SPEED COUPLED WITH THE FORCES OF THE SUPER-EMERALD CAUSES TIME ITSELF TO MOVE FORWARD AT A FAR GREATER RATE--AS NATE MORGAN PREDICTED!
MEANWHILE, BACK AT MOBOTROPOLIS' CASTLE ACORN...
WHAT IS IT, ELIAS?
FATHER--LOOK!
THE TIME-BEAM IS MOVING AWAY FROM KNOTHOLE VILLAGE VALLEY...
"...BUT WHERE IS IT GOING?!"
THE TIME-BEAM--I GOT IT TO FOLLOW ME AND NOW IT'S HOT ON MY TRAIL! I'VE GOTTA DO EXACTLY LIKE NATE SAID AND--

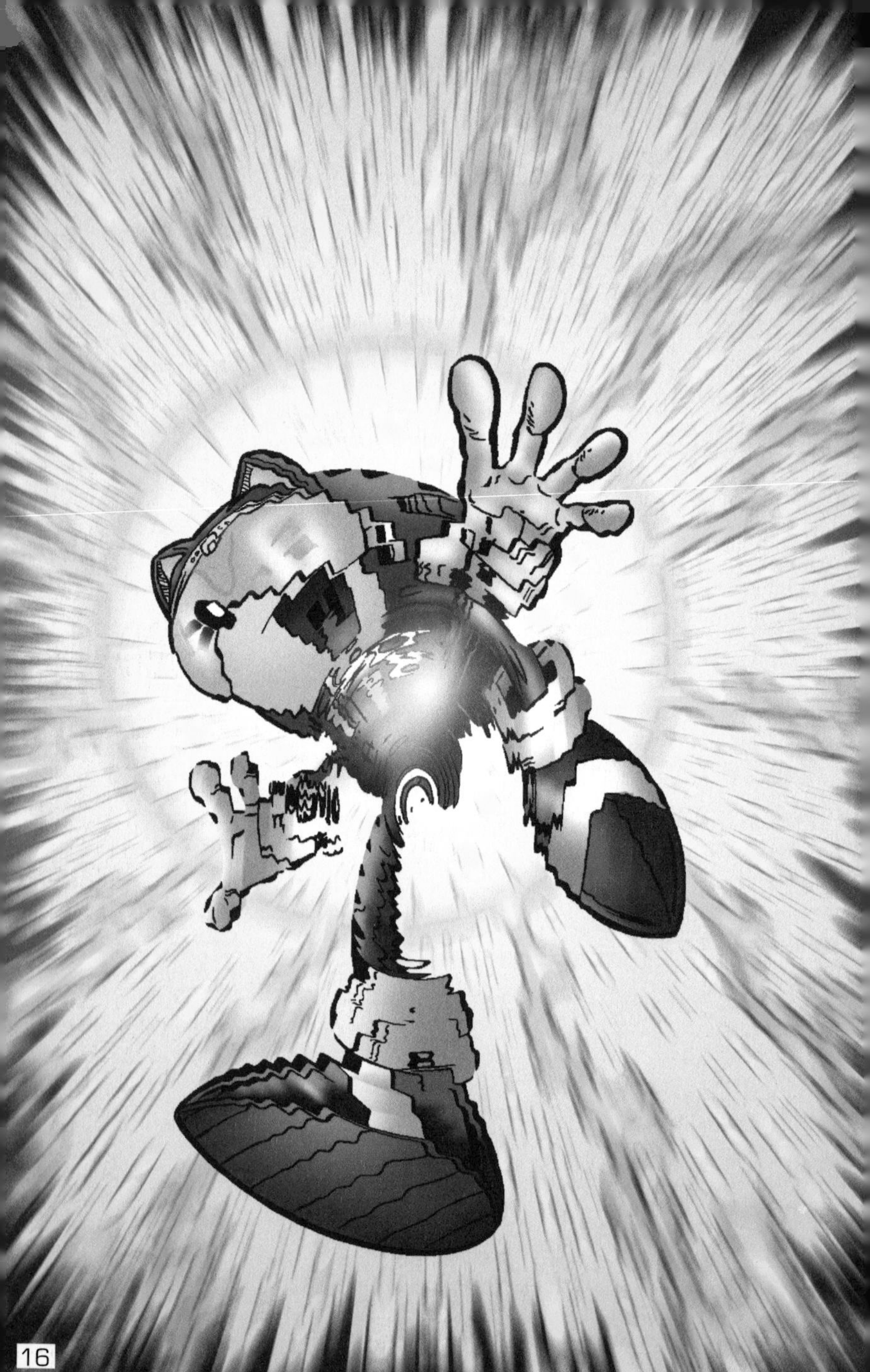

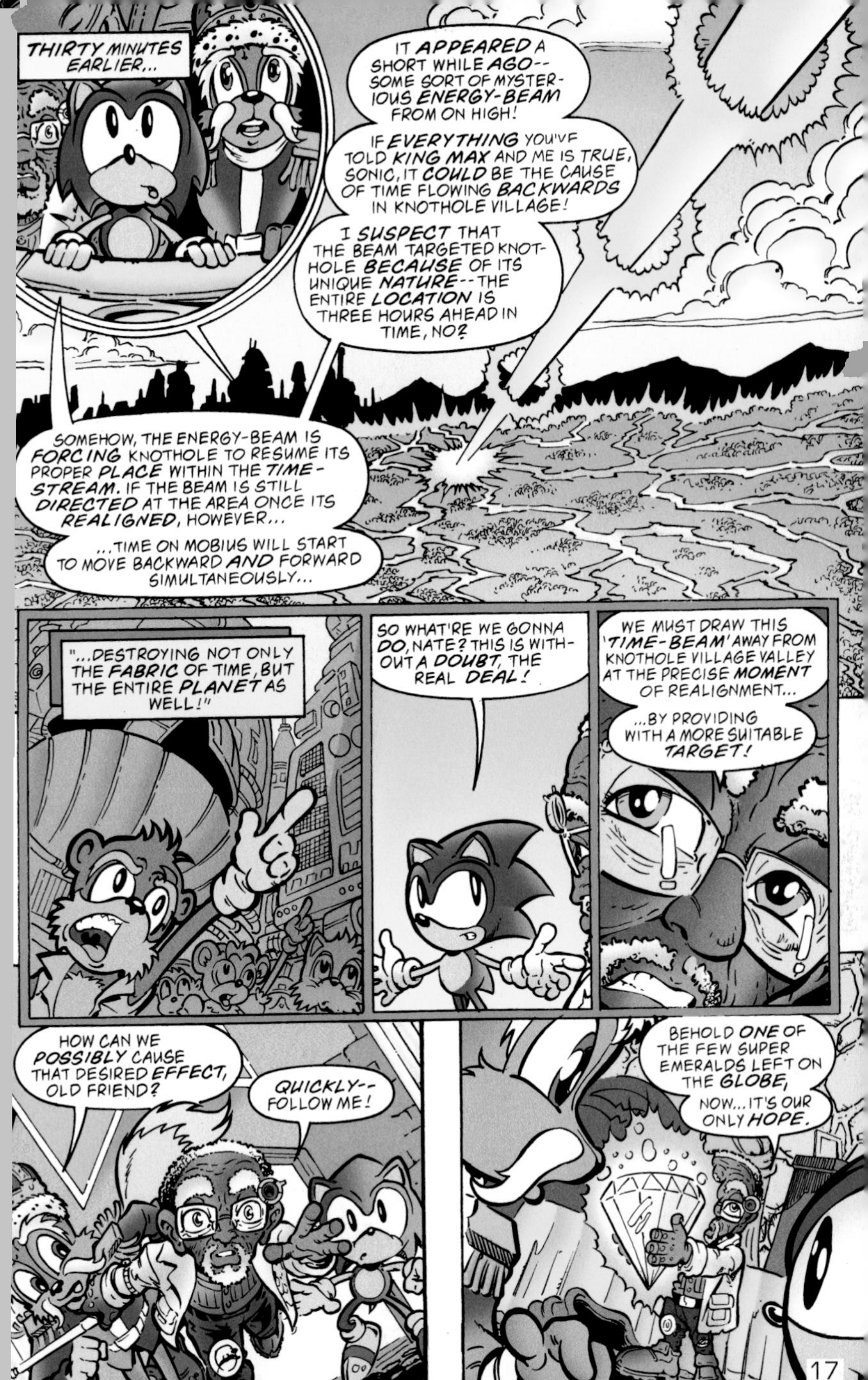
THIRTY MINUTES EARLIER...
IT APPEARED A SHORT WHILE AGO-- SOME SORT OF MYSTERIOUS ENERGY-BEAM FROM ON HIGH!
IF EVERYTHING YOU'VE TOLD KING MAX AND ME IS TRUE, SONIC, IT COULD BE THE CAUSE OF TIME FLOWING BACKWARDS IN KNOTHOLE VILLAGE!
I SUSPECT THAT THE BEAM TARGETED KNOTHOLE BECAUSE OF ITS UNIQUE NATURE--THE ENTIRE LOCATION IS THREE HOURS AHEAD IN TIME, NO?
SOMEHOW, THE ENERGY-BEAM IS FORCING KNOTHOLE TO RESUME ITS PROPER PLACE WITHIN THE TIME-STREAM. IF THE BEAM IS STILL DIRECTED AT THE AREA ONCE ITS REALIGNED, HOWEVER...
...TIME ON MOBIUS WILL START TO MOVE BACKWARD AND FORWARD SIMULTANEOUSLY...
"...DESTROYING NOT ONLY THE FABRIC OF TIME, BUT THE ENTIRE PLANET AS WELL!"
SO WHAT'RE WE GONNA DO, NATE? THIS IS WITHOUT A DOUBT, THE REAL DEAL!
WE MUST DRAW THIS 'TIME-BEAM' AWAY FROM KNOTHOLE VILLAGE VALLEY AT THE PRECISE MOMENT OF REALIGNMENT...
...BY PROVIDING WITH A MORE SUITABLE TARGET!
HOW CAN WE POSSIBLY CAUSE THAT DESIRED EFFECT, OLD FRIEND?
QUICKLY-- FOLLOW ME!
BEHOLD ONE OF THE FEW SUPER EMERALDS LEFT ON THE GLOBE,
NOW... IT'S OUR ONLY HOPE.

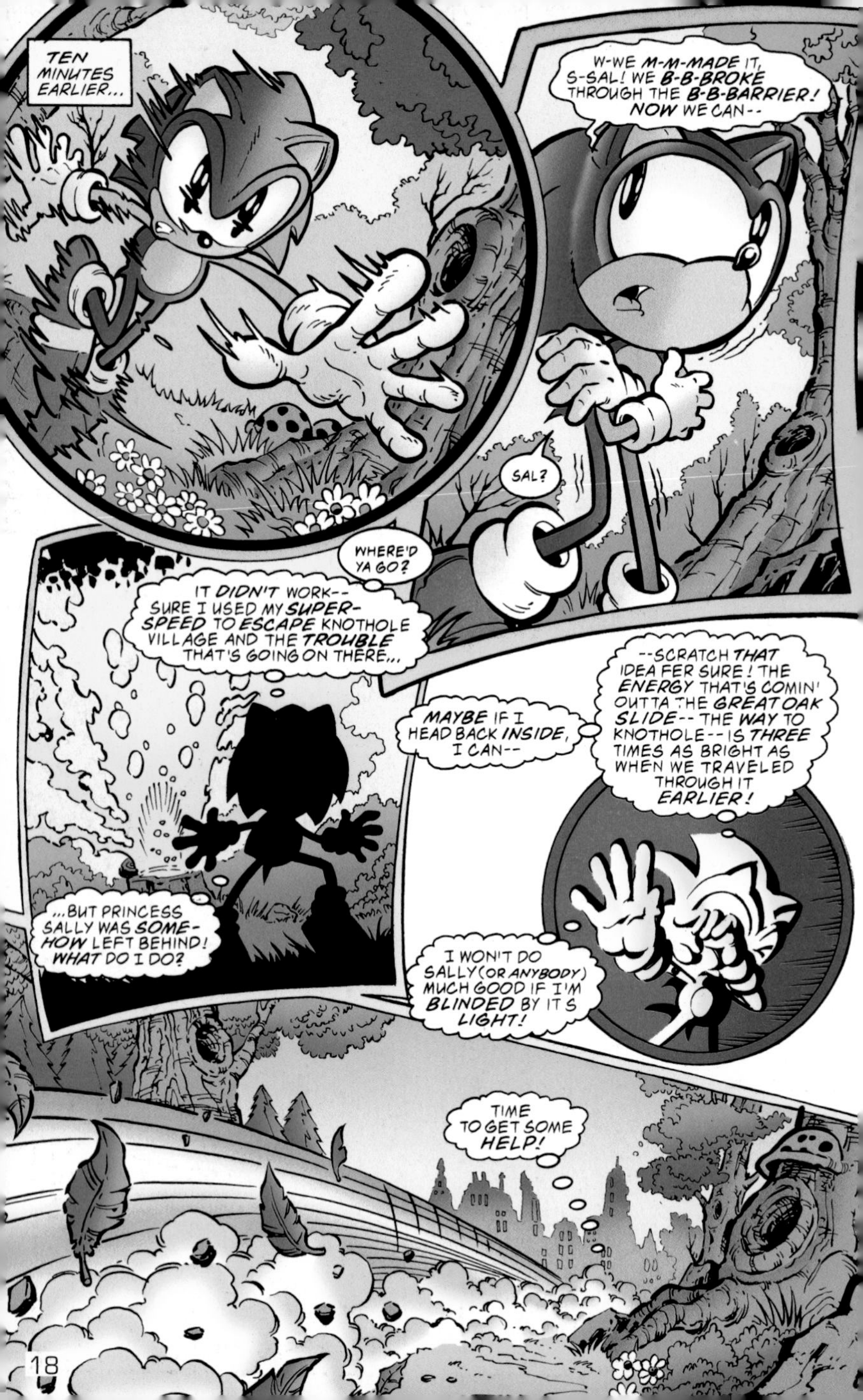

TEN MINUTES EARLIER...
W-WE M-M-MADE IT, S-SAL! WE B-B-BROKE THROUGH THE B-B-BARRIER! NOW WE CAN--
SAL?
WHERE'D YA GO?
IT DIDN'T WORK-- SURE I USED MY SUPER-SPEED TO ESCAPE KNOTHOLE VILLAGE AND THE TROUBLE THAT'S GOING ON THERE...
...BUT PRINCESS SALLY WAS SOME-HOW LEFT BEHIND! WHAT DO I DO?
MAYBE IF I HEAD BACK INSIDE, I CAN--
--SCRATCH THAT IDEA FER SURE! THE ENERGY THAT'S COMIN' OUTTA THE GREAT OAK SLIDE-- THE WAY TO KNOTHOLE--IS THREE TIMES AS BRIGHT AS WHEN WE TRAVELED THROUGH IT EARLIER!
I WON'T DO SALLY (OR ANYBODY) MUCH GOOD IF I'M BLINDED BY IT'S LIGHT!
TIME TO GET SOME HELP!

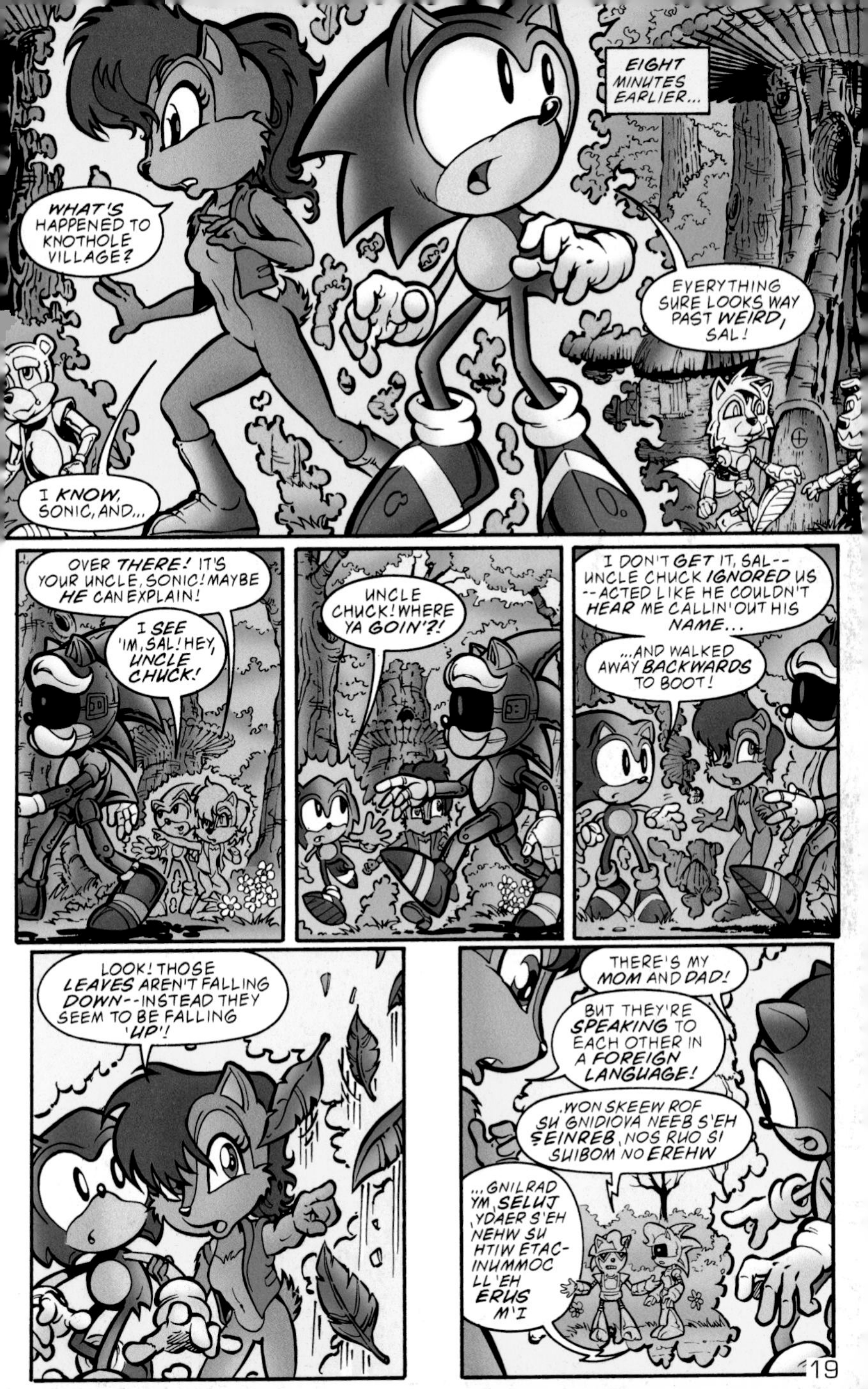
EIGHT MINUTES EARLIER...
WHAT'S HAPPENED TO KNOTHOLE VILLAGE?
EVERYTHING SURE LOOKS WAY PAST WEIRD, SAL!
I KNOW, SONIC, AND...
OVER THERE! IT'S YOUR UNCLE, SONIC! MAYBE HE CAN EXPLAIN!
I SEE 'IM, SAL! HEY, UNCLE CHUCK!
UNCLE CHUCK! WHERE YA GOIN'?!
I DON'T GET IT, SAL-- UNCLE CHUCK IGNORED US --ACTED LIKE HE COULDN'T HEAR ME CALLIN' OUT HIS NAME...
...AND WALKED AWAY BACKWARDS TO BOOT!
LOOK! THOSE LEAVES AREN'T FALLING DOWN--INSTEAD THEY SEEM TO BE FALLING 'UP'!
THERE'S MY MOM AND DAD!
BUT THEY'RE SPEAKING TO EACH OTHER IN A FOREIGN LANGUAGE!
.WON SKEEW ROF SU GNIDIOVA NEEB S'EH SEINREB ,NOS RUO SI SUIBOM NO EREHW
...GNILRAD YM ,SELUJ YDAER S'EH NEHW SU HTIW ETAC-INUMMOC LL'EH ERUS M'I

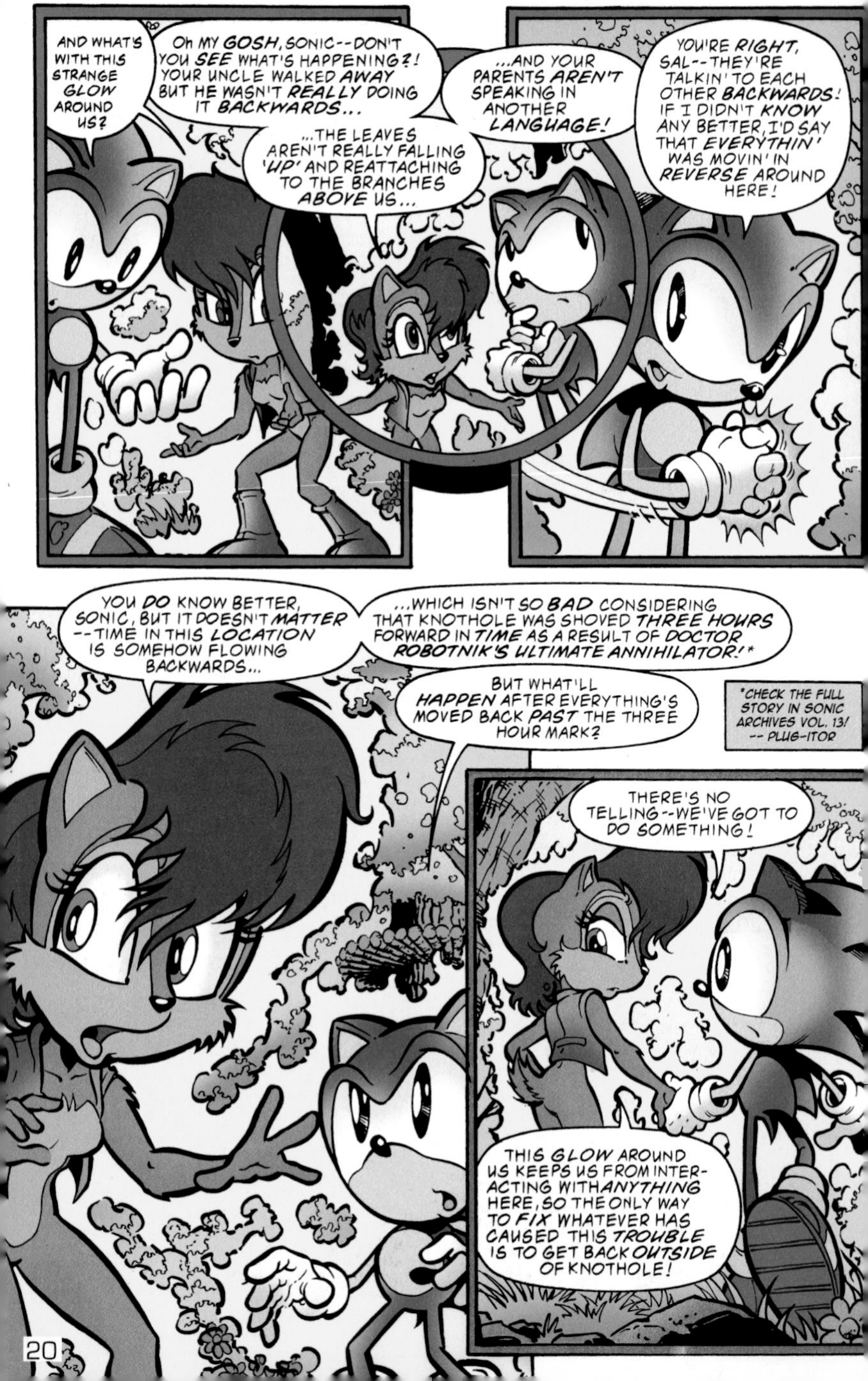
AND WHAT'S WITH THIS STRANGE GLOW AROUND US?
Oh MY GOSH, SONIC--DON'T YOU SEE WHAT'S HAPPENING?! YOUR UNCLE WALKED AWAY BUT HE WASN'T REALLY DOING IT BACKWARDS...
...THE LEAVES AREN'T REALLY FALLING 'UP' AND REATTACHING TO THE BRANCHES ABOVE US...
...AND YOUR PARENTS AREN'T SPEAKING IN ANOTHER LANGUAGE!
YOU'RE RIGHT, SAL--THEY'RE TALKIN' TO EACH OTHER BACKWARDS! IF I DIDN'T KNOW ANY BETTER, I'D SAY THAT EVERYTHIN' WAS MOVIN' IN REVERSE AROUND HERE!
YOU DO KNOW BETTER, SONIC, BUT IT DOESN'T MATTER--TIME IN THIS LOCATION IS SOMEHOW FLOWING BACKWARDS...
...WHICH ISN'T SO BAD CONSIDERING THAT KNOTHOLE WAS SHOVED THREE HOURS FORWARD IN TIME AS A RESULT OF DOCTOR ROBOTNIK'S ULTIMATE ANNIHILATOR!*
BUT WHAT'LL HAPPEN AFTER EVERYTHING'S MOVED BACK PAST THE THREE HOUR MARK?
*CHECK THE FULL STORY IN SONIC ARCHIVES VOL. 13! --PLUG-ITOR
THERE'S NO TELLING--WE'VE GOT TO DO SOMETHING!
THIS GLOW AROUND US KEEPS US FROM INTERACTING WITH ANYTHING HERE, SO THE ONLY WAY TO FIX WHATEVER HAS CAUSED THIS TROUBLE IS TO GET BACK OUTSIDE OF KNOTHOLE!

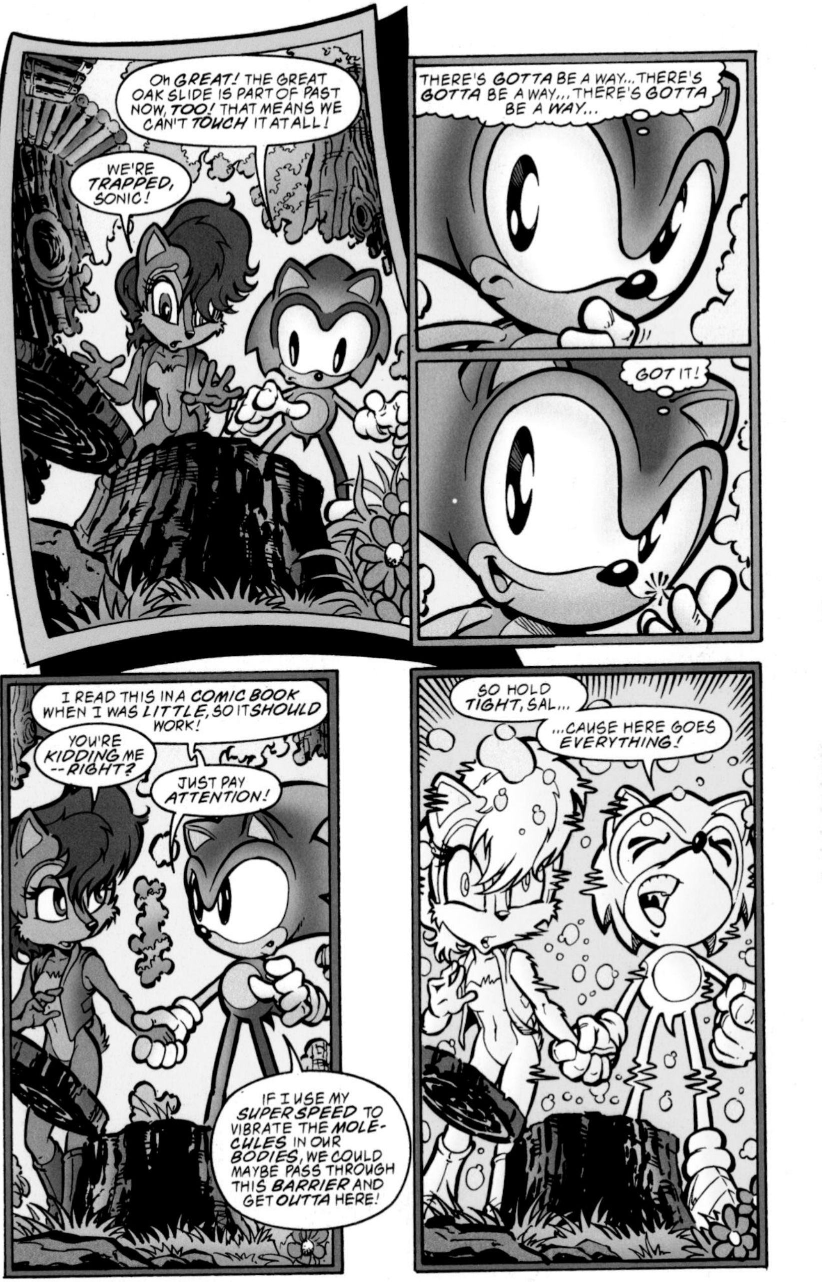
Oh GREAT! THE GREAT OAK SLIDE IS PART OF PAST NOW, TOO! THAT MEANS WE CAN'T TOUCH IT AT ALL!
WE'RE TRAPPED, SONIC!
THERE'S GOTTA BE A WAY... THERE'S GOTTA BE A WAY... THERE'S GOTTA BE A WAY...
GOT IT!
I READ THIS IN A COMIC BOOK WHEN I WAS LITTLE, SO IT SHOULD WORK!
YOU'RE KIDDING ME --RIGHT?
JUST PAY ATTENTION!
IF I USE MY SUPERSPEED TO VIBRATE THE MOLE-CULES IN OUR BODIES, WE COULD MAYBE PASS THROUGH THIS BARRIER AND GET OUTTA HERE!
SO HOLD TIGHT, SAL...
...CAUSE HERE GOES EVERYTHING!

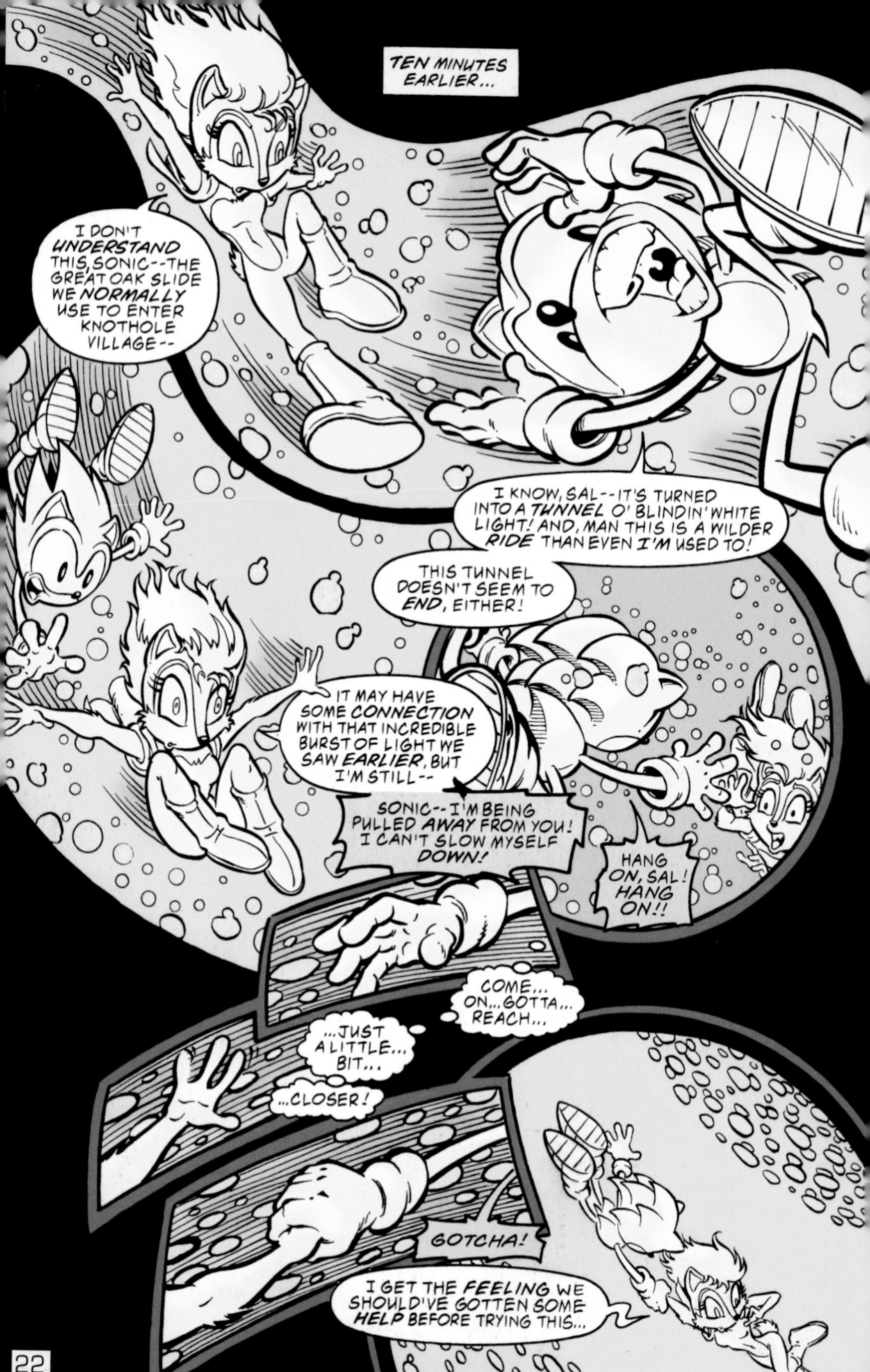
TEN MINUTES EARLIER...
I DON'T UNDERSTAND THIS, SONIC--THE GREAT OAK SLIDE WE NORMALLY USE TO ENTER KNOTHOLE VILLAGE--
I KNOW, SAL--IT'S TURNED INTO A TUNNEL O' BLINDIN' WHITE LIGHT! AND, MAN THIS IS A WILDER RIDE THAN EVEN I'M USED TO!
THIS TUNNEL DOESN'T SEEM TO END, EITHER!
IT MAY HAVE SOME CONNECTION WITH THAT INCREDIBLE BURST OF LIGHT WE SAW EARLIER, BUT I'M STILL--
SONIC--I'M BEING PULLED AWAY FROM YOU! I CAN'T SLOW MYSELF DOWN!
HANG ON, SAL! HANG ON!!
COME... ON... GOTTA... REACH...
...JUST A LITTLE... BIT...
...CLOSER!
GOTCHA!
I GET THE FEELING WE SHOULD'VE GOTTEN SOME HELP BEFORE TRYING THIS...

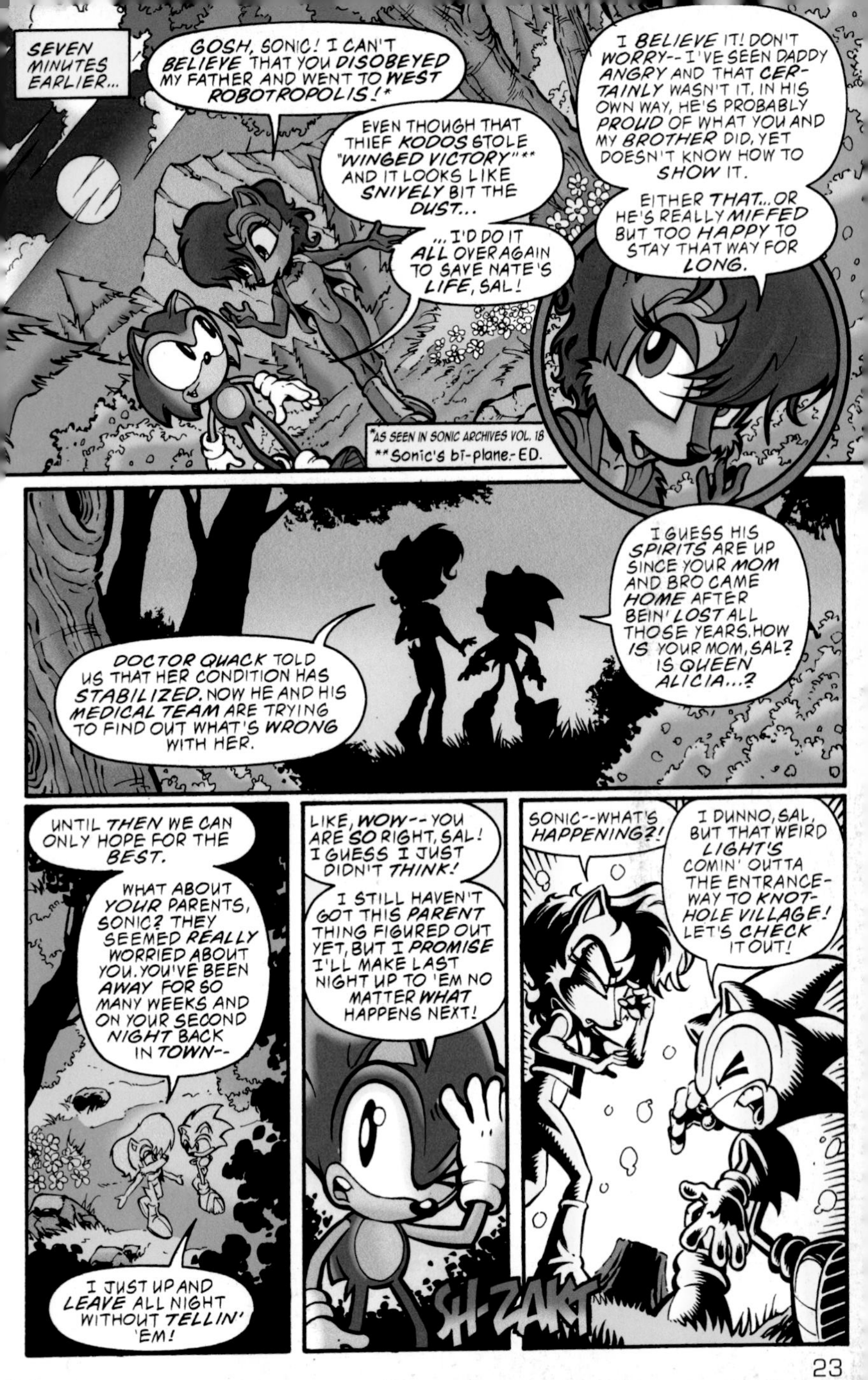
SEVEN MINUTES EARLIER...
GOSH, SONIC! I CAN'T BELIEVE THAT YOU DISOBEYED MY FATHER AND WENT TO WEST ROBOTROPOLIS!*
EVEN THOUGH THAT THIEF KODOS STOLE "WINGED VICTORY"** AND IT LOOKS LIKE SNIVELY BIT THE DUST...
...I'D DO IT ALL OVER AGAIN TO SAVE NATE'S LIFE, SAL!
I BELIEVE IT! DON'T WORRY-- I'VE SEEN DADDY ANGRY AND THAT CERTAINLY WASN'T IT. IN HIS OWN WAY, HE'S PROBABLY PROUD OF WHAT YOU AND MY BROTHER DID, YET DOESN'T KNOW HOW TO SHOW IT.
EITHER THAT...OR HE'S REALLY MIFFED BUT TOO HAPPY TO STAY THAT WAY FOR LONG.
*AS SEEN IN SONIC ARCHIVES VOL. 18
**Sonic's bi-plane.-ED.
I GUESS HIS SPIRITS ARE UP SINCE YOUR MOM AND BRO CAME HOME AFTER BEIN' LOST ALL THOSE YEARS. HOW IS YOUR MOM, SAL? IS QUEEN ALICIA...?
DOCTOR QUACK TOLD US THAT HER CONDITION HAS STABILIZED. NOW HE AND HIS MEDICAL TEAM ARE TRYING TO FIND OUT WHAT'S WRONG WITH HER.
UNTIL THEN WE CAN ONLY HOPE FOR THE BEST.
WHAT ABOUT YOUR PARENTS, SONIC? THEY SEEMED REALLY WORRIED ABOUT YOU. YOU'VE BEEN AWAY FOR SO MANY WEEKS AND ON YOUR SECOND NIGHT BACK IN TOWN--
I JUST UP AND LEAVE ALL NIGHT WITHOUT TELLIN' 'EM!
LIKE, WOW-- YOU ARE SO RIGHT, SAL! I GUESS I JUST DIDN'T THINK!
I STILL HAVEN'T GOT THIS PARENT THING FIGURED OUT YET, BUT I PROMISE I'LL MAKE LAST NIGHT UP TO 'EM NO MATTER WHAT HAPPENS NEXT!
SH-ZAKT
SONIC--WHAT'S HAPPENING?!
I DUNNO, SAL, BUT THAT WEIRD LIGHT'S COMIN' OUTTA THE ENTRANCE-WAY TO KNOTHOLE VILLAGE! LET'S CHECK IT OUT!

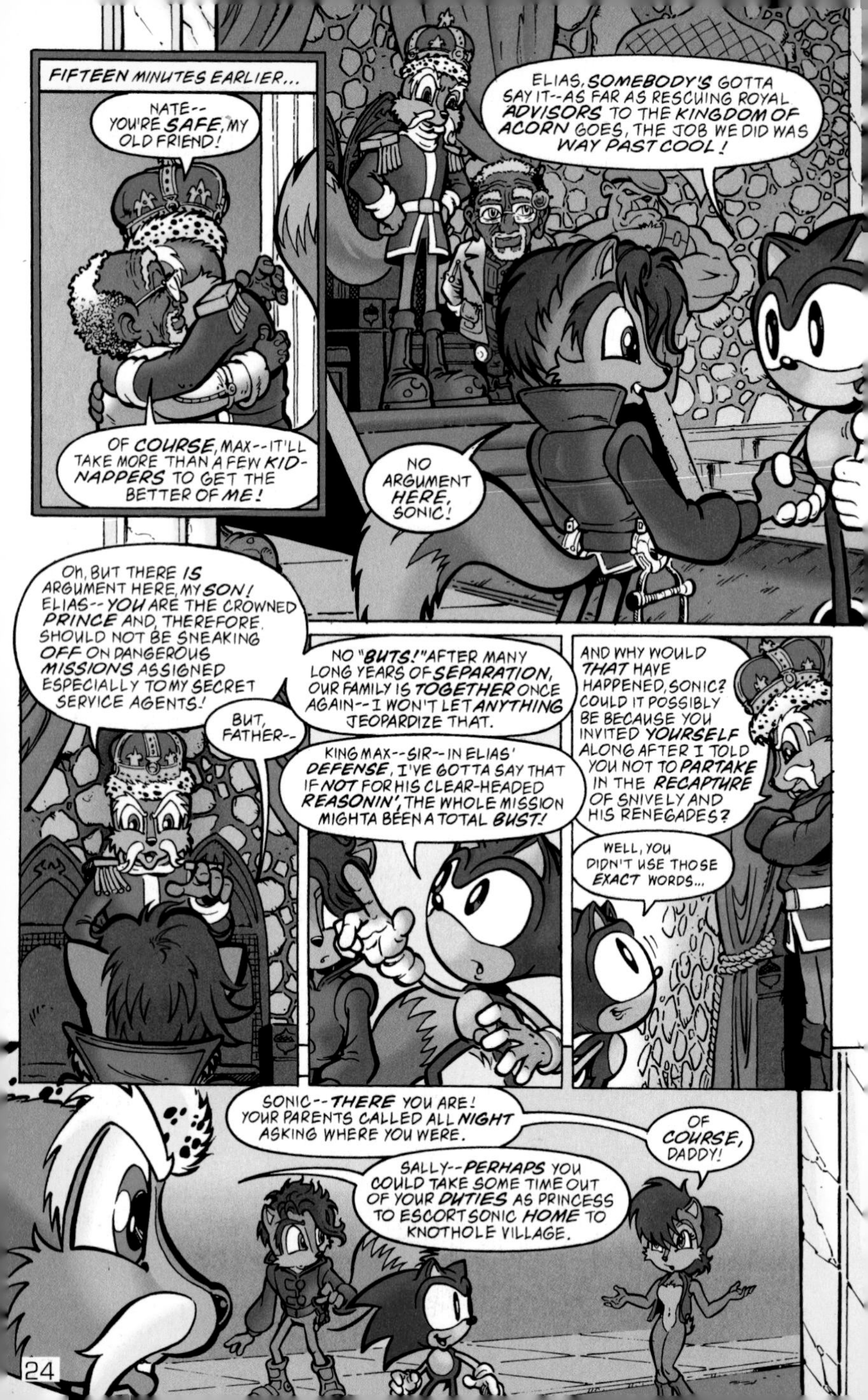
FIFTEEN MINUTES EARLIER...
NATE--YOU'RE SAFE, MY OLD FRIEND!
OF COURSE, MAX--IT'LL TAKE MORE THAN A FEW KID-NAPPERS TO GET THE BETTER OF ME!
ELIAS, SOMEBODY'S GOTTA SAY IT--AS FAR AS RESCUING ROYAL ADVISORS TO THE KINGDOM OF ACORN GOES, THE JOB WE DID WAS WAY PAST COOL!
NO ARGUMENT HERE, SONIC!
Oh, BUT THERE IS ARGUMENT HERE, MY SON! ELIAS--YOU ARE THE CROWNED PRINCE AND, THEREFORE, SHOULD NOT BE SNEAKING OFF ON DANGEROUS MISSIONS ASSIGNED ESPECIALLY TO MY SECRET SERVICE AGENTS!
BUT, FATHER--
NO "BUTS!" AFTER MANY LONG YEARS OF SEPARATION, OUR FAMILY IS TOGETHER ONCE AGAIN--I WON'T LET ANYTHING JEOPARDIZE THAT.
KING MAX--SIR--IN ELIAS' DEFENSE, I'VE GOTTA SAY THAT IF NOT FOR HIS CLEAR-HEADED REASONIN', THE WHOLE MISSION MIGHTA BEEN A TOTAL BUST!
AND WHY WOULD THAT HAVE HAPPENED, SONIC? COULD IT POSSIBLY BE BECAUSE YOU INVITED YOURSELF ALONG AFTER I TOLD YOU NOT TO PARTAKE IN THE RECAPTURE OF SNIVELY AND HIS RENEGADES?
WELL, YOU DIDN'T USE THOSE EXACT WORDS...
SONIC--THERE YOU ARE! YOUR PARENTS CALLED ALL NIGHT ASKING WHERE YOU WERE.
SALLY--PERHAPS YOU COULD TAKE SOME TIME OUT OF YOUR DUTIES AS PRINCESS TO ESCORT SONIC HOME TO KNOTHOLE VILLAGE.
OF COURSE, DADDY!

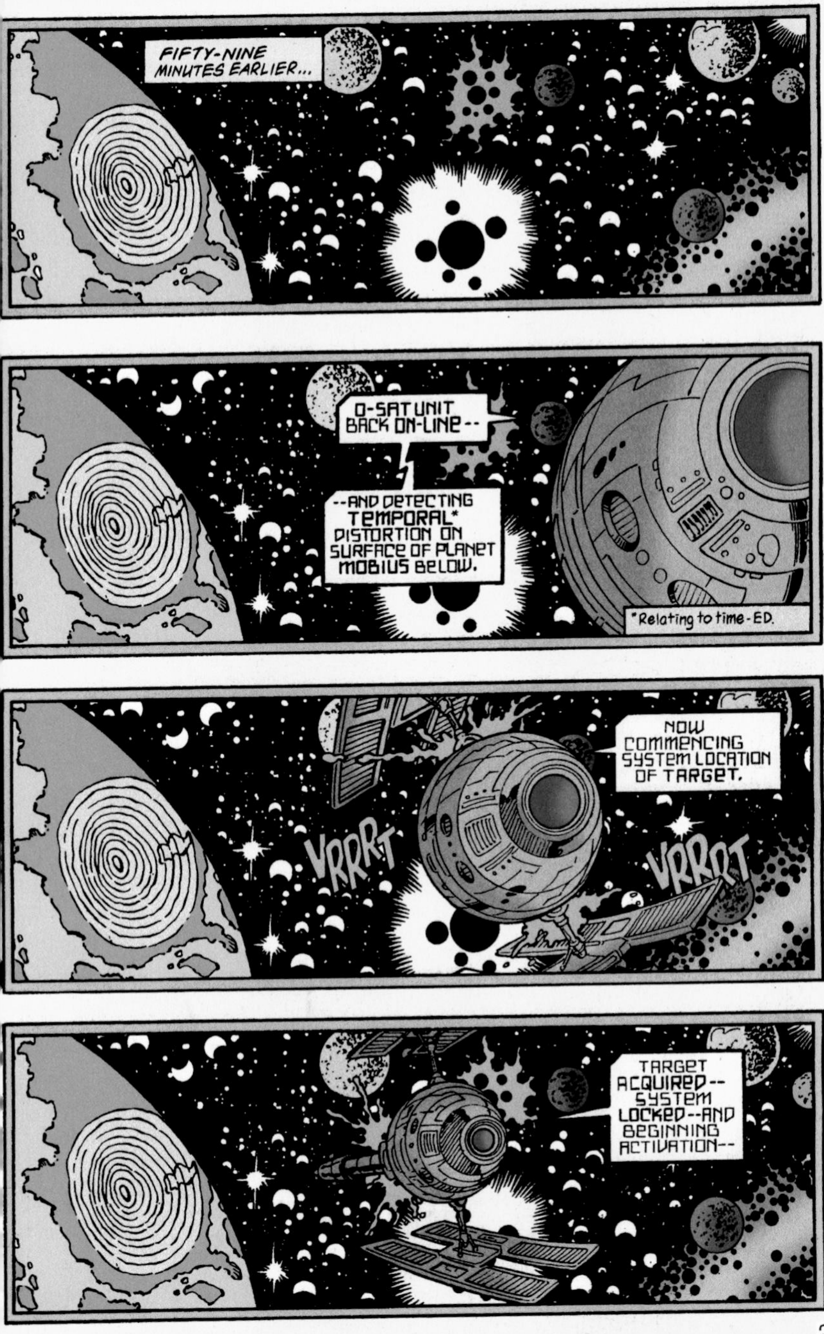
FIFTY-NINE MINUTES EARLIER...
O-SAT UNIT BACK ON-LINE--
--AND DETECTING TEMPORAL* DISTORTION ON SURFACE OF PLANET MOBIUS BELOW.
*Relating to time-ED.
NOW COMMENCING SYSTEM LOCATION OF TARGET.
VRRRT
VRRRT
TARGET ACQUIRED--SYSTEM LOCKED--AND BEGINNING ACTIVATION--

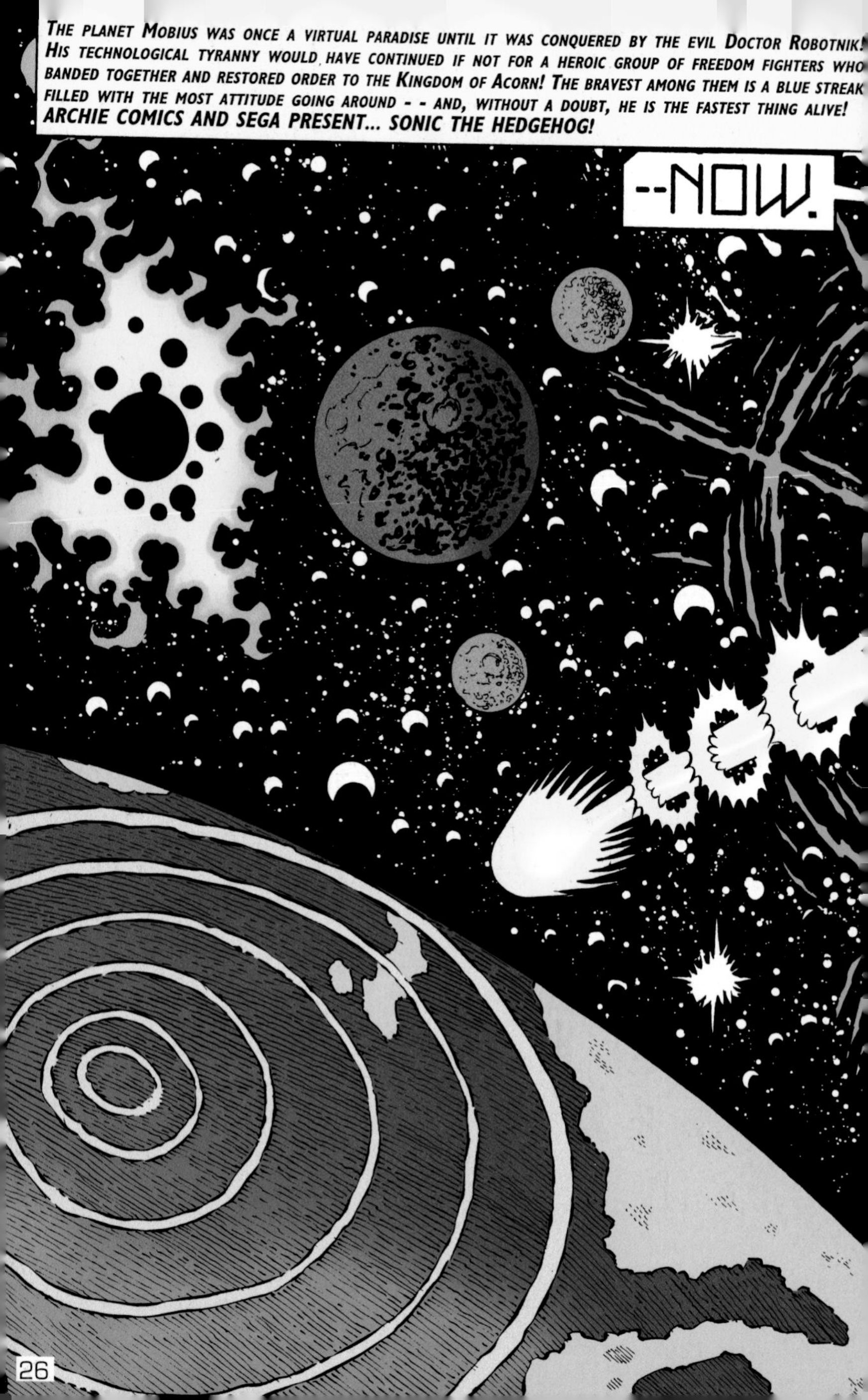
THE PLANET MOBIUS WAS ONCE A VIRTUAL PARADISE UNTIL IT WAS CONQUERED BY THE EVIL DOCTOR ROBOTNIK! HIS TECHNOLOGICAL TYRANNY WOULD HAVE CONTINUED IF NOT FOR A HEROIC GROUP OF FREEDOM FIGHTERS WHO BANDED TOGETHER AND RESTORED ORDER TO THE KINGDOM OF ACORN! THE BRAVEST AMONG THEM IS A BLUE STREAK FILLED WITH THE MOST ATTITUDE GOING AROUND - - AND, WITHOUT A DOUBT, HE IS THE FASTEST THING ALIVE!
ARCHIE COMICS AND SEGA PRESENT... SONIC THE HEDGEHOG!
--NOW.

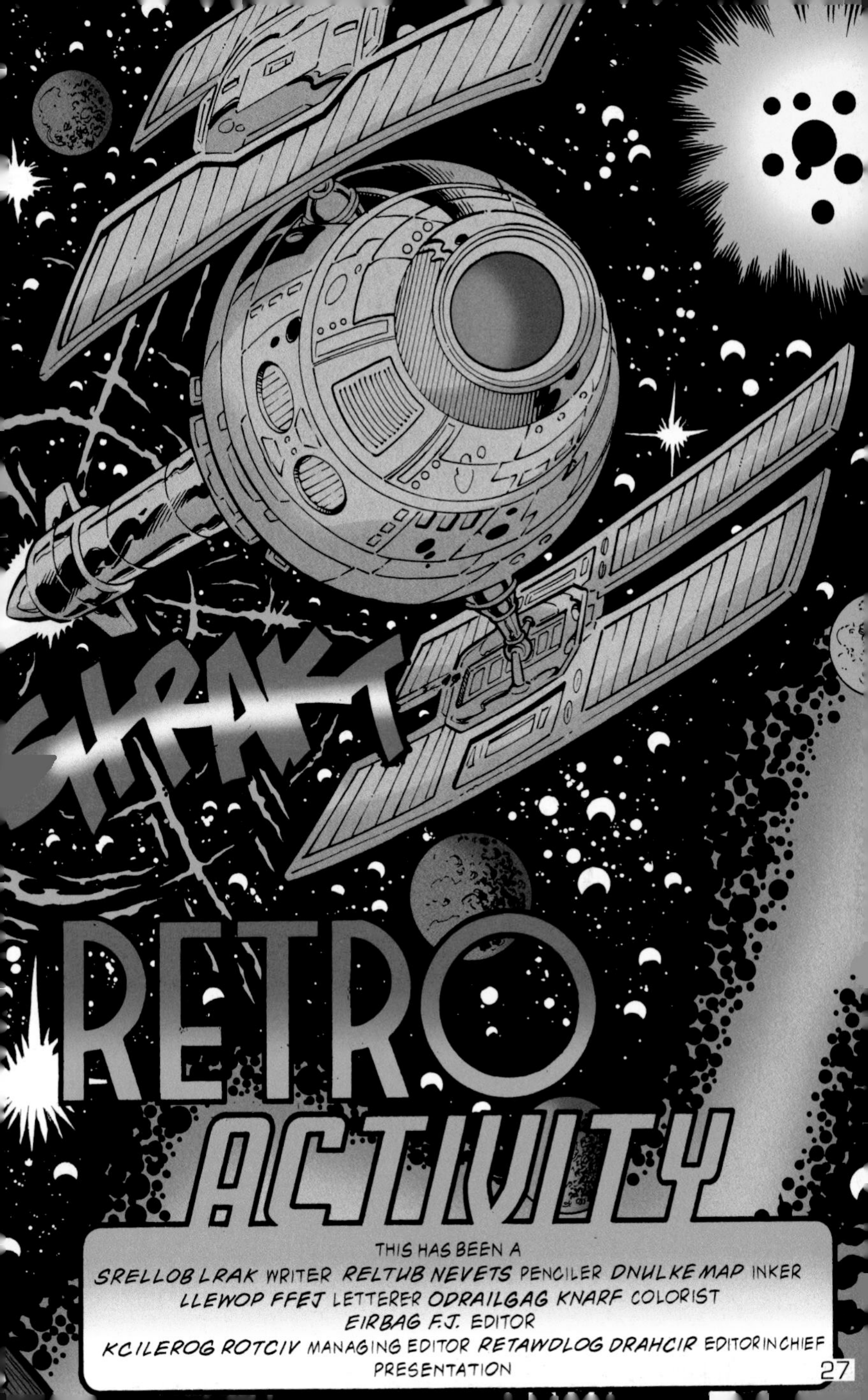
RETRO ACTIVITY
THIS HAS BEEN A
SRELLOB LRAK WRITER RELTUB NEVETS PENCILER DNULKE MAP INKER
LLEWOP FFEJ LETTERER ODRAILGAG KNARF COLORIST
EIRBAG F.J. EDITOR
KCILEROG ROTCIV MANAGING EDITOR RETAWDLOG DRAHCIR EDITOR IN CHIEF
PRESENTATION

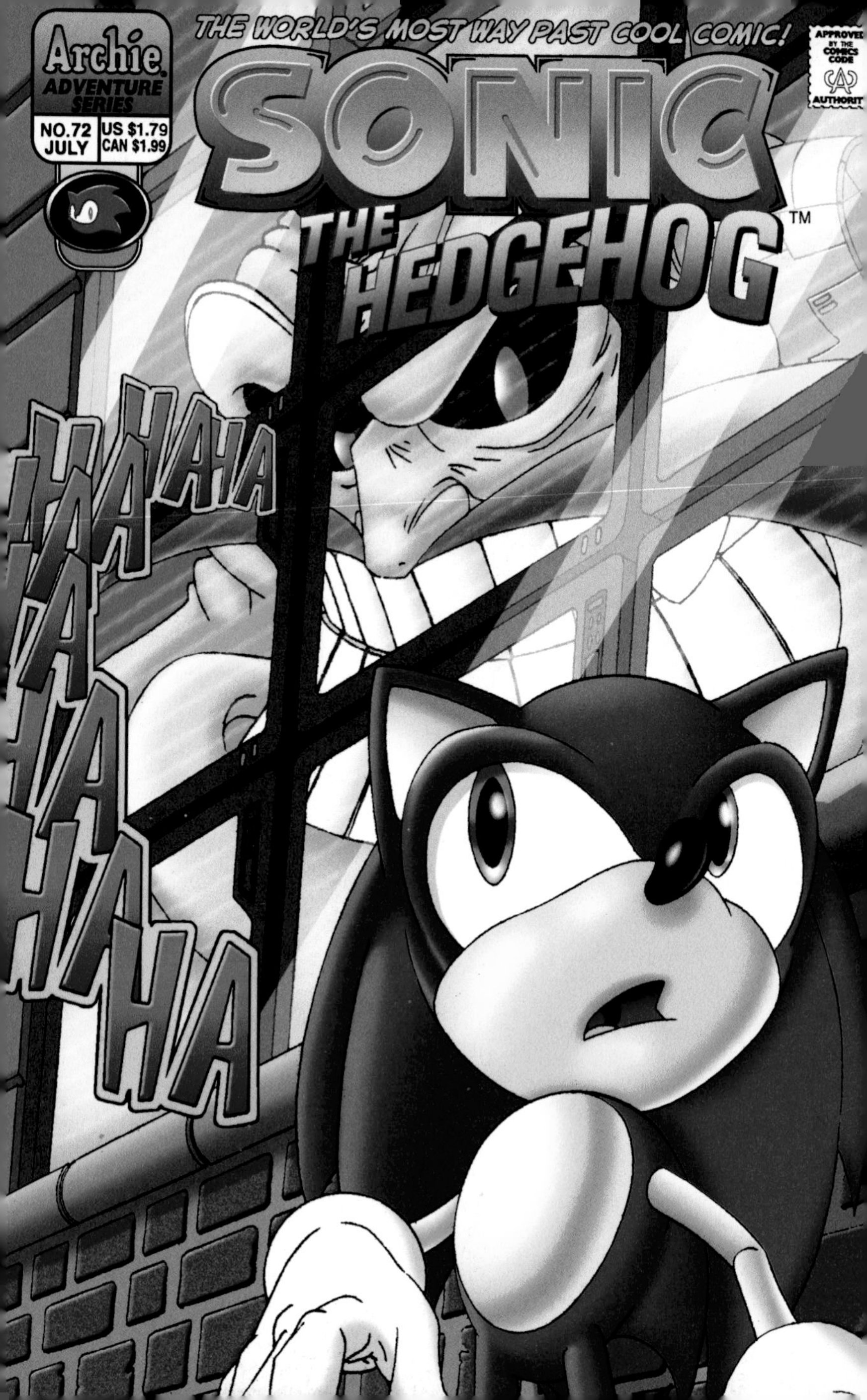

Archie
ADVENTURE SERIES
NO.72
JULY
US $1.79
CAN $1.99
THE WORLD'S MOST WAY PAST COOL COMIC!
APPROVED BY THE COMICS CODE AUTHORIT
SONIC THE HEDGEHOG™
HAHAHA
HA HA HA HA HA HA HA HA

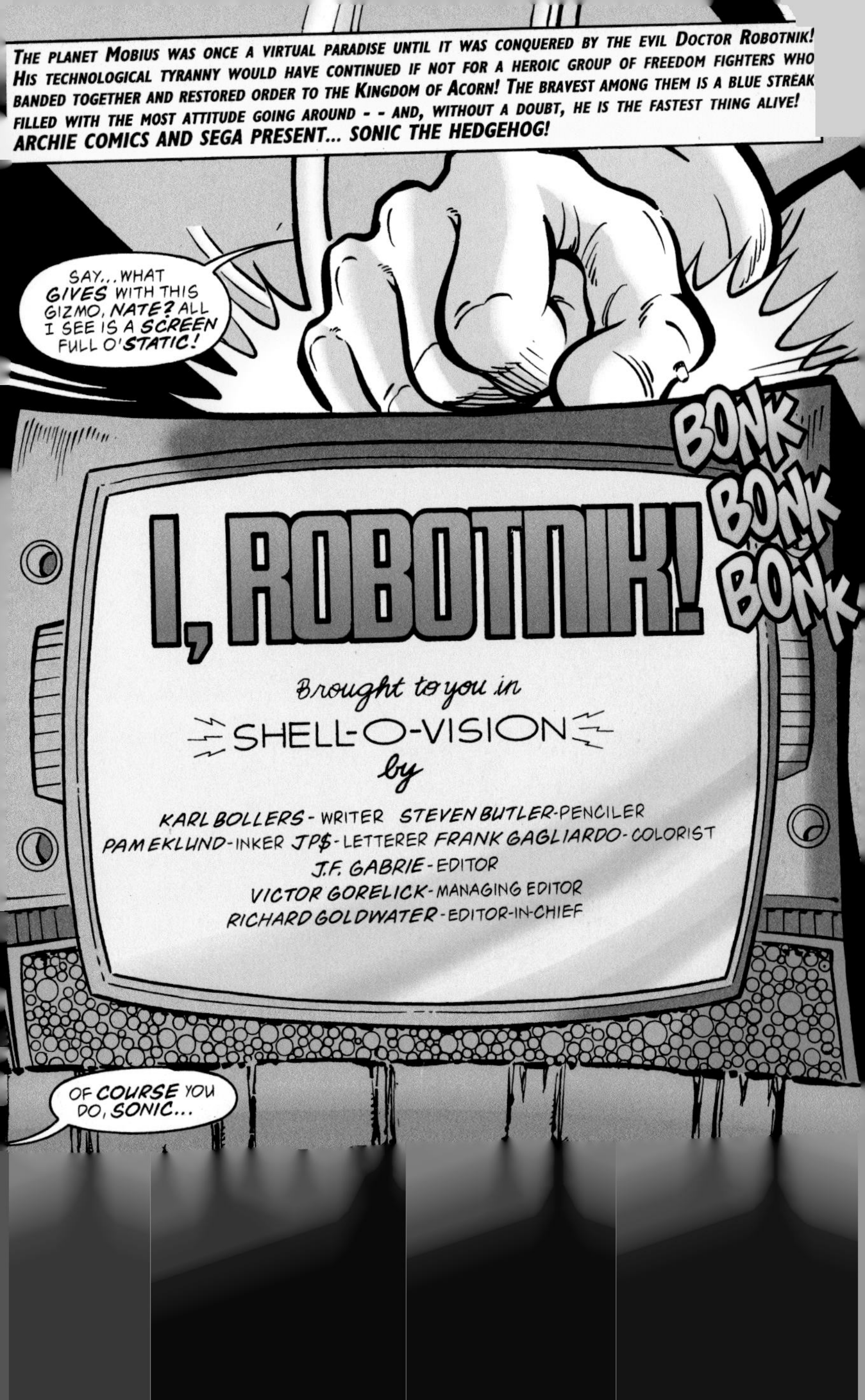

THE PLANET MOBIUS WAS ONCE A VIRTUAL PARADISE UNTIL IT WAS CONQUERED BY THE EVIL DOCTOR ROBOTNIK! HIS TECHNOLOGICAL TYRANNY WOULD HAVE CONTINUED IF NOT FOR A HEROIC GROUP OF FREEDOM FIGHTERS WHO BANDED TOGETHER AND RESTORED ORDER TO THE KINGDOM OF ACORN! THE BRAVEST AMONG THEM IS A BLUE STREAK FILLED WITH THE MOST ATTITUDE GOING AROUND - - AND, WITHOUT A DOUBT, HE IS THE FASTEST THING ALIVE!
ARCHIE COMICS AND SEGA PRESENT... SONIC THE HEDGEHOG!
SAY...WHAT GIVES WITH THIS GIZMO, NATE? ALL I SEE IS A SCREEN FULL O'STATIC!
BONK BONK BONK
I, ROBOTNIK!
Brought to you in
SHELL-O-VISION
by
KARL BOLLERS - WRITER STEVEN BUTLER - PENCILER
PAM EKLUND - INKER JP$ - LETTERER FRANK GAGLIARDO - COLORIST
J.F. GABRIE - EDITOR
VICTOR GORELICK - MANAGING EDITOR
RICHARD GOLDWATER - EDITOR-IN-CHIEF
OF COURSE YOU DO, SONIC...

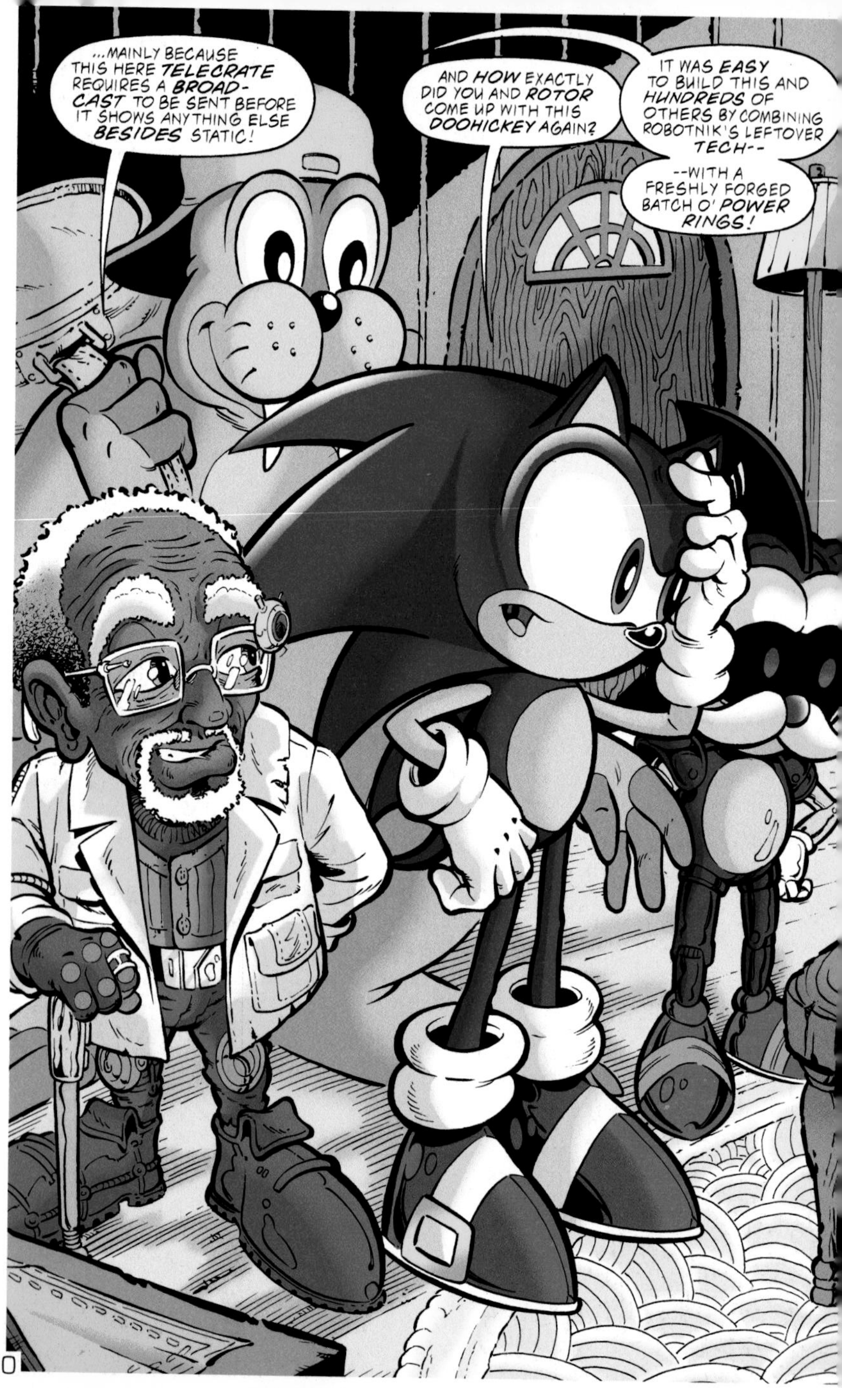
...MAINLY BECAUSE THIS HERE TELECRATE REQUIRES A BROAD-CAST TO BE SENT BEFORE IT SHOWS ANYTHING ELSE BESIDES STATIC!
AND HOW EXACTLY DID YOU AND ROTOR COME UP WITH THIS DOOHICKEY AGAIN?
IT WAS EASY TO BUILD THIS AND HUNDREDS OF OTHERS BY COMBINING ROBOTNIK'S LEFTOVER TECH--
--WITH A FRESHLY FORGED BATCH O' POWER RINGS!

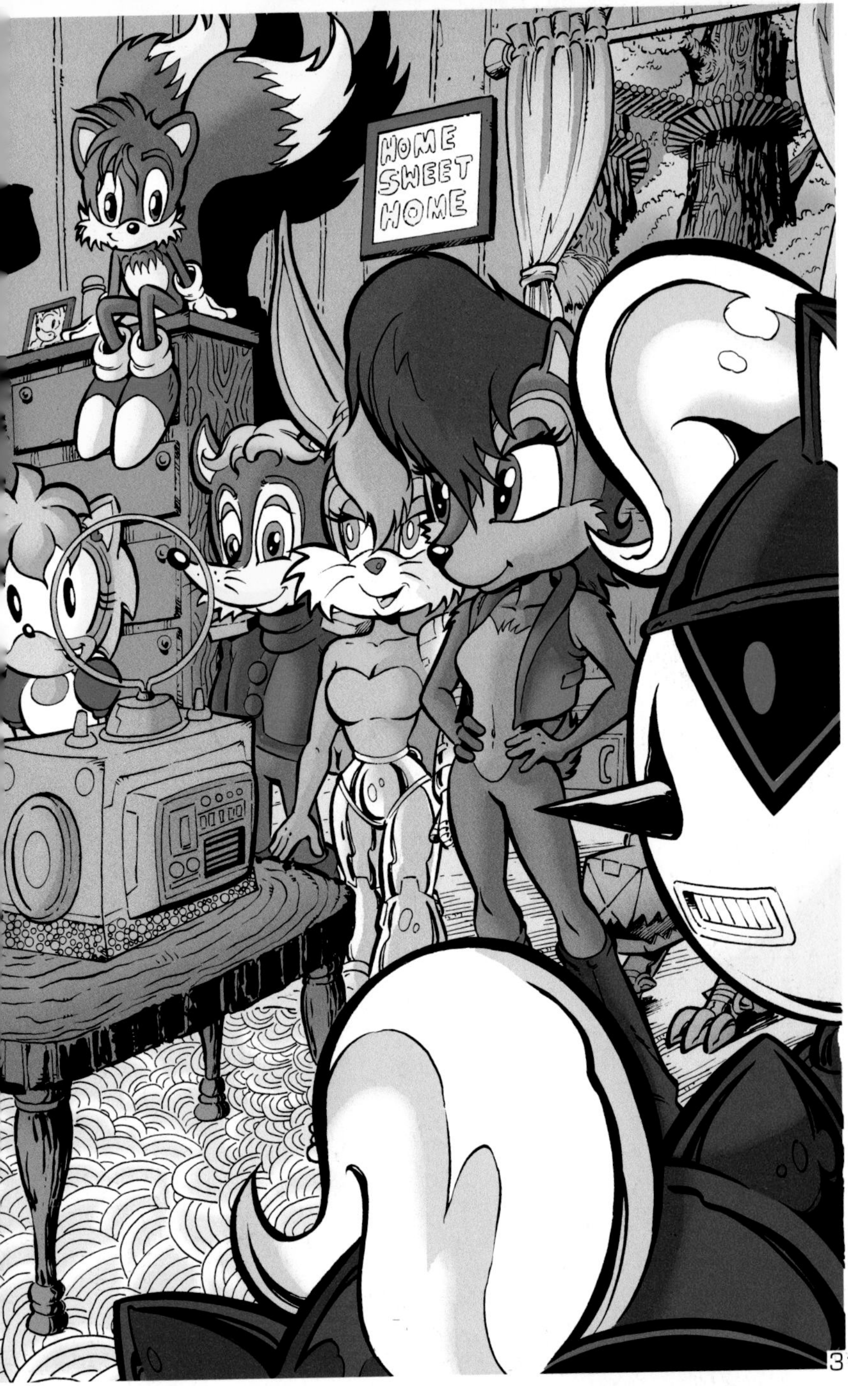
HOME SWEET HOME

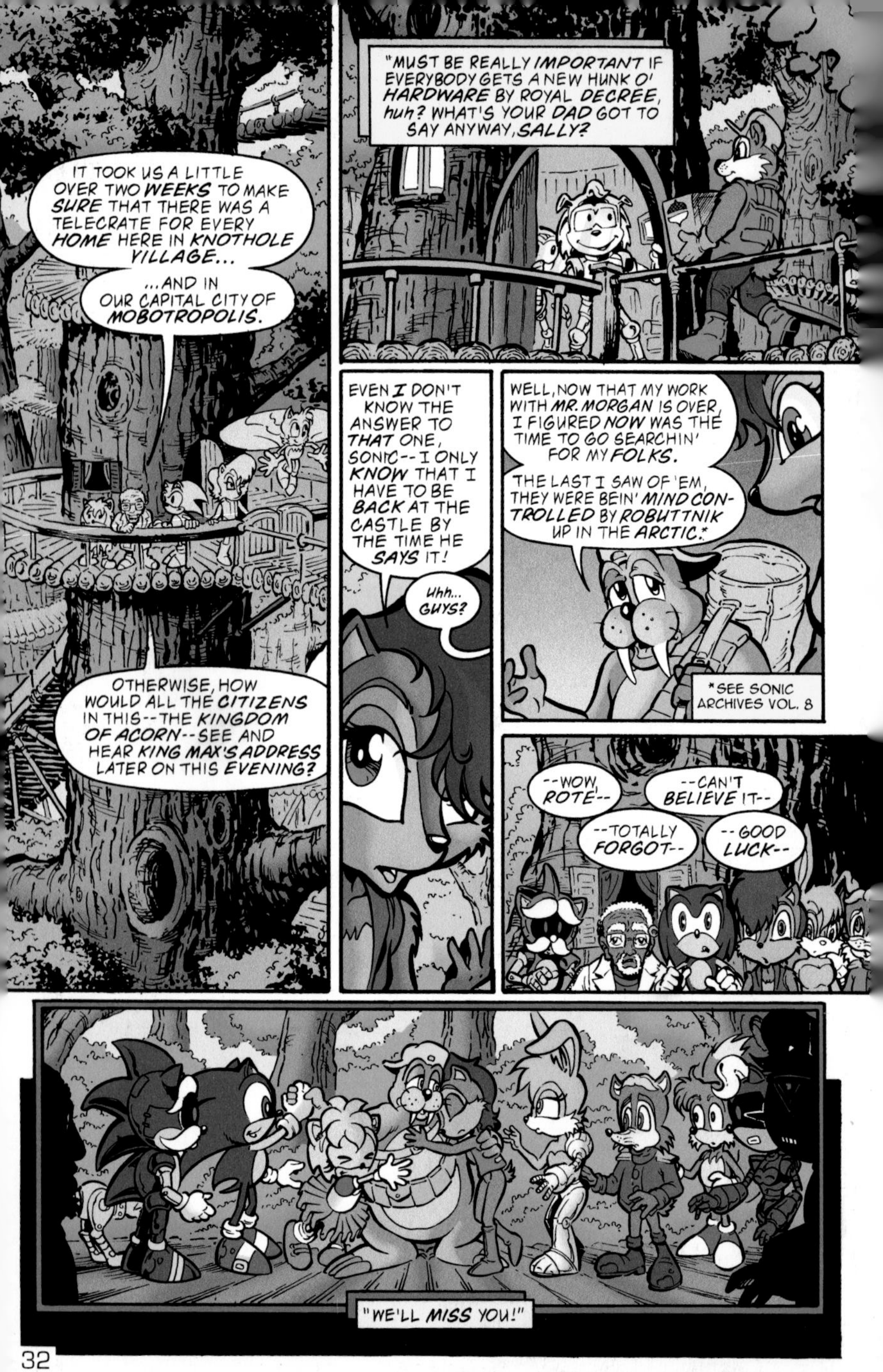
IT TOOK US A LITTLE OVER TWO WEEKS TO MAKE SURE THAT THERE WAS A TELECRATE FOR EVERY HOME HERE IN KNOTHOLE VILLAGE...
...AND IN OUR CAPITAL CITY OF MOBOTROPOLIS.
OTHERWISE, HOW WOULD ALL THE CITIZENS IN THIS--THE KINGDOM OF ACORN--SEE AND HEAR KING MAX'S ADDRESS LATER ON THIS EVENING?
"MUST BE REALLY IMPORTANT IF EVERYBODY GETS A NEW HUNK O' HARDWARE BY ROYAL DECREE, huh? WHAT'S YOUR DAD GOT TO SAY ANYWAY, SALLY?
EVEN I DON'T KNOW THE ANSWER TO THAT ONE, SONIC--I ONLY KNOW THAT I HAVE TO BE BACK AT THE CASTLE BY THE TIME HE SAYS IT!
Uhh... GUYS?
WELL, NOW THAT MY WORK WITH MR. MORGAN IS OVER, I FIGURED NOW WAS THE TIME TO GO SEARCHIN' FOR MY FOLKS.
THE LAST I SAW OF 'EM, THEY WERE BEIN' MIND CONTROLLED BY ROBUTTNIK UP IN THE ARCTIC.*
*SEE SONIC ARCHIVES VOL. 8
--WOW, ROTE--
--CAN'T BELIEVE IT--
--TOTALLY FORGOT--
--GOOD LUCK--
"WE'LL MISS YOU!"

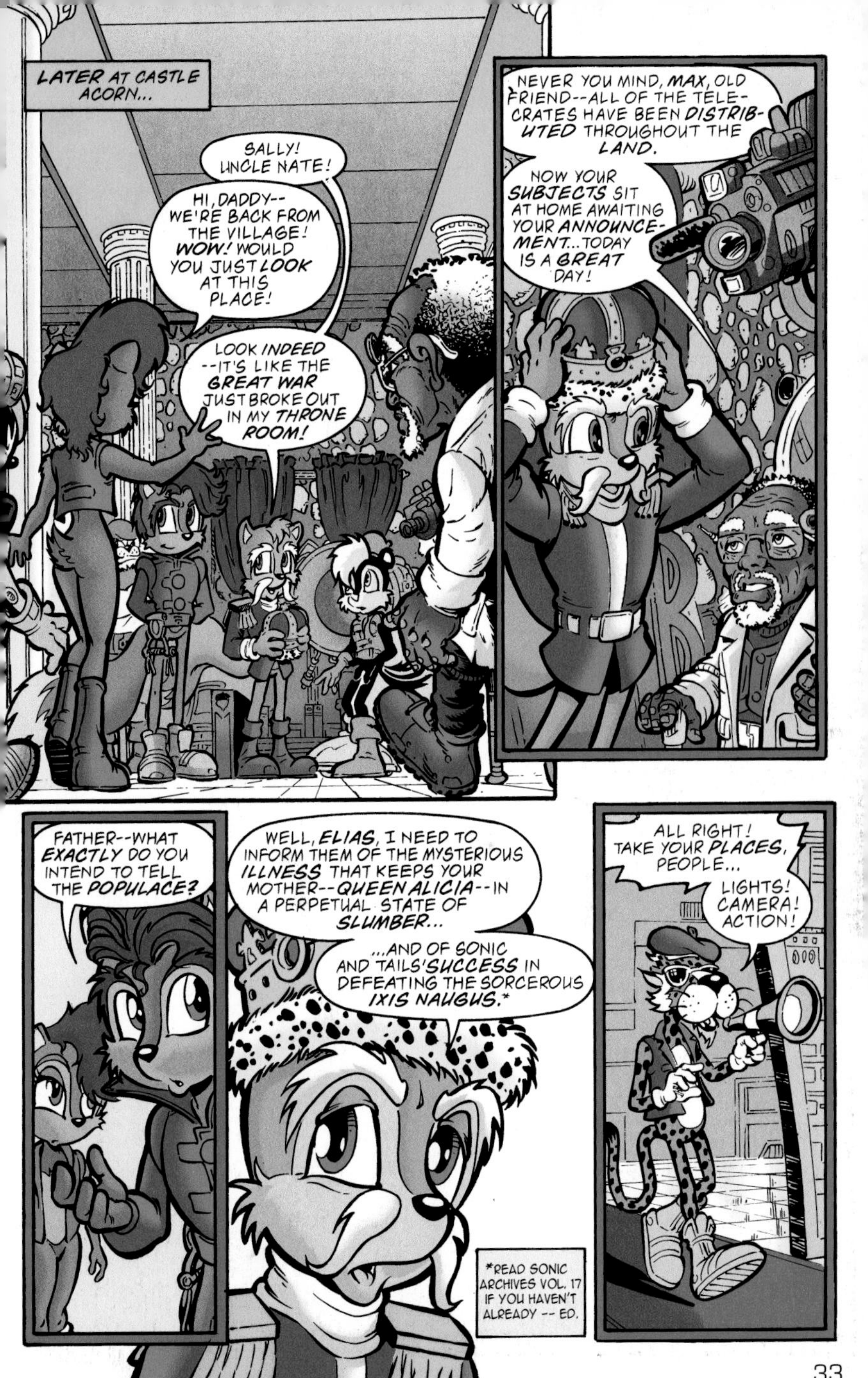
LATER AT CASTLE ACORN...
SALLY! UNCLE NATE!
HI, DADDY-- WE'RE BACK FROM THE VILLAGE! WOW! WOULD YOU JUST LOOK AT THIS PLACE!
LOOK INDEED --IT'S LIKE THE GREAT WAR JUST BROKE OUT IN MY THRONE ROOM!
NEVER YOU MIND, MAX, OLD FRIEND--ALL OF THE TELE-CRATES HAVE BEEN DISTRIB-UTED THROUGHOUT THE LAND.
NOW YOUR SUBJECTS SIT AT HOME AWAITING YOUR ANNOUNCE-MENT...TODAY IS A GREAT DAY!
FATHER--WHAT EXACTLY DO YOU INTEND TO TELL THE POPULACE?
WELL, ELIAS, I NEED TO INFORM THEM OF THE MYSTERIOUS ILLNESS THAT KEEPS YOUR MOTHER--QUEEN ALICIA--IN A PERPETUAL STATE OF SLUMBER...
...AND OF SONIC AND TAILS' SUCCESS IN DEFEATING THE SORCEROUS IXIS NAUGUS.*
*READ SONIC ARCHIVES VOL. 17 IF YOU HAVEN'T ALREADY -- ED.
ALL RIGHT! TAKE YOUR PLACES, PEOPLE...
LIGHTS! CAMERA! ACTION!

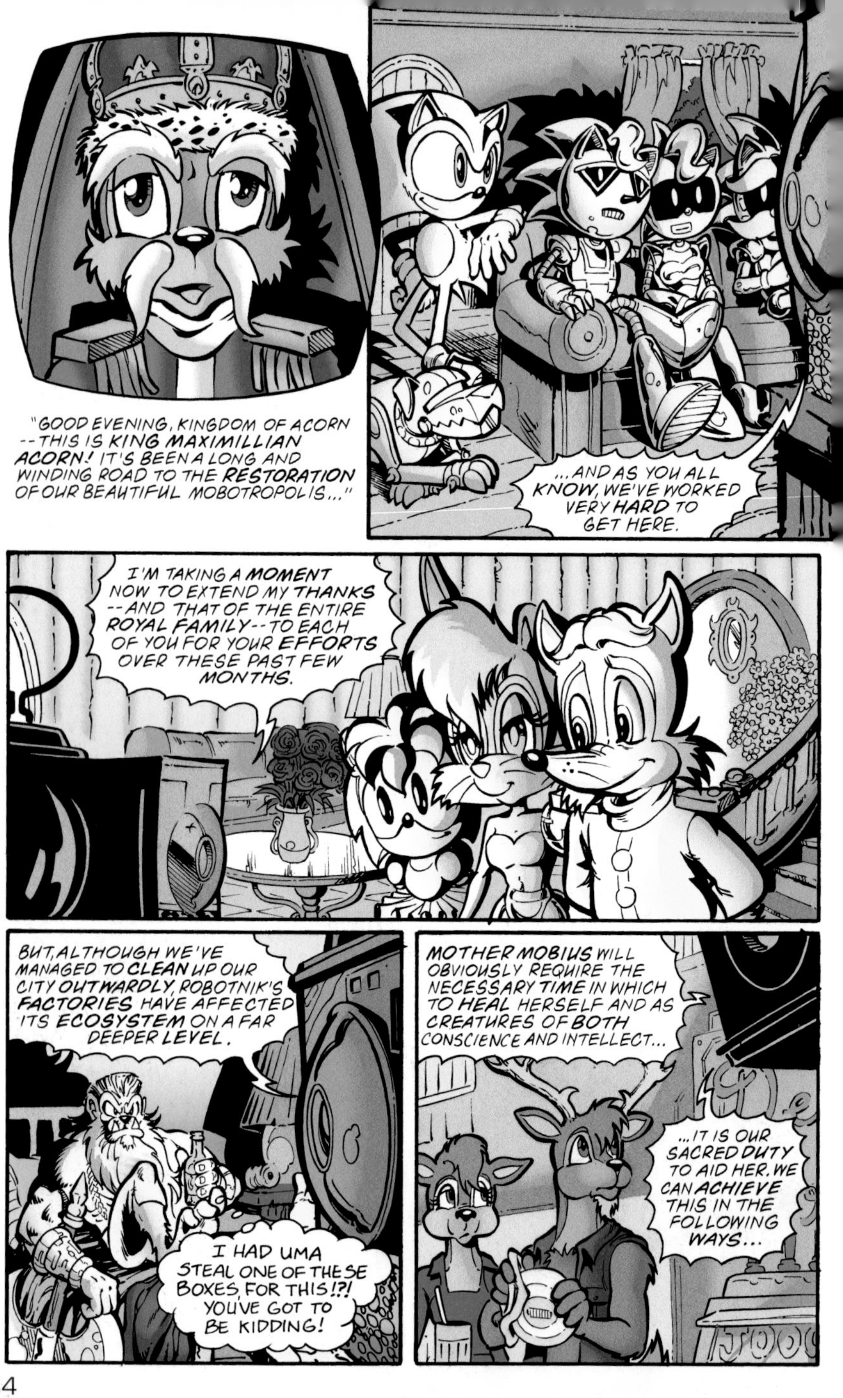
"GOOD EVENING, KINGDOM OF ACORN --THIS IS KING MAXIMILLIAN ACORN! IT'S BEEN A LONG AND WINDING ROAD TO THE RESTORATION OF OUR BEAUTIFUL MOBOTROPOLIS..."
...AND AS YOU ALL KNOW, WE'VE WORKED VERY HARD TO GET HERE.
I'M TAKING A MOMENT NOW TO EXTEND MY THANKS --AND THAT OF THE ENTIRE ROYAL FAMILY--TO EACH OF YOU FOR YOUR EFFORTS OVER THESE PAST FEW MONTHS.
BUT, ALTHOUGH WE'VE MANAGED TO CLEAN UP OUR CITY OUTWARDLY, ROBOTNIK'S FACTORIES HAVE AFFECTED ITS ECOSYSTEM ON A FAR DEEPER LEVEL.
I HAD UMA STEAL ONE OF THESE BOXES, FOR THIS!?! YOU'VE GOT TO BE KIDDING!
MOTHER MOBIUS WILL OBVIOUSLY REQUIRE THE NECESSARY TIME IN WHICH TO HEAL HERSELF AND AS CREATURES OF BOTH CONSCIENCE AND INTELLECT...
...IT IS OUR SACRED DUTY TO AID HER. WE CAN ACHIEVE THIS IN THE FOLLOWING WAYS...

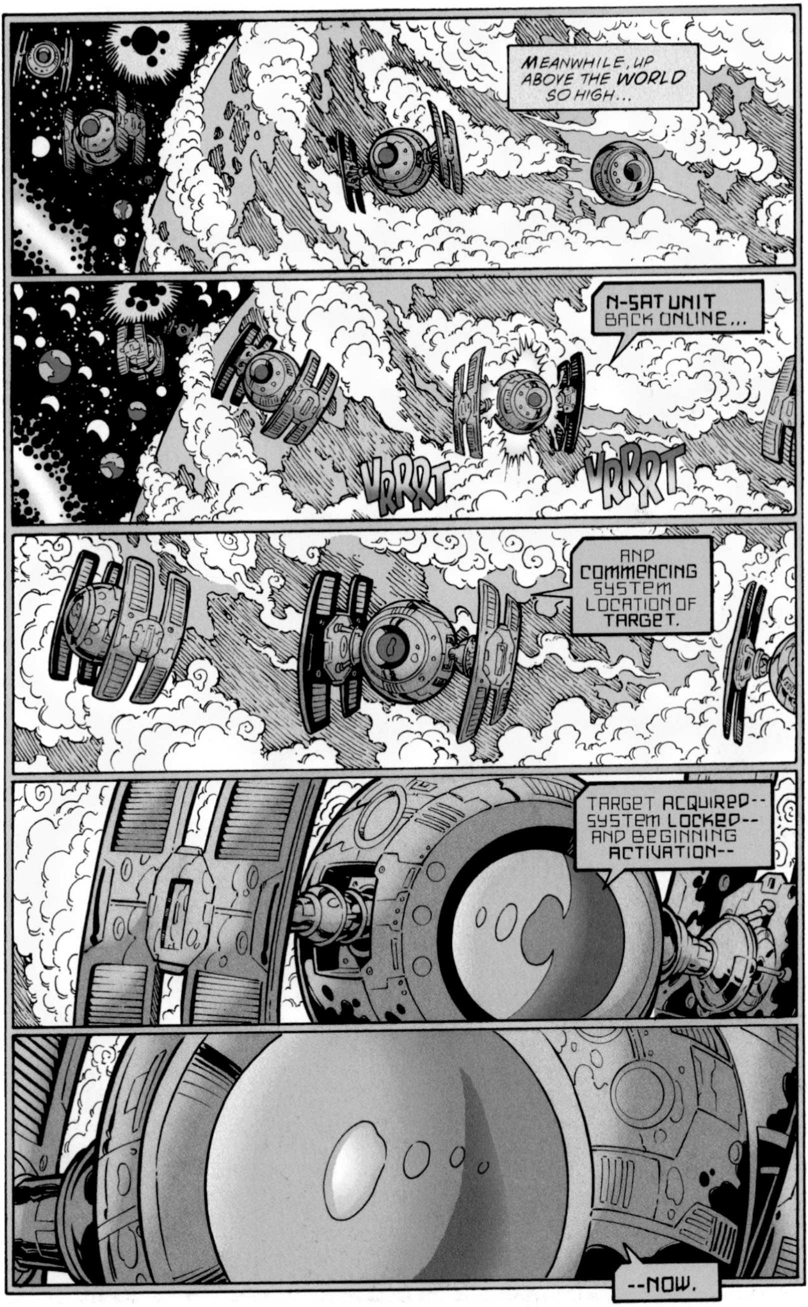
MEANWHILE, UP ABOVE THE WORLD SO HIGH...
N-SAT UNIT BACK ONLINE...
VRRRT
VRRRT
AND COMMENCING SYSTEM LOCATION OF TARGET.
TARGET ACQUIRED--SYSTEM LOCKED--AND BEGINNING ACTIVATION--
--NOW.

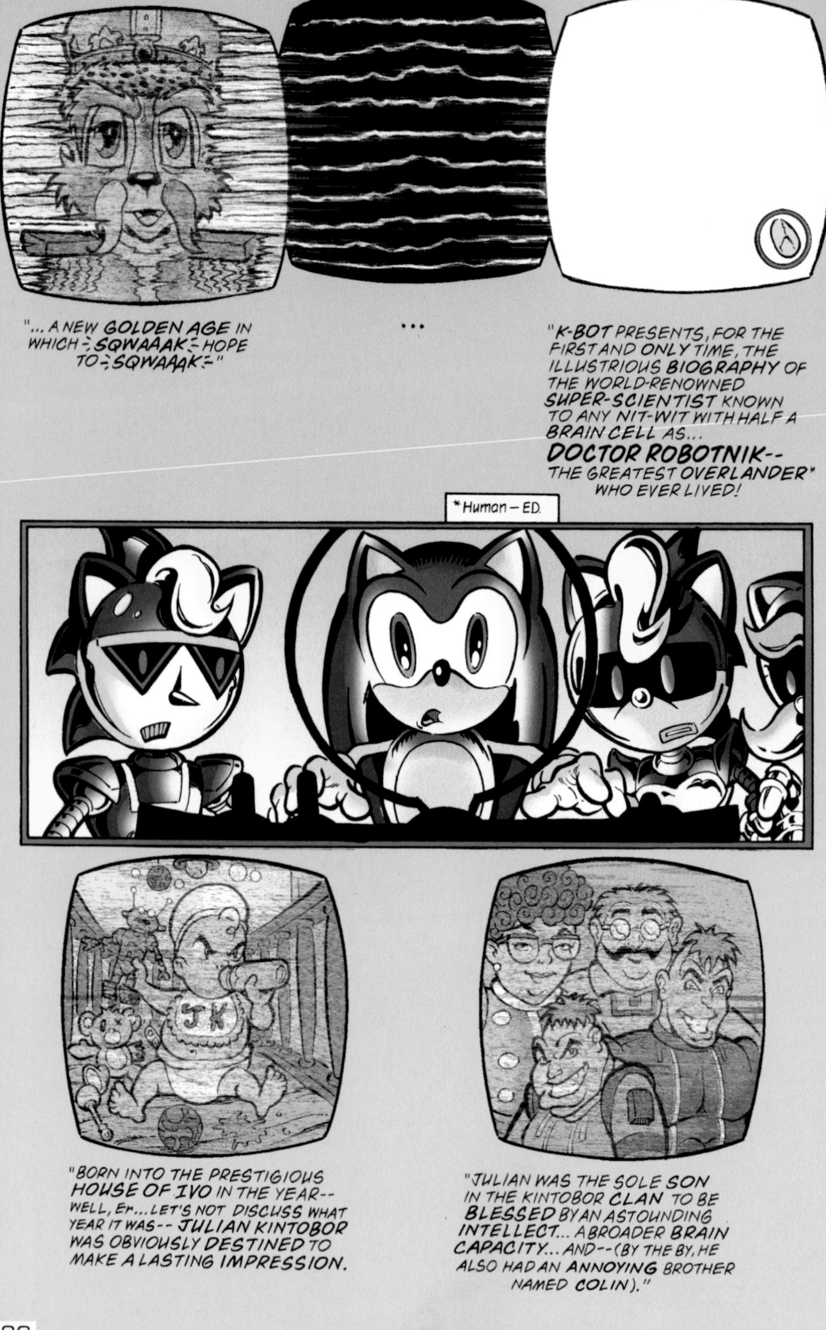
"... A NEW GOLDEN AGE IN WHICH -SQWAAAK- HOPE TO -SQWAAAK-"
...
"K-BOT PRESENTS, FOR THE FIRST AND ONLY TIME, THE ILLUSTRIOUS BIOGRAPHY OF THE WORLD-RENOWNED SUPER-SCIENTIST KNOWN TO ANY NIT-WIT WITH HALF A BRAIN CELL AS... DOCTOR ROBOTNIK-- THE GREATEST OVERLANDER* WHO EVER LIVED!
*Human – ED.
"BORN INTO THE PRESTIGIOUS HOUSE OF IVO IN THE YEAR-- WELL, Er... LET'S NOT DISCUSS WHAT YEAR IT WAS-- JULIAN KINTOBOR WAS OBVIOUSLY DESTINED TO MAKE A LASTING IMPRESSION.
"JULIAN WAS THE SOLE SON IN THE KINTOBOR CLAN TO BE BLESSED BY AN ASTOUNDING INTELLECT... A BROADER BRAIN CAPACITY... AND--(BY THE BY, HE ALSO HAD AN ANNOYING BROTHER NAMED COLIN)."

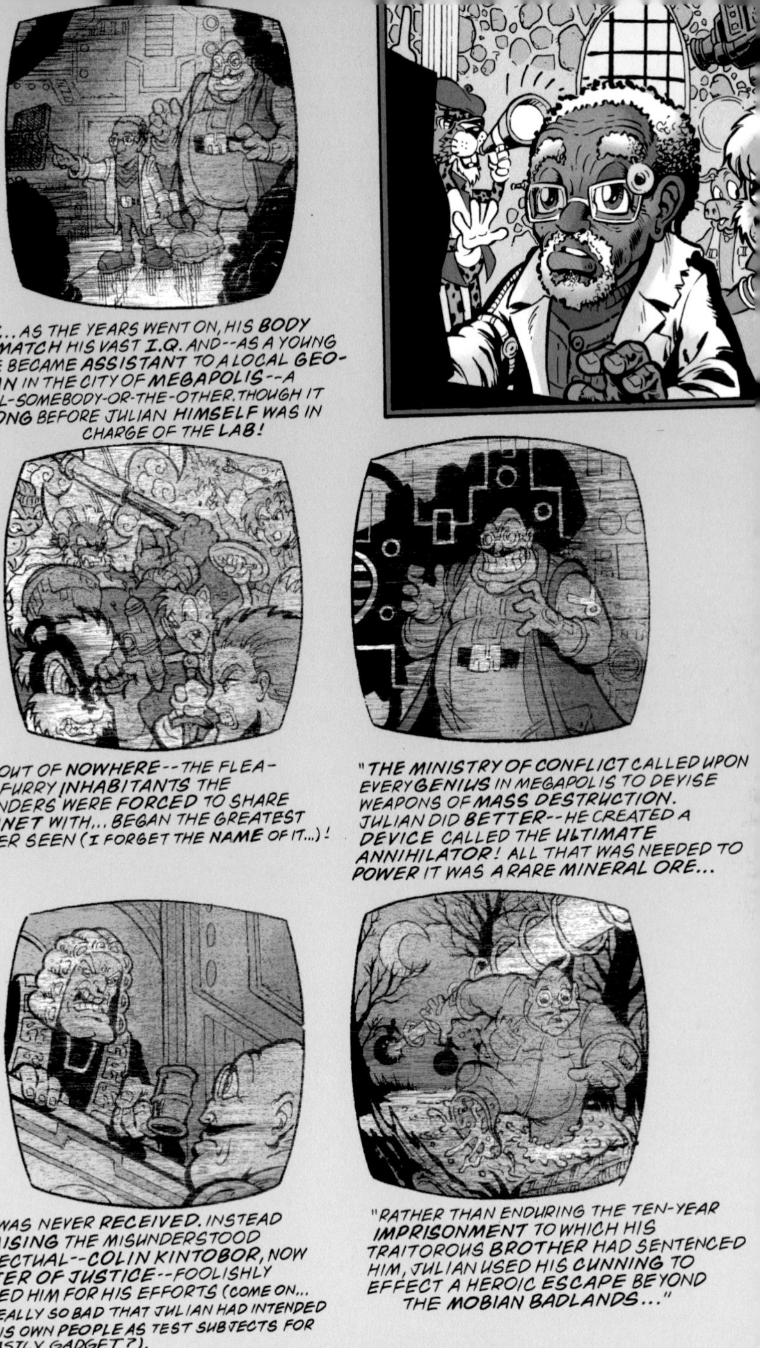
"ANYWAY... AS THE YEARS WENT ON, HIS BODY GREW TO MATCH HIS VAST I.Q. AND--AS A YOUNG MAN--HE BECAME ASSISTANT TO A LOCAL GEO-PHYSICIAN IN THE CITY OF MEGAPOLIS--A NATHANIEL-SOMEBODY-OR-THE-OTHER. THOUGH IT WASN'T LONG BEFORE JULIAN HIMSELF WAS IN CHARGE OF THE LAB!
"THEN--OUT OF NOWHERE--THE FLEA-BITTEN, FURRY INHABITANTS THE OVERLANDERS WERE FORCED TO SHARE THE PLANET WITH... BEGAN THE GREATEST WAR EVER SEEN (I FORGET THE NAME OF IT...)!
"THE MINISTRY OF CONFLICT CALLED UPON EVERY GENIUS IN MEGAPOLIS TO DEVISE WEAPONS OF MASS DESTRUCTION. JULIAN DID BETTER--HE CREATED A DEVICE CALLED THE ULTIMATE ANNIHILATOR! ALL THAT WAS NEEDED TO POWER IT WAS A RARE MINERAL ORE...
"...THAT WAS NEVER RECEIVED. INSTEAD OF PRAISING THE MISUNDERSTOOD INTELLECTUAL--COLIN KINTOBOR, NOW MINISTER OF JUSTICE--FOOLISHLY PUNISHED HIM FOR HIS EFFORTS (COME ON... WAS IT REALLY SO BAD THAT JULIAN HAD INTENDED TO USE HIS OWN PEOPLE AS TEST SUBJECTS FOR THE GHASTLY GADGET?).
"RATHER THAN ENDURING THE TEN-YEAR IMPRISONMENT TO WHICH HIS TRAITOROUS BROTHER HAD SENTENCED HIM, JULIAN USED HIS CUNNING TO EFFECT A HEROIC ESCAPE BEYOND THE MOBIAN BADLANDS..."

"...WHERE HE WAS FOUND BY TWO MOBIAN *SAVAGES.* THEY DIDN'T DO HIM ANY *HARM*--THEY WERE HEDGEHOGS--NO *REAL* THREAT! AS A MATTER OF *FACT*...

"...THEY TOOK HIM TO THEIR *LEADER*-- KING MAX! NOW HERE WAS A *SUCKER* WHO COULD SPOT GREATNESS IN A *SPLIT-SECOND.* IT WASN'T LONG BEFORE OL' MAXIE PRACTICALLY HANDED OVER CONTROL OF HIS *REALM* TO JULIAN!

"FIRST THAT WASH-UP OF A *WARLORD*-- *KODOS*--WAS ORDERED TO INSTRUCT THE NEW *ARRIVAL* IN THE ART OF *WARFARE.* AFTER ALL, WHO KNEW THE OVERLANDERS' *WEAKNESSES* BETTER THAN JULIAN?

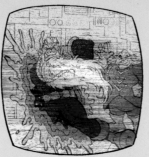

"AND SECOND, IT WAS JULIAN WHO *REPLACED* KODOS AFTER *LEARNING* EVERYTHING HE HAD TO *TEACH.* GO AHEAD AND *ASK* YOURSELVES--*WASN'T HE* THE BEST MAN FOR THE *JOB*?"

"FOR THE FIRST *TIME*, THE INFERIOR MOBIAN *GROUND TROOPS* HAD THE NECESSARY *BRAINS AND BRAWN* REQUIRED TO SHIFT THE WAR IN MOBOTROPOLIS' *FAVOR*.

"DAYS *LATER*, JULIAN'S DIM-WIT NEPHEW-- *SNIVELY*--ARRIVED AT THE *WAR MINISTRY BUILDING* TO PLEDGE HIS ALLEGIANCE TO HIS UNCLE.

"BUT JULIAN--NEVER *CONTENT* TO JUST REST ON HIS *LAURELS*-- DECIDED THAT *BEATING BACK* THE *OVERLANDERS* WASN'T *ENOUGH*. HE DESIRED NOW TO *REMODEL* THE FACE OF MOBIUS. IT WOULD TAKE AN *ARTIFICAL ARMY*...

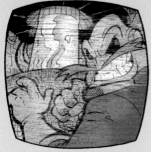

"...AND THE *SABOTAGE* OF SIR CHARLES HEDGEHOG'S *RO-BOTICIZER*, A NEWLY-INVENTED *DEVICE* THAT WAS SUPPOSED TO HELP CURE THE WOUNDED."

"AND SO, IT **WAS** ON THAT MORNING MORE THAN A **DECADE** AGO, A MASSIVE, METAL **FLAGSHIP** APPEARED OVER THE MOBOTROPOLIS SKYLINE, FOREVER ALTERING IT. AND WHO CLAIMED RESPONSIBILITY FOR THIS NEW INDUSTRIAL AGE? WAS IT JULIAN KINTOBOR? NO-- IT WAS...

"...DOCTOR ROBOTNIK-- THE GREATEST SCIENTIFIC **MIND** OF ALL TIME!

"BUT THERE WERE THE IGNORANT **FEW** WHO ADHERED TO THE WAYS OF **TRADITION** AND OPPOSED ROBOTNIK'S **REFORMS**-- THEY WERE **DEALT** WITH...

"...WHILE THE **OTHER** MOBIANS TOOK **ADVANTAGE** OF ALL THE NEW **JOBS** THAT THE GOOD DOCTOR HAD CREATED AND WILLINGLY **VOLUNTEERED** THEMSELVES TO UNDERGO THE **CHANGES** NEEDED TO WORK IN HIS POSH FACTORIES.

"AS IF BEING ABSOLUTE **RULER** OF AN ENTIRE WORLD WASN'T DIFFICULT ENOUGH, THERE WERE ALSO UPSTART **REBEL GROUPS** TO CONTEND WITH-- NOTABLY, SONIC THE HEDGEHOG AND HIS RABBLE ROUSERS!"

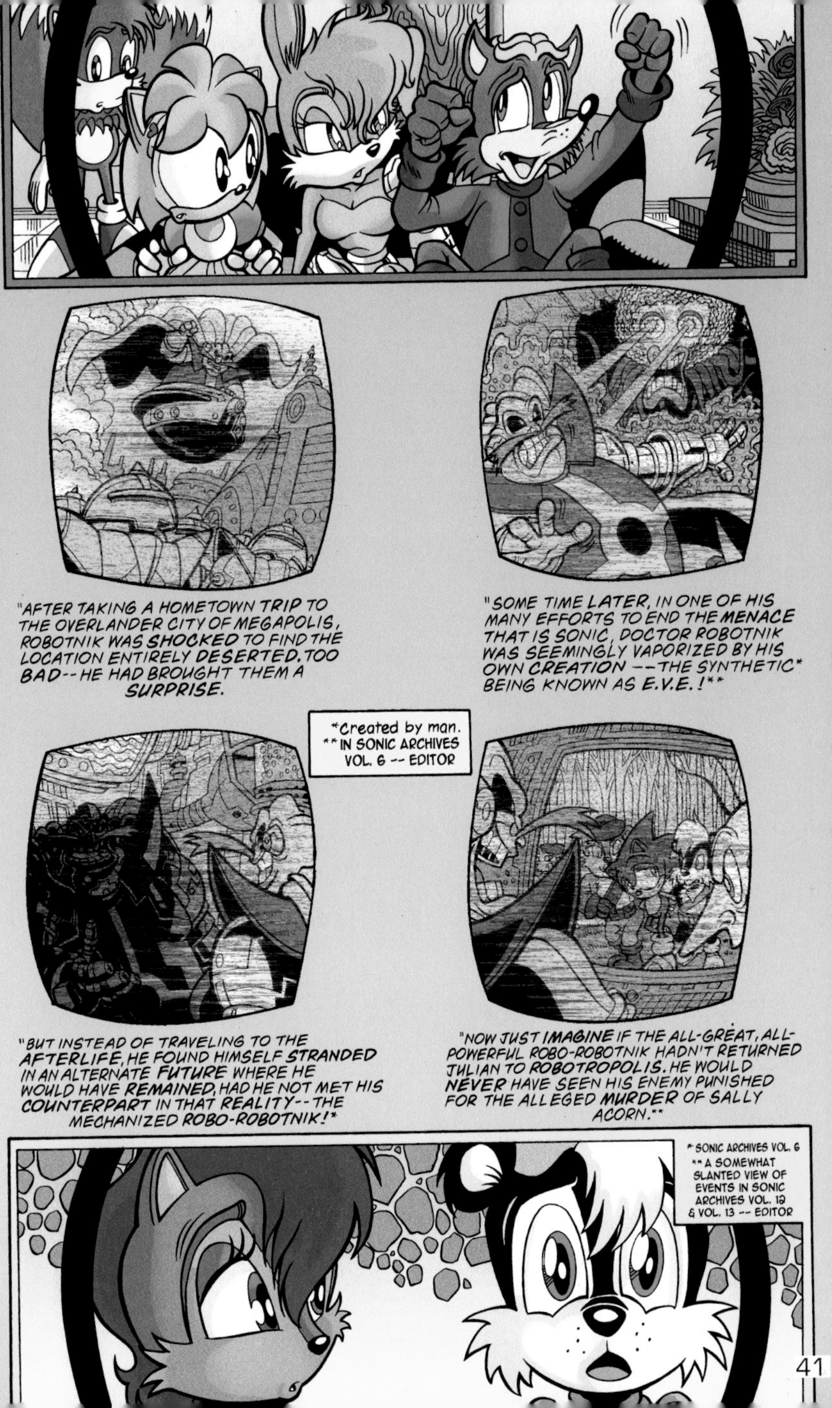
"AFTER TAKING A HOMETOWN TRIP TO THE OVERLANDER CITY OF MEGAPOLIS, ROBOTNIK WAS SHOCKED TO FIND THE LOCATION ENTIRELY DESERTED. TOO BAD--HE HAD BROUGHT THEM A SURPRISE.
"SOME TIME LATER, IN ONE OF HIS MANY EFFORTS TO END THE MENACE THAT IS SONIC, DOCTOR ROBOTNIK WAS SEEMINGLY VAPORIZED BY HIS OWN CREATION --THE SYNTHETIC* BEING KNOWN AS E.V.E.!**
*Created by man. ** IN SONIC ARCHIVES VOL. 6 -- EDITOR
"BUT INSTEAD OF TRAVELING TO THE AFTERLIFE, HE FOUND HIMSELF STRANDED IN AN ALTERNATE FUTURE WHERE HE WOULD HAVE REMAINED, HAD HE NOT MET HIS COUNTERPART IN THAT REALITY--THE MECHANIZED ROBO-ROBOTNIK!*
"NOW JUST IMAGINE IF THE ALL-GREAT, ALL-POWERFUL ROBO-ROBOTNIK HADN'T RETURNED JULIAN TO ROBOTROPOLIS. HE WOULD NEVER HAVE SEEN HIS ENEMY PUNISHED FOR THE ALLEGED MURDER OF SALLY ACORN.**
* SONIC ARCHIVES VOL. 6 ** A SOMEWHAT SLANTED VIEW OF EVENTS IN SONIC ARCHIVES VOL. 12 & VOL. 13 -- EDITOR

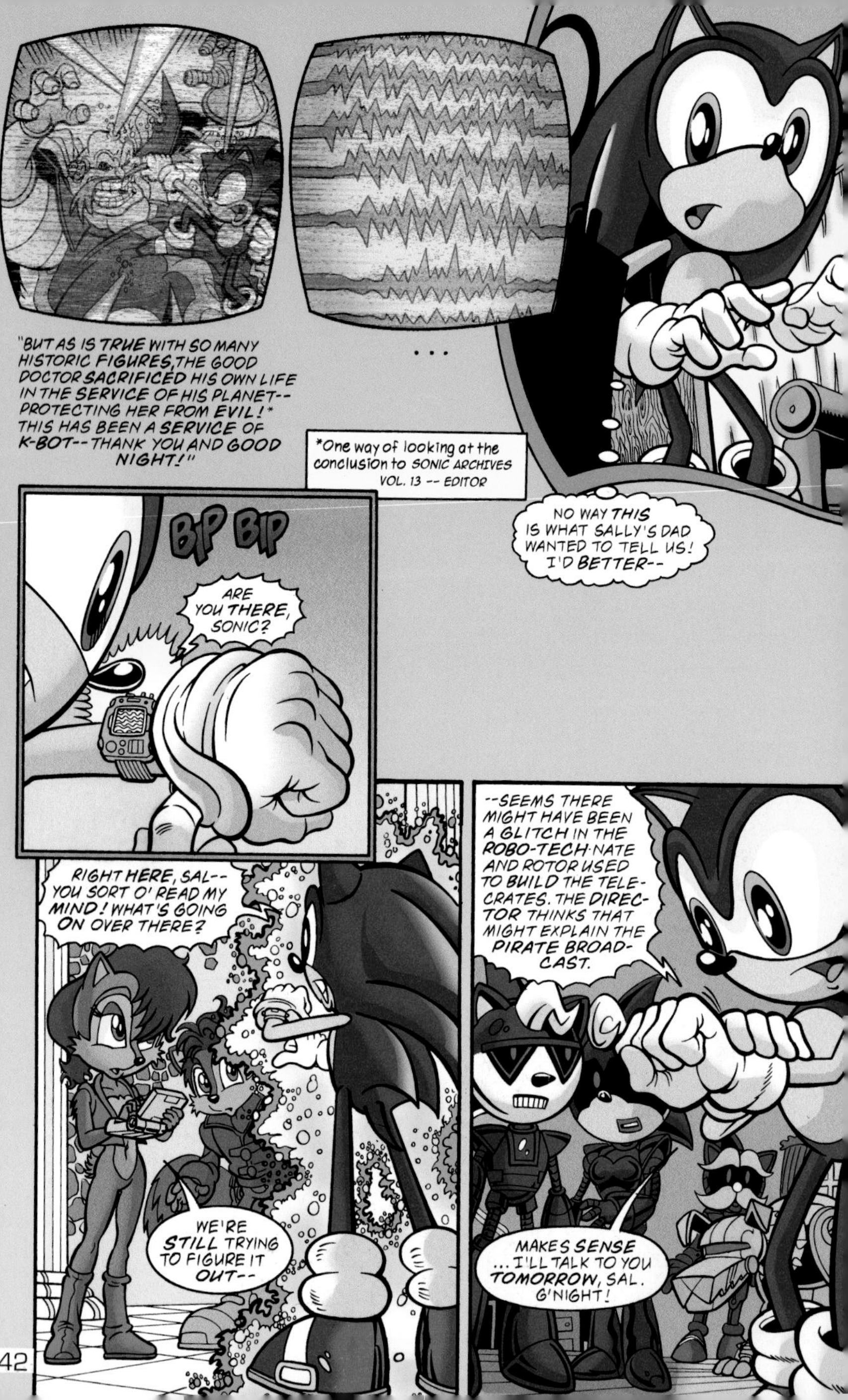

"BUT AS IS TRUE WITH SO MANY HISTORIC FIGURES, THE GOOD DOCTOR SACRIFICED HIS OWN LIFE IN THE SERVICE OF HIS PLANET-- PROTECTING HER FROM EVIL!* THIS HAS BEEN A SERVICE OF K-BOT-- THANK YOU AND GOOD NIGHT!"
. . .
*One way of looking at the conclusion to SONIC ARCHIVES VOL. 13 -- EDITOR
NO WAY THIS IS WHAT SALLY'S DAD WANTED TO TELL US! I'D BETTER--
BIP BIP
ARE YOU THERE, SONIC?
RIGHT HERE, SAL-- YOU SORT O' READ MY MIND! WHAT'S GOING ON OVER THERE?
WE'RE STILL TRYING TO FIGURE IT OUT--
--SEEMS THERE MIGHT HAVE BEEN A GLITCH IN THE ROBO-TECH NATE AND ROTOR USED TO BUILD THE TELE-CRATES. THE DIRECTOR THINKS THAT MIGHT EXPLAIN THE PIRATE BROADCAST.
MAKES SENSE ... I'LL TALK TO YOU TOMORROW, SAL. G'NIGHT!

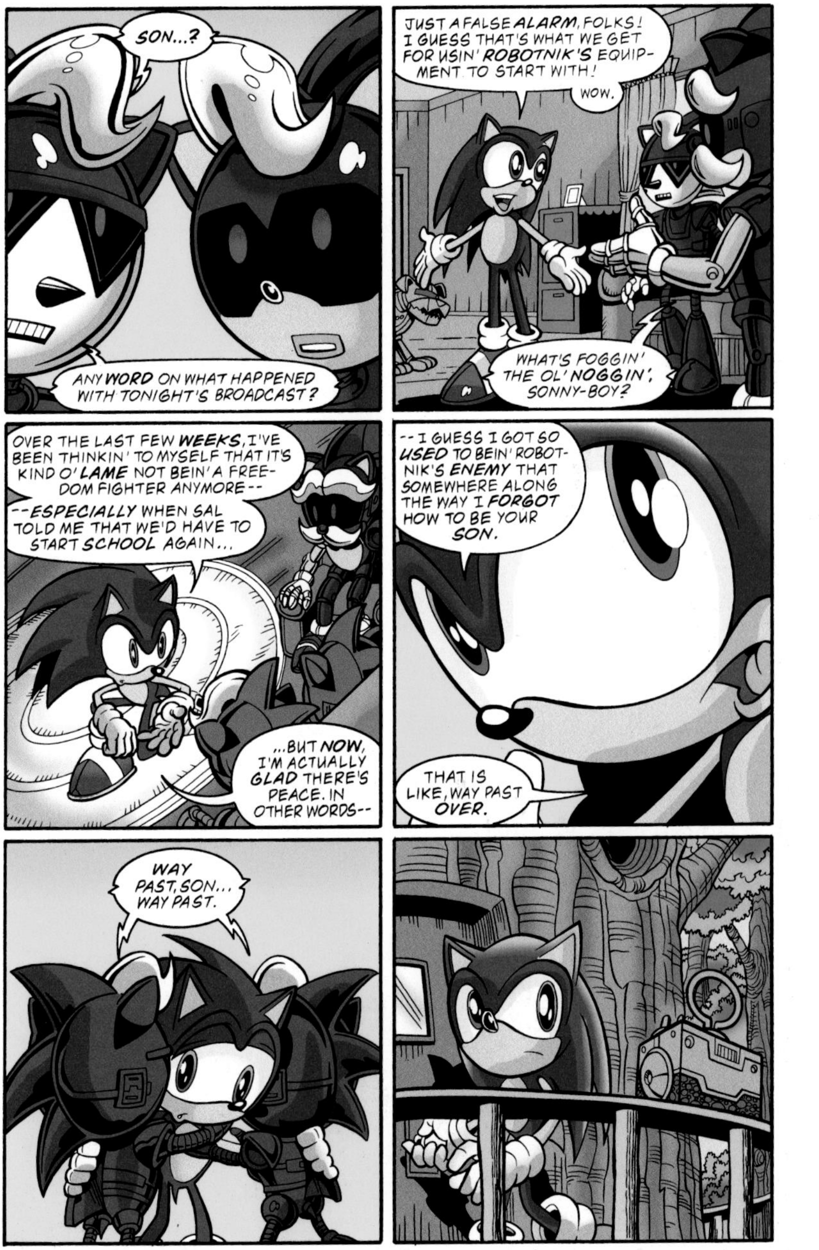
SON...?
ANY WORD ON WHAT HAPPENED WITH TONIGHT'S BROADCAST?
JUST A FALSE ALARM, FOLKS! I GUESS THAT'S WHAT WE GET FOR USIN' ROBOTNIK'S EQUIPMENT TO START WITH!
WOW.
WHAT'S FOGGIN' THE OL' NOGGIN', SONNY-BOY?
OVER THE LAST FEW WEEKS, I'VE BEEN THINKIN' TO MYSELF THAT IT'S KIND O' LAME NOT BEIN' A FREEDOM FIGHTER ANYMORE--
--ESPECIALLY WHEN SAL TOLD ME THAT WE'D HAVE TO START SCHOOL AGAIN...
...BUT NOW, I'M ACTUALLY GLAD THERE'S PEACE. IN OTHER WORDS--
--I GUESS I GOT SO USED TO BEIN' ROBOTNIK'S ENEMY THAT SOMEWHERE ALONG THE WAY I FORGOT HOW TO BE YOUR SON.
THAT IS LIKE, WAY PAST OVER.
WAY PAST, SON... WAY PAST.

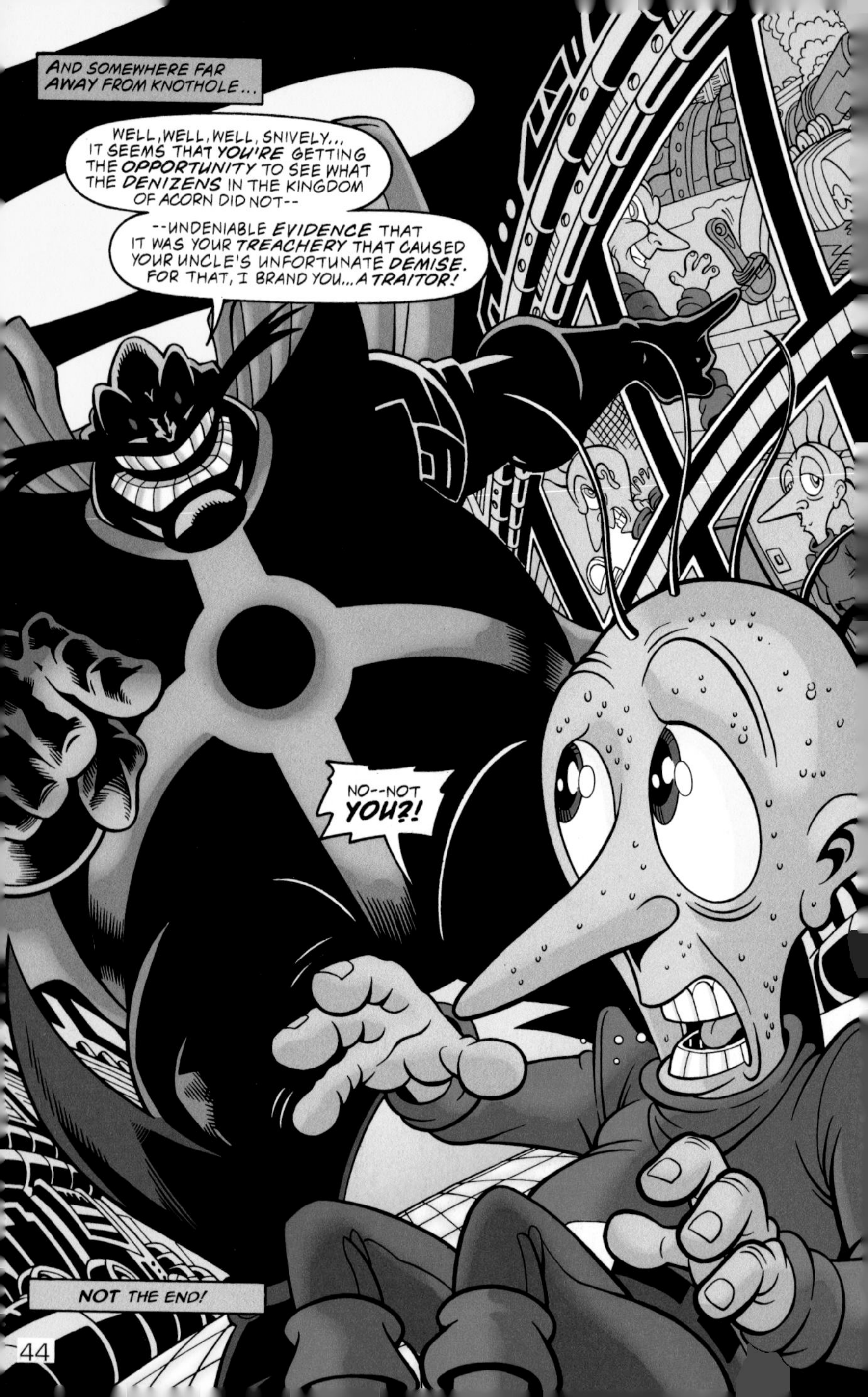
AND SOMEWHERE FAR AWAY FROM KNOTHOLE...
WELL, WELL, WELL, SNIVELY... IT SEEMS THAT YOU'RE GETTING THE OPPORTUNITY TO SEE WHAT THE DENIZENS IN THE KINGDOM OF ACORN DID NOT--
--UNDENIABLE EVIDENCE THAT IT WAS YOUR TREACHERY THAT CAUSED YOUR UNCLE'S UNFORTUNATE DEMISE. FOR THAT, I BRAND YOU... A TRAITOR!
NO--NOT YOU?!
NOT THE END!

TALES OF THE GREAT WAR

PART ONE

"SINCE THE TIME OF *ALEXANDER*, MOBIANS LIVED IN RELATIVE PEACE AND TRANQUILITY.

"OF ALL WHO DWELLED IN THE LANDS SURROUNDING THE KINGDOM, THE MOST *MYSTERIOUS* WERE THE *OVERLANDERS*.

KEN PENDERS	WRITER
ART MAWHINNY	PENCILER
JIM AMASH	INKER
BARRY GROSSMAN	COLORIST
JEFF POWELL	LETTERER
J.F. GABRIE	EDITOR

"*CONTACT* WITH THEM WAS FEW AND FAR BETWEEN, AND QUITE *BENIGN*, UNTIL ONE FATEFUL DAY, WHEN *PRINCE EMERSON* STOOD FACING A YOUNG OVERLANDER BOY ACROSS *ROUNDABOUT CREEK*...

HELLO!

WHO ARE YOU?

THE SHOT HEARD ROUND THE WORLD!

45

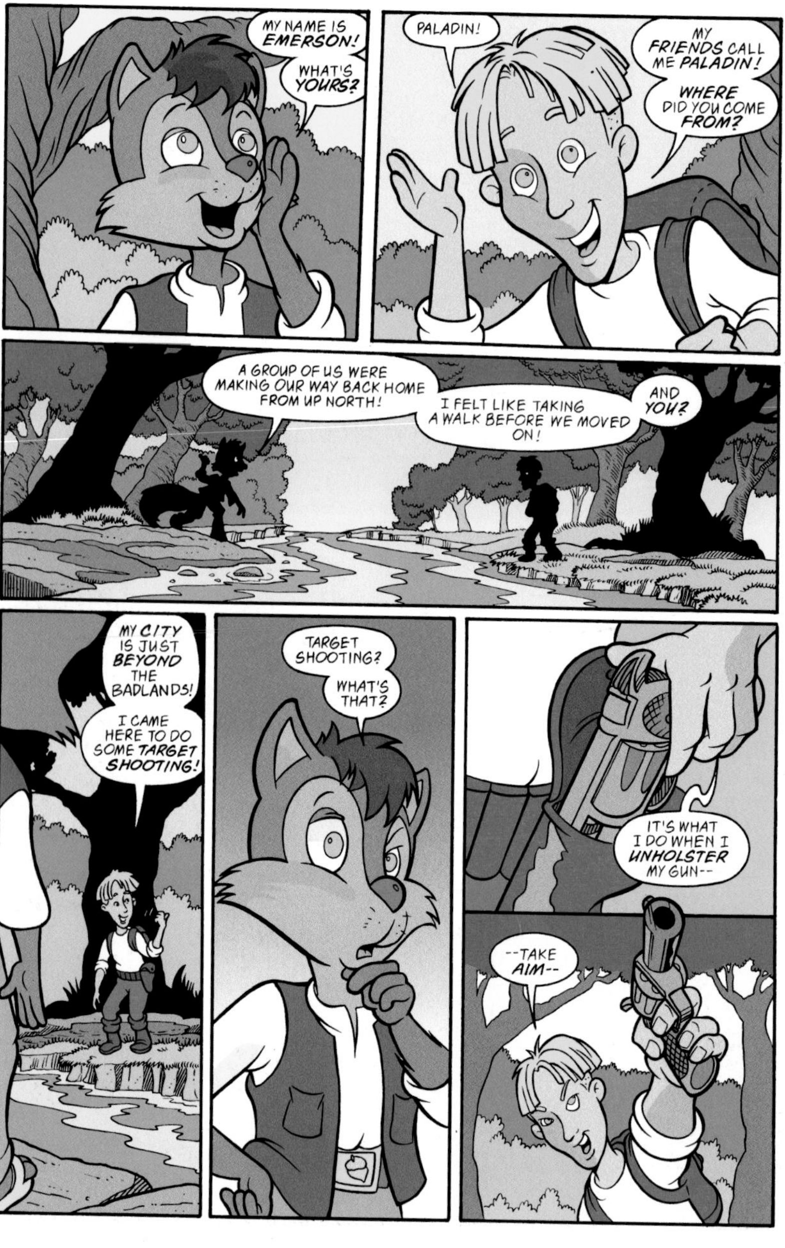
MY NAME IS EMERSON!
WHAT'S YOURS?
PALADIN!
MY FRIENDS CALL ME PALADIN!
WHERE DID YOU COME FROM?
A GROUP OF US WERE MAKING OUR WAY BACK HOME FROM UP NORTH!
I FELT LIKE TAKING A WALK BEFORE WE MOVED ON!
AND YOU?
MY CITY IS JUST BEYOND THE BADLANDS!
I CAME HERE TO DO SOME TARGET SHOOTING!
TARGET SHOOTING?
WHAT'S THAT?
IT'S WHAT I DO WHEN I UNHOLSTER MY GUN--
--TAKE AIM--

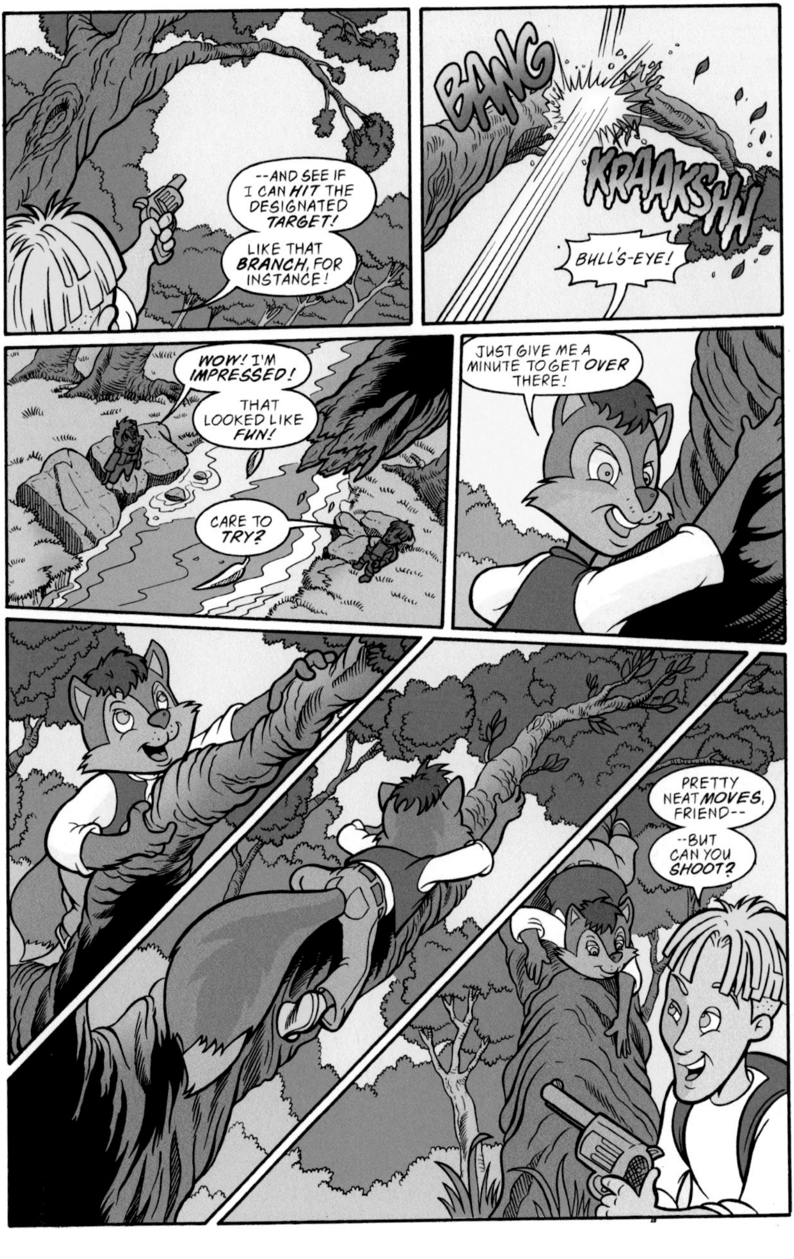
--AND SEE IF I CAN HIT THE DESIGNATED TARGET!
LIKE THAT BRANCH, FOR INSTANCE!
BANG
KRAAKSHH
BULL'S-EYE!
WOW! I'M IMPRESSED!
THAT LOOKED LIKE FUN!
CARE TO TRY?
JUST GIVE ME A MINUTE TO GET OVER THERE!
PRETTY NEAT MOVES, FRIEND--
--BUT CAN YOU SHOOT?

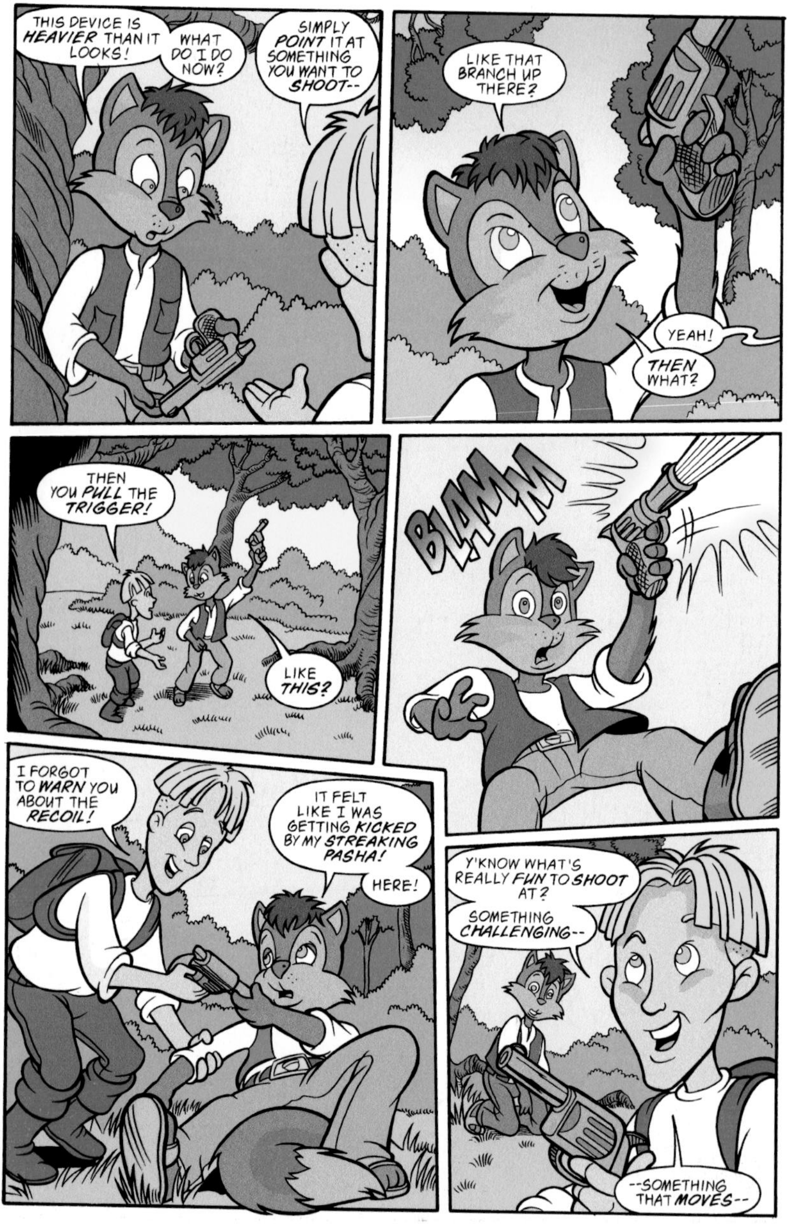
THIS DEVICE IS HEAVIER THAN IT LOOKS!
WHAT DO I DO NOW?
SIMPLY POINT IT AT SOMETHING YOU WANT TO SHOOT--
LIKE THAT BRANCH UP THERE?
YEAH!
THEN WHAT?
THEN YOU PULL THE TRIGGER!
LIKE THIS?
BLAMM
I FORGOT TO WARN YOU ABOUT THE RECOIL!
IT FELT LIKE I WAS GETTING KICKED BY MY STREAKING PASHA!
HERE!
Y'KNOW WHAT'S REALLY FUN TO SHOOT AT?
SOMETHING CHALLENGING--
--SOMETHING THAT MOVES--

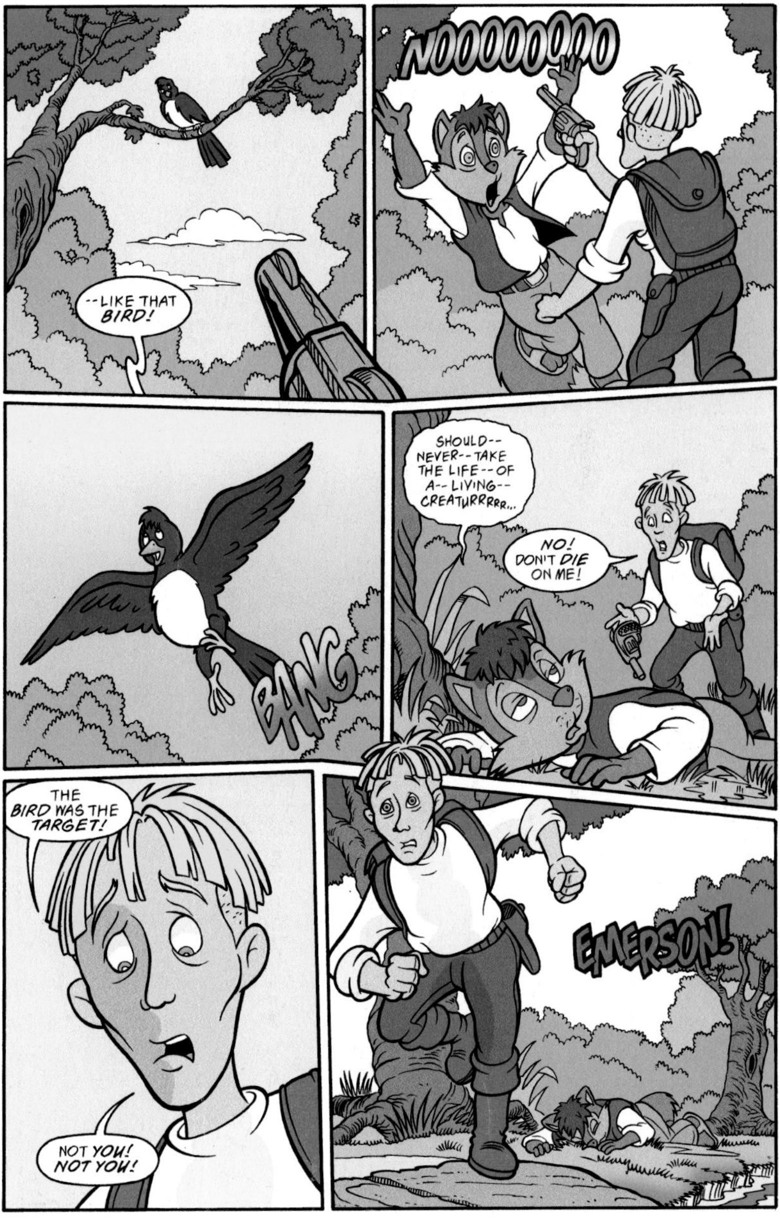
--LIKE THAT BIRD!
NOOOOOOOO
BANG
SHOULD-- NEVER--TAKE THE LIFE--OF A--LIVING-- CREATURRRRR...
NO! DON'T DIE ON ME!
THE BIRD WAS THE TARGET!
NOT YOU! NOT YOU!
EMERSON!

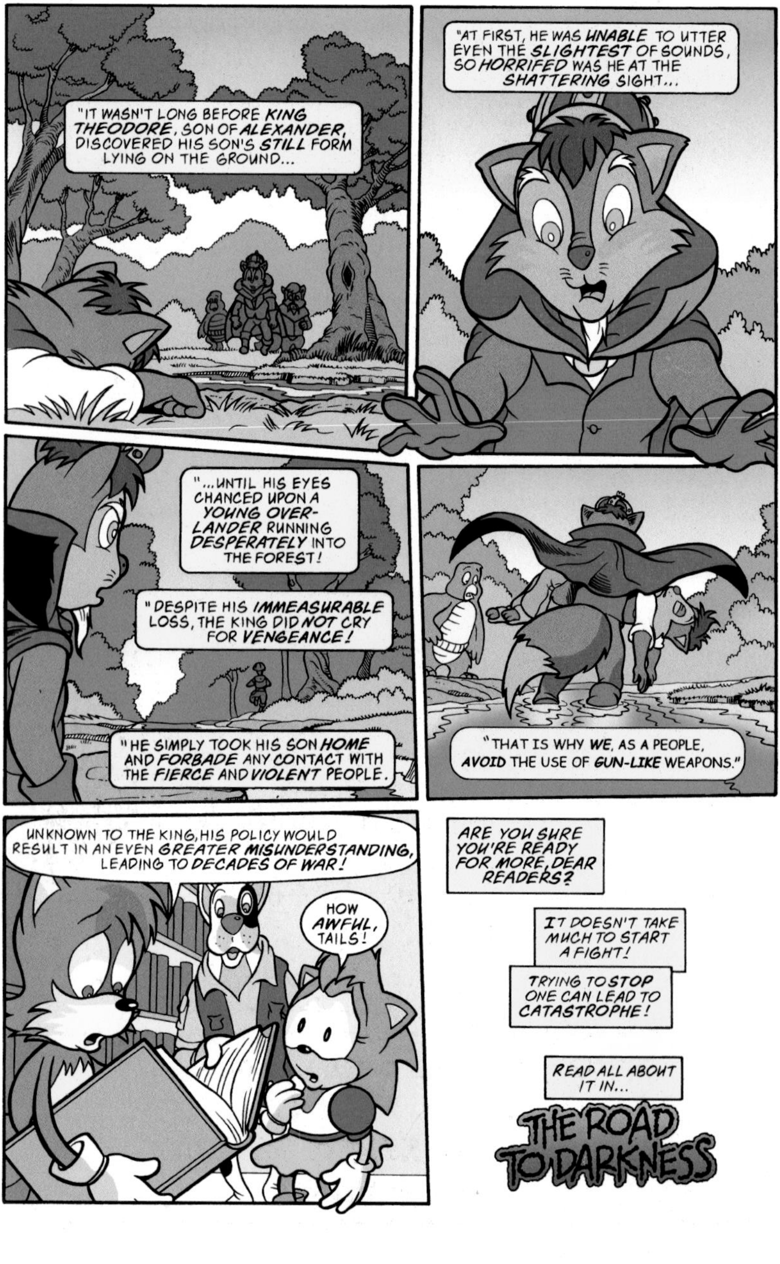
"IT WASN'T LONG BEFORE KING THEODORE, SON OF ALEXANDER, DISCOVERED HIS SON'S STILL FORM LYING ON THE GROUND...
"AT FIRST, HE WAS UNABLE TO UTTER EVEN THE SLIGHTEST OF SOUNDS, SO HORRIFED WAS HE AT THE SHATTERING SIGHT...
"...UNTIL HIS EYES CHANCED UPON A YOUNG OVER-LANDER RUNNING DESPERATELY INTO THE FOREST!
"DESPITE HIS IMMEASURABLE LOSS, THE KING DID NOT CRY FOR VENGEANCE!
"HE SIMPLY TOOK HIS SON HOME AND FORBADE ANY CONTACT WITH THE FIERCE AND VIOLENT PEOPLE.
"THAT IS WHY WE, AS A PEOPLE, AVOID THE USE OF GUN-LIKE WEAPONS."
UNKNOWN TO THE KING, HIS POLICY WOULD RESULT IN AN EVEN GREATER MISUNDERSTANDING, LEADING TO DECADES OF WAR!
HOW AWFUL, TAILS!
ARE YOU SURE YOU'RE READY FOR MORE, DEAR READERS?
IT DOESN'T TAKE MUCH TO START A FIGHT!
TRYING TO STOP ONE CAN LEAD TO CATASTROPHE!
READ ALL ABOUT IT IN...
THE ROAD TO DARKNESS

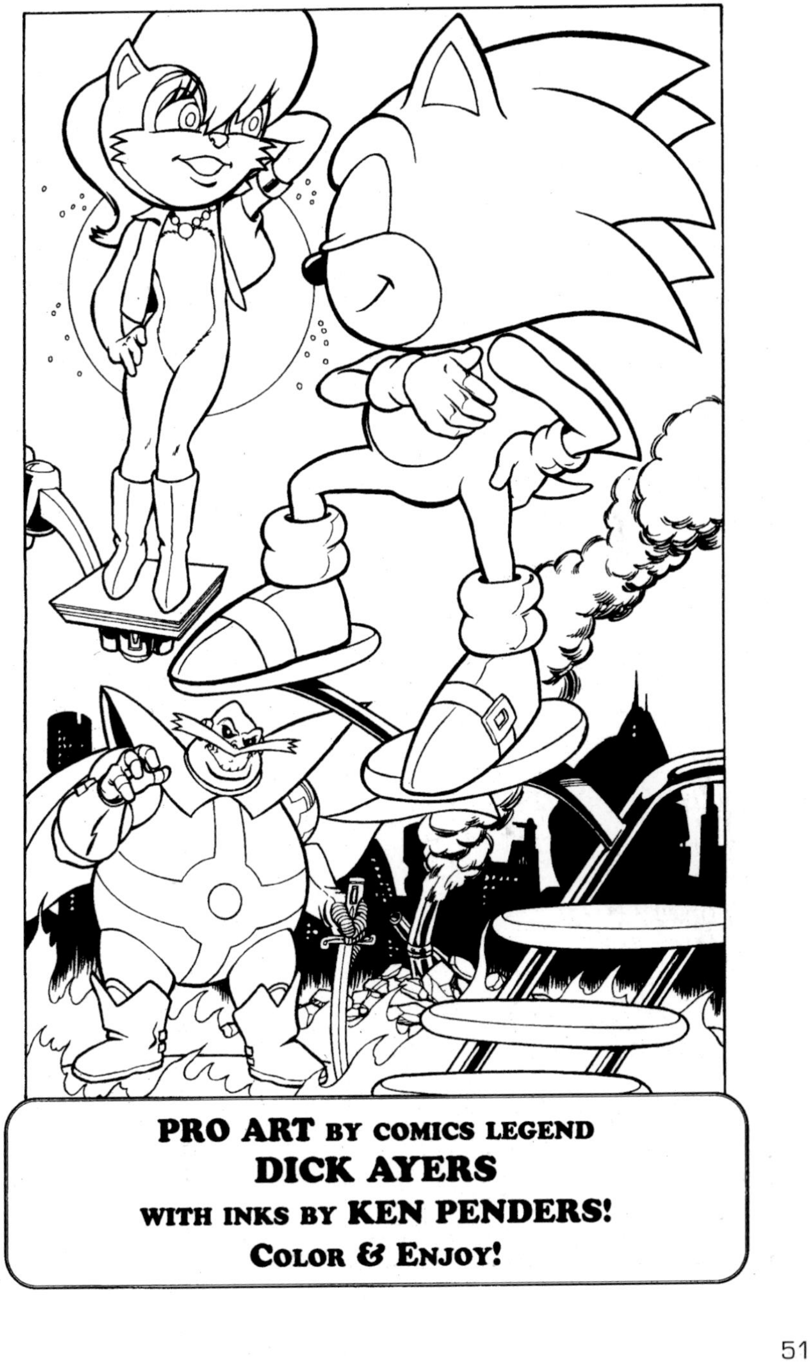

PRO ART BY COMICS LEGEND
DICK AYERS
WITH INKS BY **KEN PENDERS!**
COLOR & ENJOY!

PRO ART BY
SUZANNE PADDOCK & PAM EKLUND!
COLOR & ENJOY!

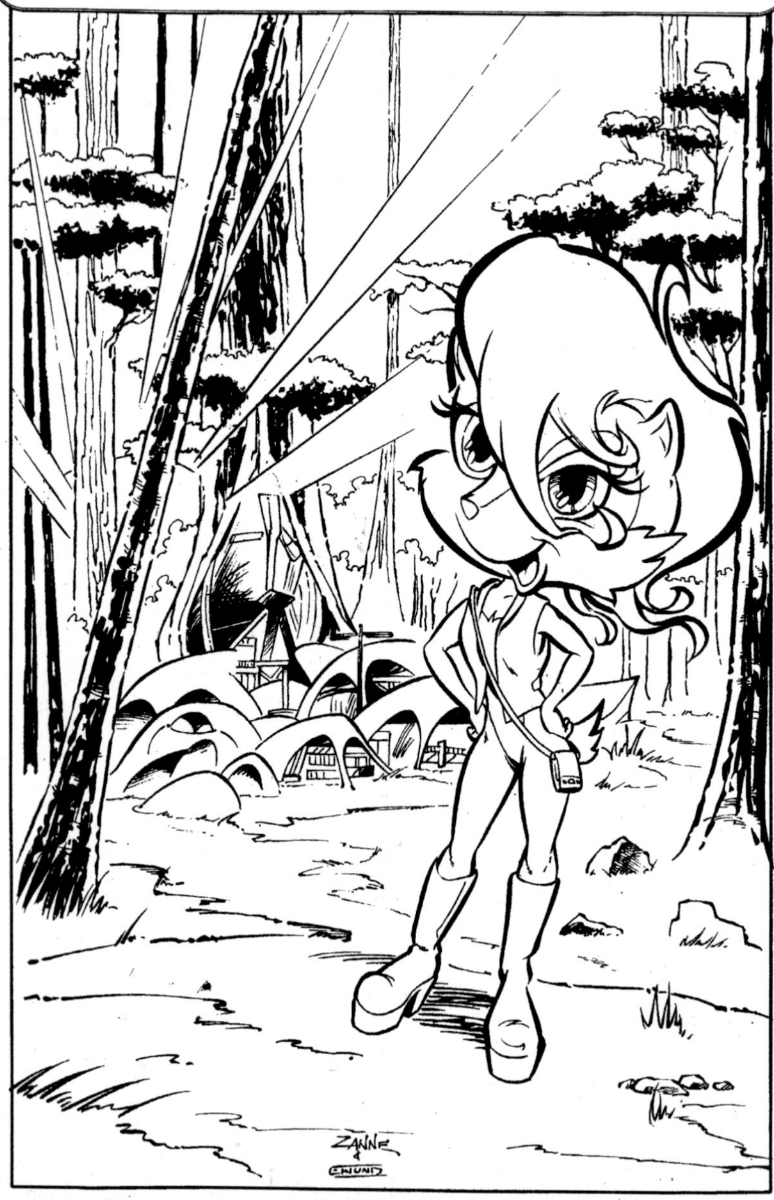
ZANNE
&
EKLUND

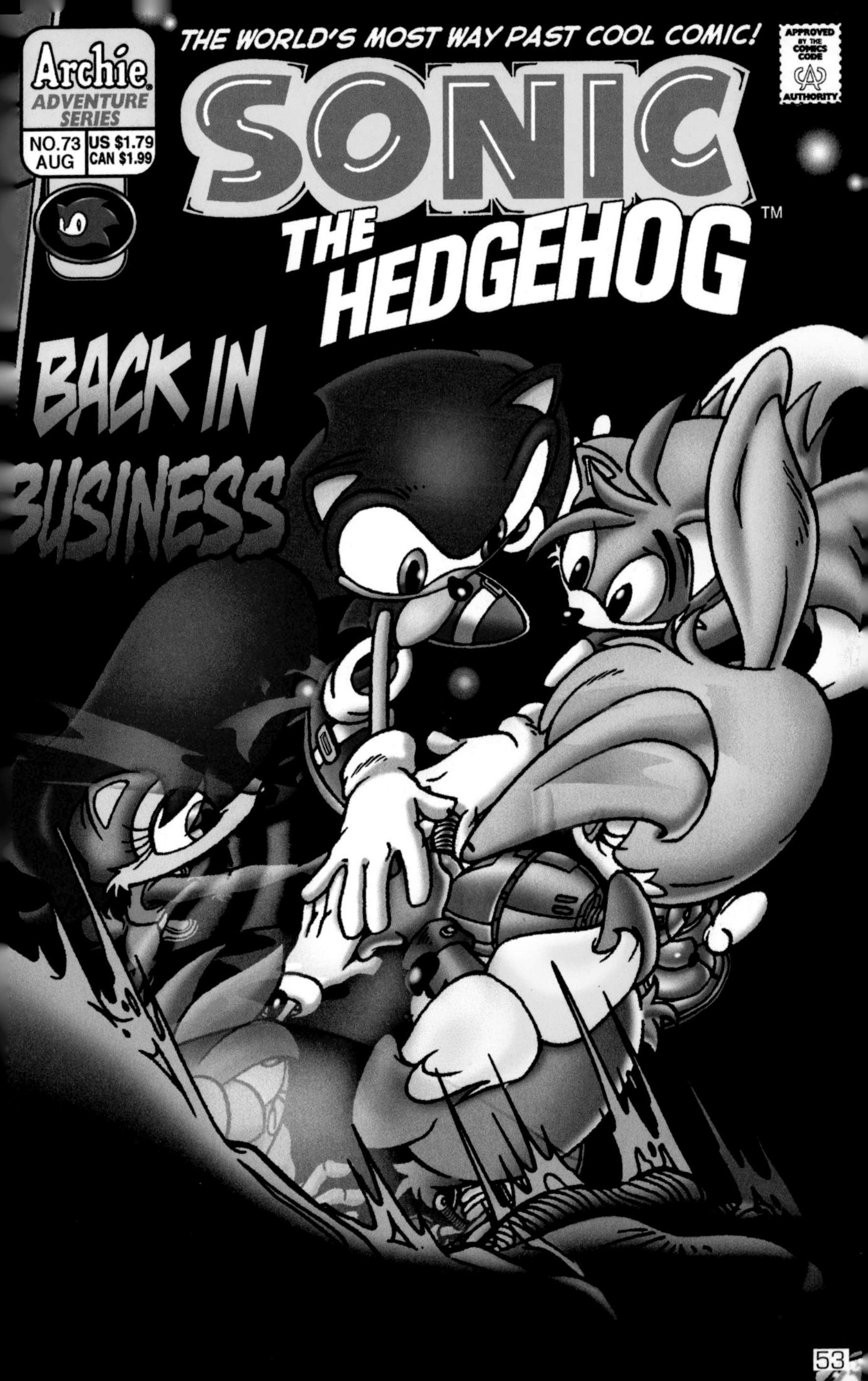
THE WORLD'S MOST WAY PAST COOL COMIC!
Archie ADVENTURE SERIES
NO.73 AUG
US $1.79 CAN $1.99
APPROVED BY THE COMICS CODE AUTHORITY
SONIC THE HEDGEHOG™
BACK IN BUSINESS

THE PLANET MOBIUS WAS ONCE A VIRTUAL PARADISE UNTIL IT WAS CONQUERED BY THE EVIL DOCTOR ROBOTNIK! HIS TECHNOLOGICAL TYRANNY WOULD HAVE CONTINUED IF NOT FOR A HEROIC GROUP OF FREEDOM FIGHTERS WHO BANDED TOGETHER AND RESTORED ORDER TO THE KINGDOM OF ACORN! THE BRAVEST AMONG THEM IS A BLUE STREAK FILLED WITH THE MOST ATTITUDE GOING AROUND -- AND, WITHOUT A DOUBT, HE IS THE FASTEST THING ALIVE! ARCHIE COMICS AND SEGA PRESENT... SONIC THE HEDGEHOG!

MORNING IN KNOTHOLE VILLAGE...

WELL, MOM 'N DAD, DO YOU LIKE 'EM?

"LIKE 'EM?" "LIKE 'EM?"

SONIC-- THESE WEDDING BANDS ARE ABSOLUTELY BEAUTIFUL!

THE TRUTH IS OUT THERE

KARL BOLLERS	STEVEN BUTLER	PAM EKLUND	FRANK GAGLIARDO	JEFF POWELL	J.F. GABRIE	VICTOR GORELICK	RICHARD GOLDWATER
WRITER	PENCILER	INKER	COLORIST	LETTERER	EDITOR\ ART DIRECTOR	MNG. EDITOR	EDITOR-IN-CHIEF

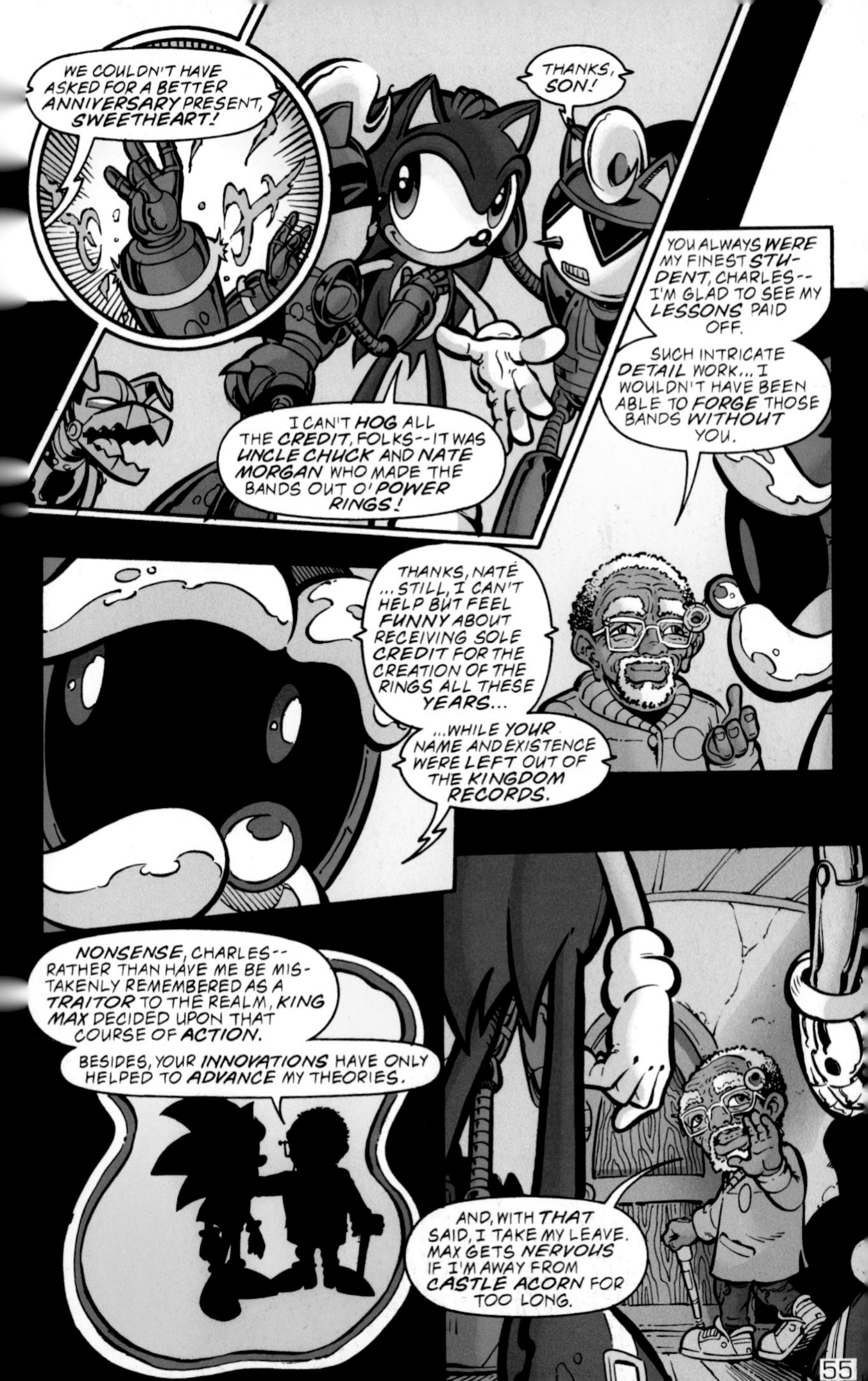
WE COULDN'T HAVE ASKED FOR A BETTER ANNIVERSARY PRESENT, SWEETHEART!
THANKS, SON!
I CAN'T HOG ALL THE CREDIT, FOLKS--IT WAS UNCLE CHUCK AND NATE MORGAN WHO MADE THE BANDS OUT O' POWER RINGS!
YOU ALWAYS WERE MY FINEST STUDENT, CHARLES--I'M GLAD TO SEE MY LESSONS PAID OFF.
SUCH INTRICATE DETAIL WORK... I WOULDN'T HAVE BEEN ABLE TO FORGE THOSE BANDS WITHOUT YOU.
THANKS, NATE ...STILL, I CAN'T HELP BUT FEEL FUNNY ABOUT RECEIVING SOLE CREDIT FOR THE CREATION OF THE RINGS ALL THESE YEARS...
...WHILE YOUR NAME AND EXISTENCE WERE LEFT OUT OF THE KINGDOM RECORDS.
NONSENSE, CHARLES--RATHER THAN HAVE ME BE MISTAKENLY REMEMBERED AS A TRAITOR TO THE REALM, KING MAX DECIDED UPON THAT COURSE OF ACTION.
BESIDES, YOUR INNOVATIONS HAVE ONLY HELPED TO ADVANCE MY THEORIES.
AND, WITH THAT SAID, I TAKE MY LEAVE. MAX GETS NERVOUS IF I'M AWAY FROM CASTLE ACORN FOR TOO LONG.

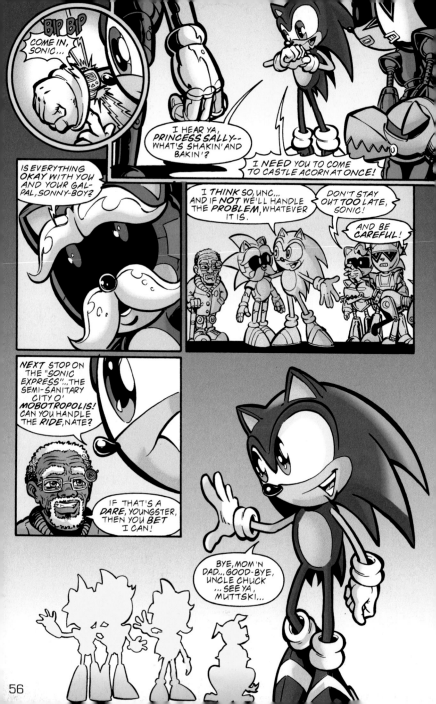

BIP BIP

COME IN, SONIC...

I HEAR YA, *PRINCESS SALLY*-- WHAT'S *SHAKIN'* AND *BAKIN'*?

I NEED YOU TO COME TO CASTLE ACORN AT ONCE!

IS EVERYTHING *OKAY* WITH YOU AND YOUR GAL-PAL, SONNY-BOY?

I *THINK* SO, UNC... AND IF *NOT* WE'LL HANDLE THE *PROBLEM*, WHATEVER IT IS.

DON'T STAY OUT *TOO* LATE, SONIC!

AND BE *CAREFUL!*

NEXT STOP ON THE "SONIC EXPRESS"...THE SEMI-SANITARY CITY O' MOBOTROPOLIS! CAN YOU HANDLE THE *RIDE*, NATE?

IF THAT'S A *DARE*, YOUNGSTER, THEN YOU *BET* I CAN!

BYE, MOM 'N DAD... GOOD-BYE, UNCLE CHUCK ...SEE YA, MUTTSKI...

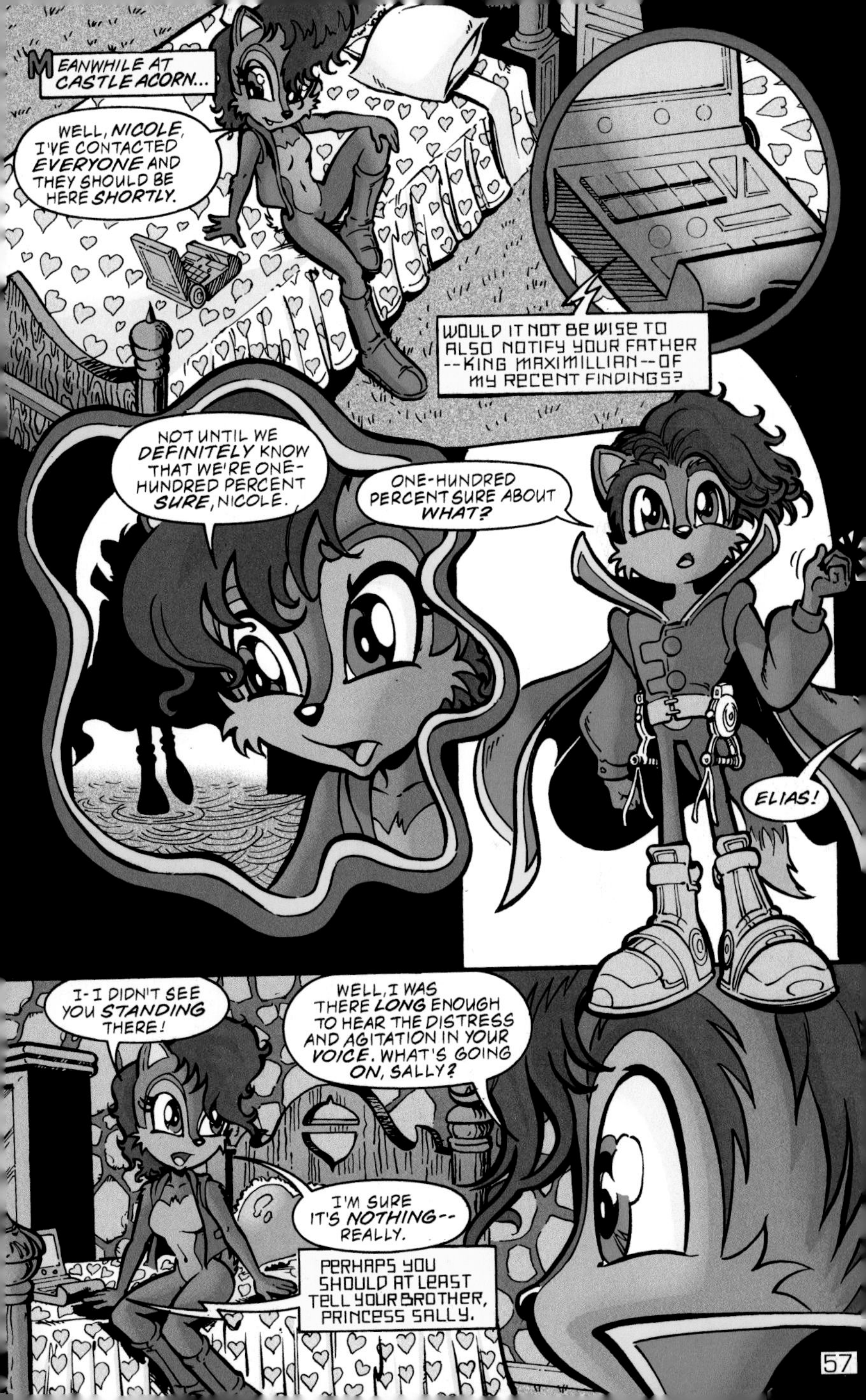
MEANWHILE AT CASTLE ACORN...
WELL, NICOLE, I'VE CONTACTED EVERYONE AND THEY SHOULD BE HERE SHORTLY.
WOULD IT NOT BE WISE TO ALSO NOTIFY YOUR FATHER --KING MAXIMILLIAN--OF MY RECENT FINDINGS?
NOT UNTIL WE DEFINITELY KNOW THAT WE'RE ONE-HUNDRED PERCENT SURE, NICOLE.
ONE-HUNDRED PERCENT SURE ABOUT WHAT?
ELIAS!
I-I DIDN'T SEE YOU STANDING THERE!
WELL, I WAS THERE LONG ENOUGH TO HEAR THE DISTRESS AND AGITATION IN YOUR VOICE. WHAT'S GOING ON, SALLY?
I'M SURE IT'S NOTHING-- REALLY.
PERHAPS YOU SHOULD AT LEAST TELL YOUR BROTHER, PRINCESS SALLY.

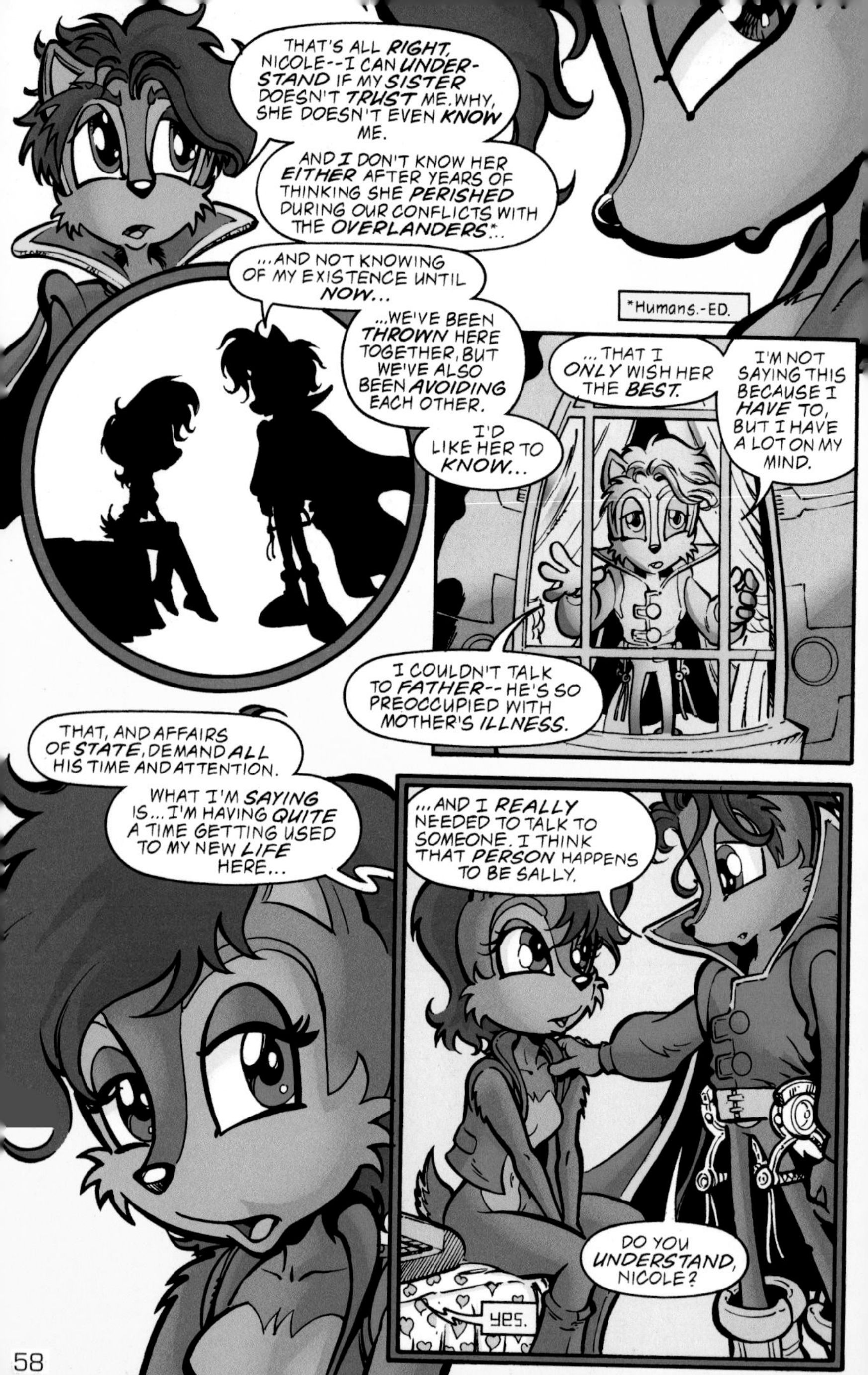

THAT'S ALL RIGHT, NICOLE--I CAN UNDERSTAND IF MY SISTER DOESN'T TRUST ME. WHY, SHE DOESN'T EVEN KNOW ME.
AND I DON'T KNOW HER EITHER AFTER YEARS OF THINKING SHE PERISHED DURING OUR CONFLICTS WITH THE OVERLANDERS*...
...AND NOT KNOWING OF MY EXISTENCE UNTIL NOW...
*Humans.-ED.
...WE'VE BEEN THROWN HERE TOGETHER, BUT WE'VE ALSO BEEN AVOIDING EACH OTHER.
I'D LIKE HER TO KNOW...
...THAT I ONLY WISH HER THE BEST.
I'M NOT SAYING THIS BECAUSE I HAVE TO, BUT I HAVE A LOT ON MY MIND.
I COULDN'T TALK TO FATHER--HE'S SO PREOCCUPIED WITH MOTHER'S ILLNESS.
THAT, AND AFFAIRS OF STATE, DEMAND ALL HIS TIME AND ATTENTION.
WHAT I'M SAYING IS... I'M HAVING QUITE A TIME GETTING USED TO MY NEW LIFE HERE...
...AND I REALLY NEEDED TO TALK TO SOMEONE. I THINK THAT PERSON HAPPENS TO BE SALLY.
DO YOU UNDERSTAND, NICOLE?
YES.

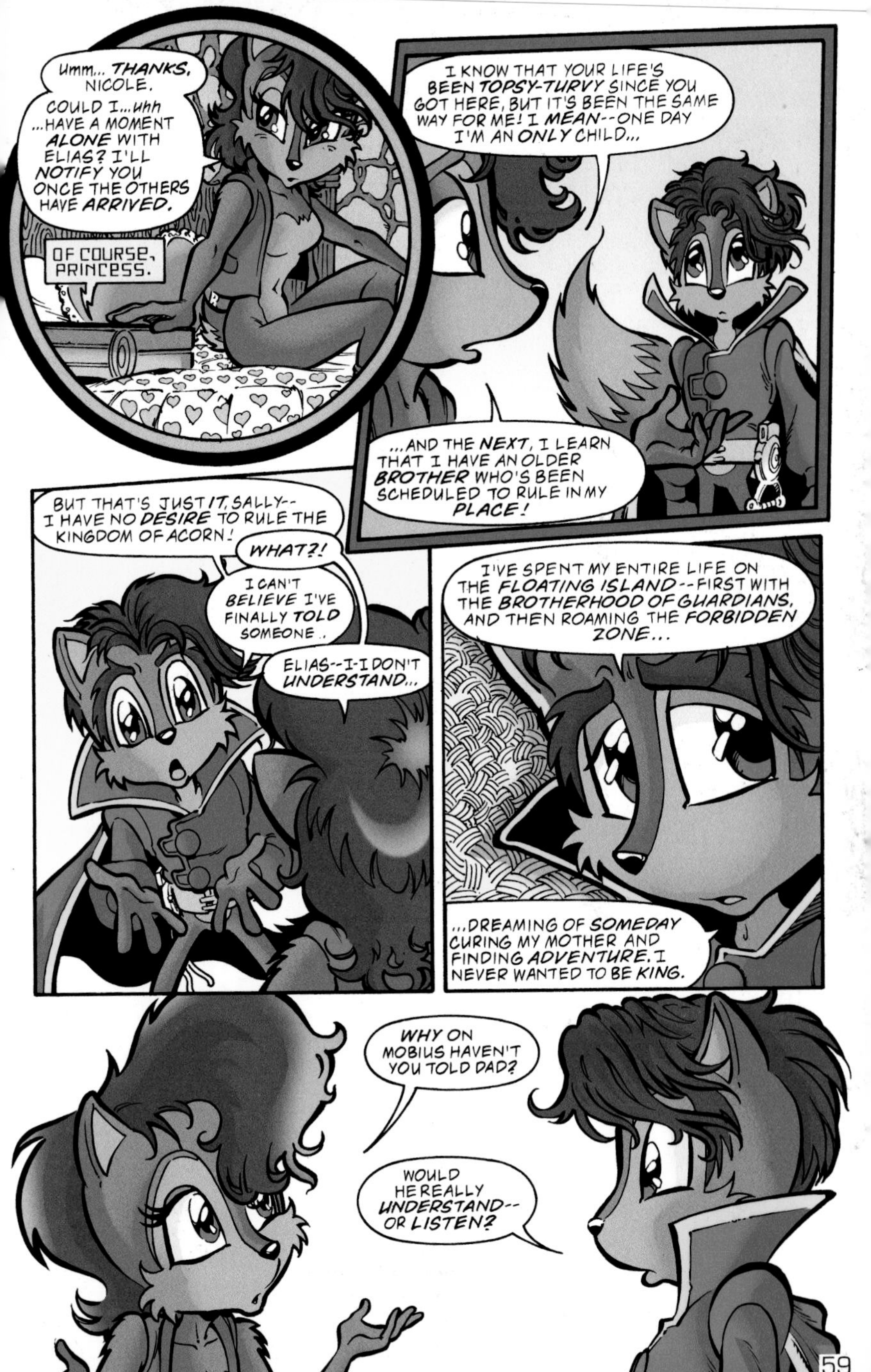
Umm... THANKS, NICOLE.
COULD I...uhh ...HAVE A MOMENT ALONE WITH ELIAS? I'LL NOTIFY YOU ONCE THE OTHERS HAVE ARRIVED.
OF COURSE, PRINCESS.
I KNOW THAT YOUR LIFE'S BEEN TOPSY-TURVY SINCE YOU GOT HERE, BUT IT'S BEEN THE SAME WAY FOR ME! I MEAN--ONE DAY I'M AN ONLY CHILD...
...AND THE NEXT, I LEARN THAT I HAVE AN OLDER BROTHER WHO'S BEEN SCHEDULED TO RULE IN MY PLACE!
BUT THAT'S JUST IT, SALLY-- I HAVE NO DESIRE TO RULE THE KINGDOM OF ACORN!
WHAT?!
I CAN'T BELIEVE I'VE FINALLY TOLD SOMEONE..
ELIAS--I-I DON'T UNDERSTAND...
I'VE SPENT MY ENTIRE LIFE ON THE FLOATING ISLAND--FIRST WITH THE BROTHERHOOD OF GUARDIANS, AND THEN ROAMING THE FORBIDDEN ZONE...
...DREAMING OF SOMEDAY CURING MY MOTHER AND FINDING ADVENTURE. I NEVER WANTED TO BE KING.
WHY ON MOBIUS HAVEN'T YOU TOLD DAD?
WOULD HE REALLY UNDERSTAND-- OR LISTEN?

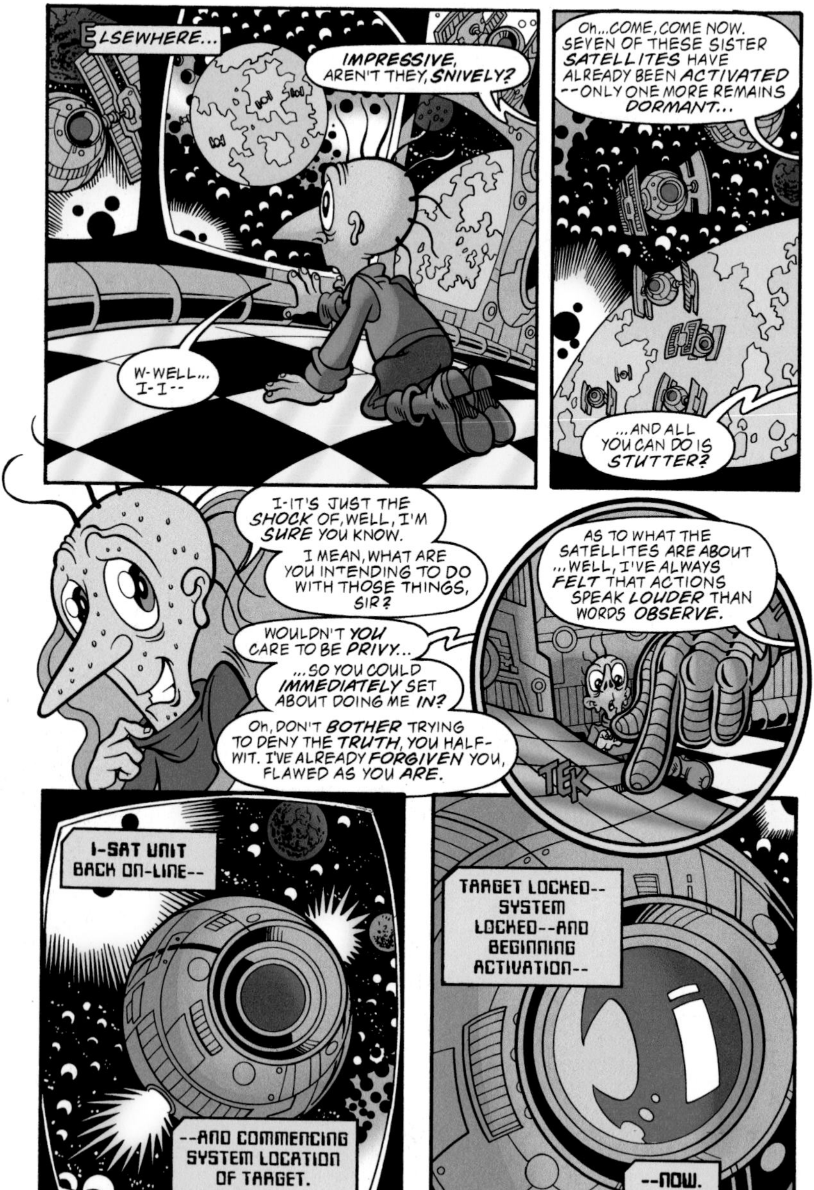
ELSEWHERE...
IMPRESSIVE, AREN'T THEY, SNIVELY?
W-WELL... I-I--
Oh...COME, COME NOW. SEVEN OF THESE SISTER SATELLITES HAVE ALREADY BEEN ACTIVATED --ONLY ONE MORE REMAINS DORMANT...
...AND ALL YOU CAN DO IS STUTTER?
I-IT'S JUST THE SHOCK OF, WELL, I'M SURE YOU KNOW.
I MEAN, WHAT ARE YOU INTENDING TO DO WITH THOSE THINGS, SIR?
WOULDN'T YOU CARE TO BE PRIVY...
...SO YOU COULD IMMEDIATELY SET ABOUT DOING ME IN?
Oh, DON'T BOTHER TRYING TO DENY THE TRUTH, YOU HALF-WIT. I'VE ALREADY FORGIVEN YOU, FLAWED AS YOU ARE.
AS TO WHAT THE SATELLITES ARE ABOUT ...WELL, I'VE ALWAYS FELT THAT ACTIONS SPEAK LOUDER THAN WORDS OBSERVE.
TEK
I-SAT UNIT BACK ON-LINE--
--AND COMMENCING SYSTEM LOCATION OF TARGET.
TARGET LOCKED-- SYSTEM LOCKED--AND BEGINNING ACTIVATION--
--NOW.

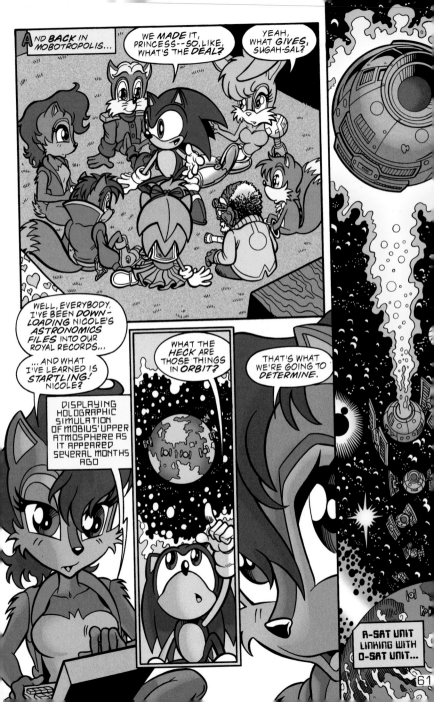

AND **BACK** IN MOBOTROPOLIS...

WE **MADE** IT, PRINCESS--SO, LIKE, WHAT'S THE **DEAL?**

YEAH, WHAT **GIVES**, SUGAH-SAL?

WELL, EVERYBODY, I'VE BEEN **DOWN-LOADING** NICOLE'S **ASTRONOMICS** FILES INTO OUR **ROYAL** RECORDS...

...AND WHAT I'VE LEARNED IS **STARTLING!** NICOLE?

DISPLAYING HOLOGRAPHIC SIMULATION OF MOBIUS' UPPER ATMOSPHERE AS IT APPEARED SEVERAL MONTHS AGO

WHAT THE HECK ARE THOSE THINGS IN **ORBIT?**

THAT'S WHAT WE'RE GOING TO DETERMINE.

R-SAT UNIT LINKING WITH O-SAT UNIT...

61

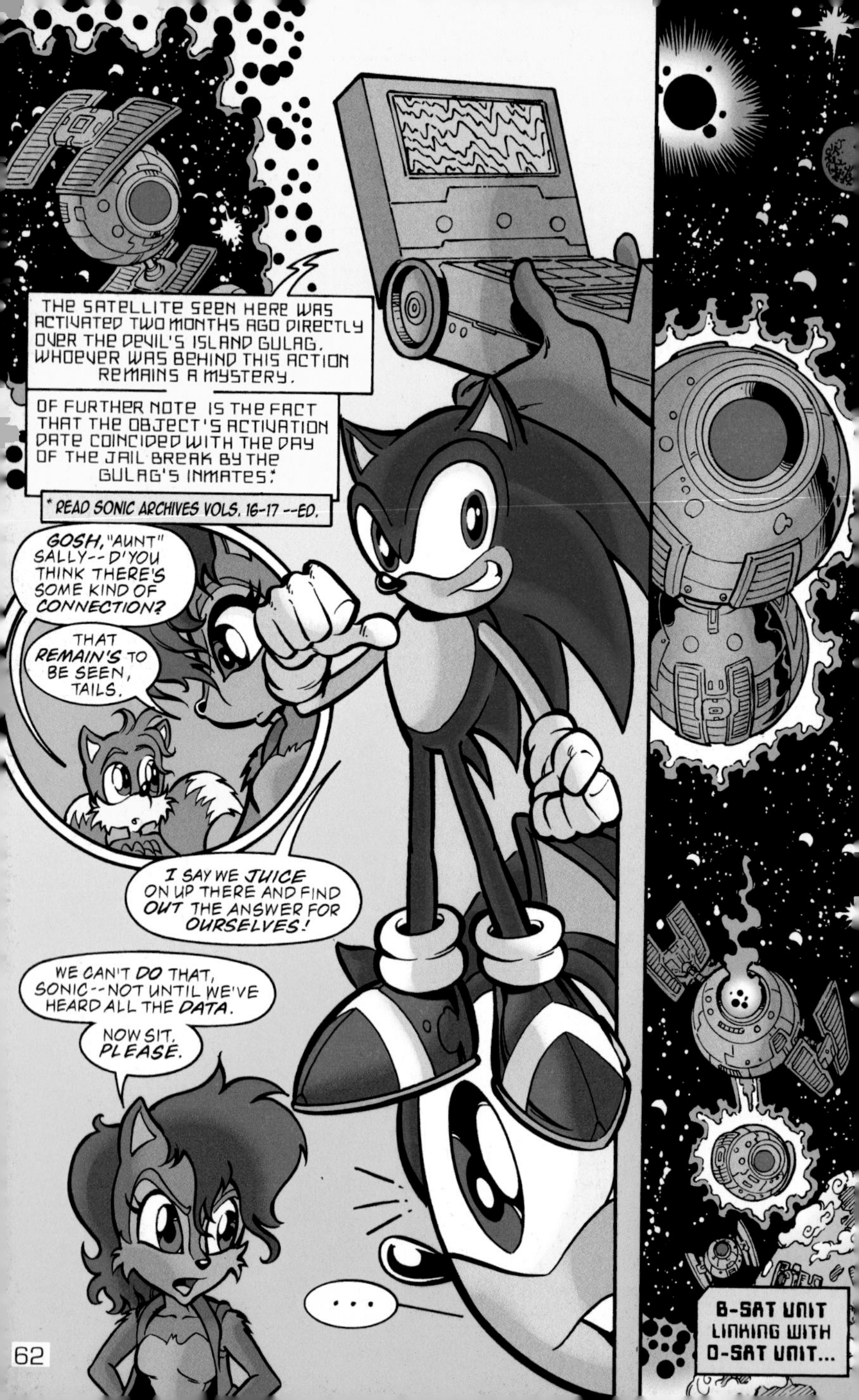
THE SATELLITE SEEN HERE WAS ACTIVATED TWO MONTHS AGO DIRECTLY OVER THE DEVIL'S ISLAND GULAG. WHOEVER WAS BEHIND THIS ACTION REMAINS A MYSTERY.
OF FURTHER NOTE IS THE FACT THAT THE OBJECT'S ACTIVATION DATE COINCIDED WITH THE DAY OF THE JAIL BREAK BY THE GULAG'S INMATES.*
* READ SONIC ARCHIVES VOLS. 16-17 --ED.
GOSH, "AUNT" SALLY-- D'YOU THINK THERE'S SOME KIND OF CONNECTION?
THAT REMAIN'S TO BE SEEN, TAILS.
I SAY WE JUICE ON UP THERE AND FIND OUT THE ANSWER FOR OURSELVES!
WE CAN'T DO THAT, SONIC--NOT UNTIL WE'VE HEARD ALL THE DATA.
NOW SIT, PLEASE.
...
B-SAT UNIT LINKING WITH D-SAT UNIT...

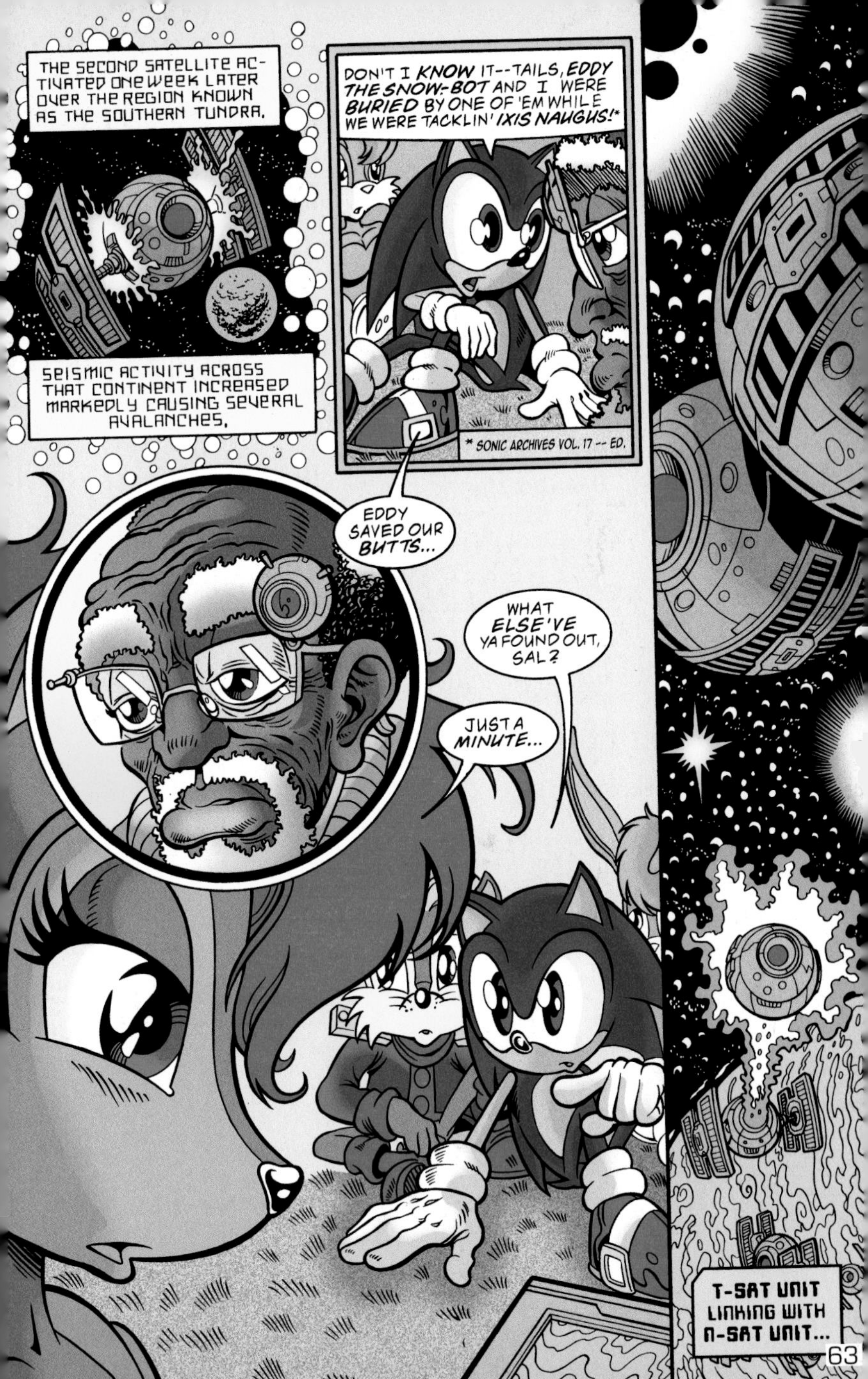
THE SECOND SATELLITE ACTIVATED ONE WEEK LATER OVER THE REGION KNOWN AS THE SOUTHERN TUNDRA.
SEISMIC ACTIVITY ACROSS THAT CONTINENT INCREASED MARKEDLY CAUSING SEVERAL AVALANCHES.
DON'T I KNOW IT--TAILS, EDDY THE SNOW-BOT AND I WERE BURIED BY ONE OF 'EM WHILE WE WERE TACKLIN' IXIS NAUGUS!*
* SONIC ARCHIVES VOL. 17 -- ED.
EDDY SAVED OUR BUTTS...
WHAT ELSE'VE YA FOUND OUT, SAL?
JUST A MINUTE...
T-SAT UNIT LINKING WITH N-SAT UNIT...

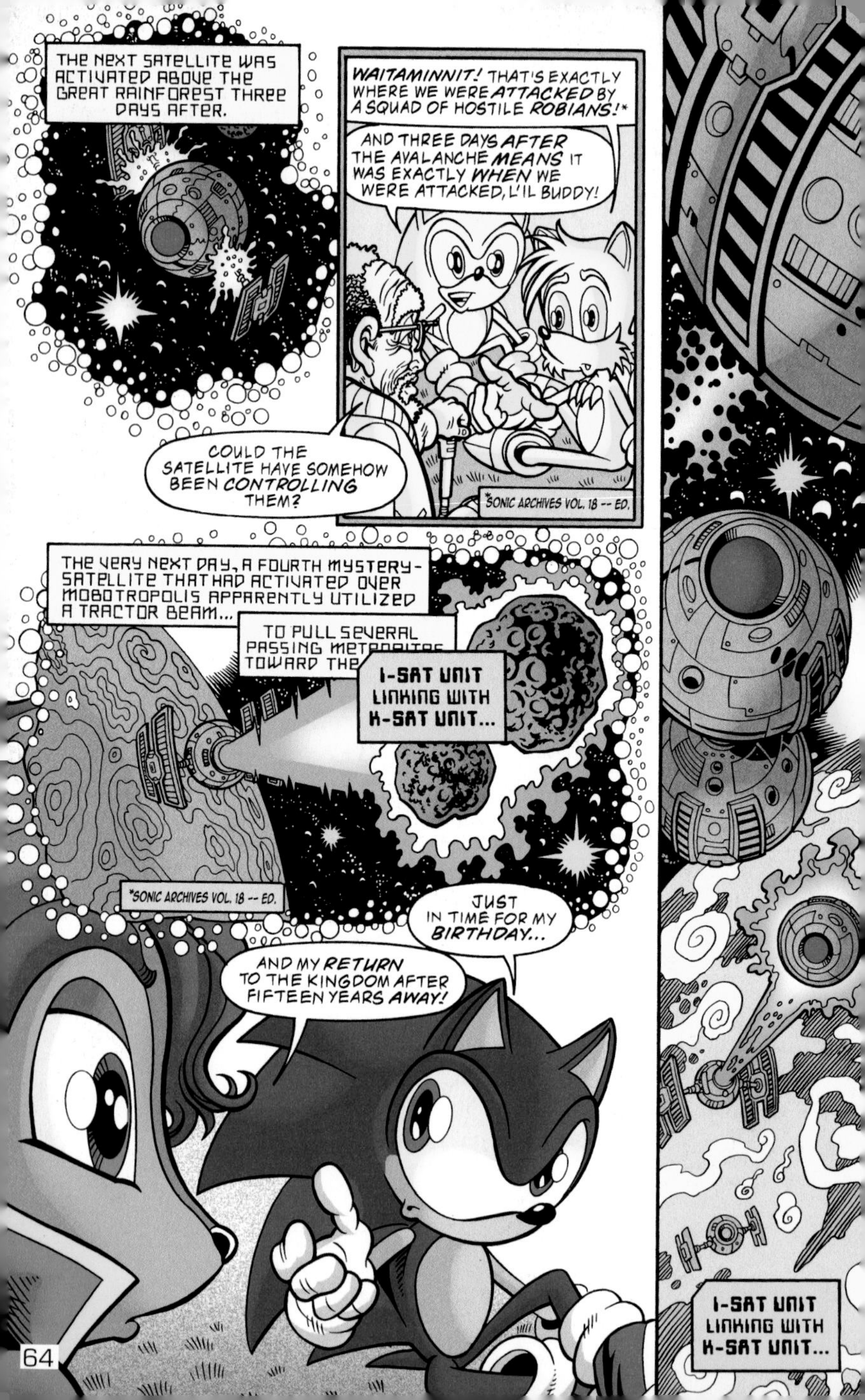
THE NEXT SATELLITE WAS ACTIVATED ABOVE THE GREAT RAINFOREST THREE DAYS AFTER.
WAITAMINNIT! THAT'S EXACTLY WHERE WE WERE ATTACKED BY A SQUAD OF HOSTILE ROBIANS!*
AND THREE DAYS AFTER THE AVALANCHE MEANS IT WAS EXACTLY WHEN WE WERE ATTACKED, L'IL BUDDY!
COULD THE SATELLITE HAVE SOMEHOW BEEN CONTROLLING THEM?
*SONIC ARCHIVES VOL. 18 -- ED.
THE VERY NEXT DAY, A FOURTH MYSTERY-SATELLITE THAT HAD ACTIVATED OVER MOBOTROPOLIS APPARENTLY UTILIZED A TRACTOR BEAM...
TO PULL SEVERAL PASSING
I-SAT UNIT LINKING WITH K-SAT UNIT...
*SONIC ARCHIVES VOL. 18 -- ED.
JUST IN TIME FOR MY BIRTHDAY...
AND MY RETURN TO THE KINGDOM AFTER FIFTEEN YEARS AWAY!
I-SAT UNIT LINKING WITH K-SAT UNIT...

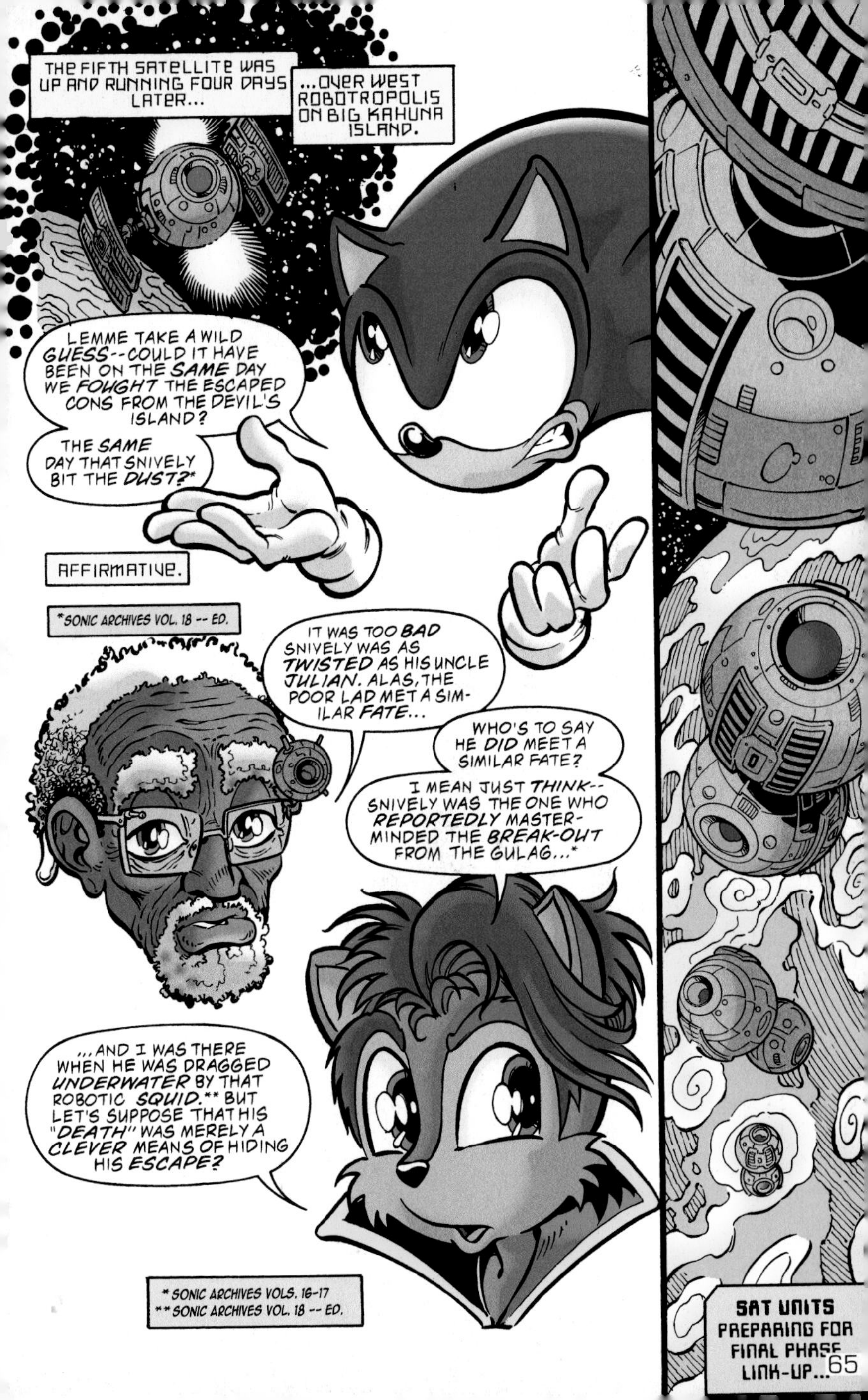
THE FIFTH SATELLITE WAS UP AND RUNNING FOUR DAYS LATER...
...OVER WEST ROBOTROPOLIS ON BIG KAHUNA ISLAND.
LEMME TAKE A WILD GUESS--COULD IT HAVE BEEN ON THE SAME DAY WE FOUGHT THE ESCAPED CONS FROM THE DEVIL'S ISLAND?
THE SAME DAY THAT SNIVELY BIT THE DUST?*
AFFIRMATIVE.
*SONIC ARCHIVES VOL. 18 -- ED.
IT WAS TOO BAD SNIVELY WAS AS TWISTED AS HIS UNCLE JULIAN. ALAS, THE POOR LAD MET A SIM-ILAR FATE...
WHO'S TO SAY HE DID MEET A SIMILAR FATE?
I MEAN JUST THINK-- SNIVELY WAS THE ONE WHO REPORTEDLY MASTER-MINDED THE BREAK-OUT FROM THE GULAG...*
...AND I WAS THERE WHEN HE WAS DRAGGED UNDERWATER BY THAT ROBOTIC SQUID.** BUT LET'S SUPPOSE THAT HIS "DEATH" WAS MERELY A CLEVER MEANS OF HIDING HIS ESCAPE?
* SONIC ARCHIVES VOLS. 16-17
** SONIC ARCHIVES VOL. 18 -- ED.
SAT UNITS PREPARING FOR FINAL PHASE LINK-UP...

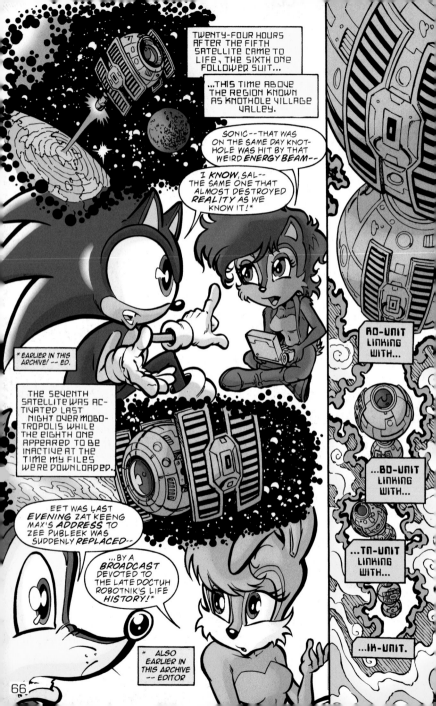

TWENTY-FOUR HOURS AFTER THE FIFTH SATELLITE CAME TO LIFE, THE SIXTH ONE FOLLOWER SUIT...

...THIS TIME ABOVE THE REGION KNOWN AS KNOTHOLE VILLAGE.

SONIC--THAT WAS ON THE SAME DAY KNOT-HOLE WAS HIT BY THAT WEIRD *ENERGY BEAM*--

I *KNOW*, SAL-- THE SAME ONE THAT ALMOST DESTROYED *REALITY* AS WE KNOW IT!*

* EARLIER IN THIS ARCHIVE! -- ED.

THE SEVENTH SATELLITE WAS AC-TIVATED LAST NIGHT OVER MOBO-TROPOLIS WHILE THE EIGHTH ONE APPEARED TO BE INACTIVE AT THE TIME MY FILES WE'RE DOWNLOADED.

EET WAS LAST *EVENING* ZAT KEENG MAX'S *ADDRESS* TO ZEE *PUBLEEK* WAS SUDDENLY *REPLACED*--

...BY A *BROADCAST* DEVOTED TO THE LATE DOCTUH ROBOTNIK'S LIFE *HISTORY*!*

* ALSO EARLIER IN THIS ARCHIVE -- EDITOR

AD-UNIT LINKING WITH...

...BD-UNIT LINKING WITH...

...TD-UNIT LINKING WITH...

...IK-UNIT.

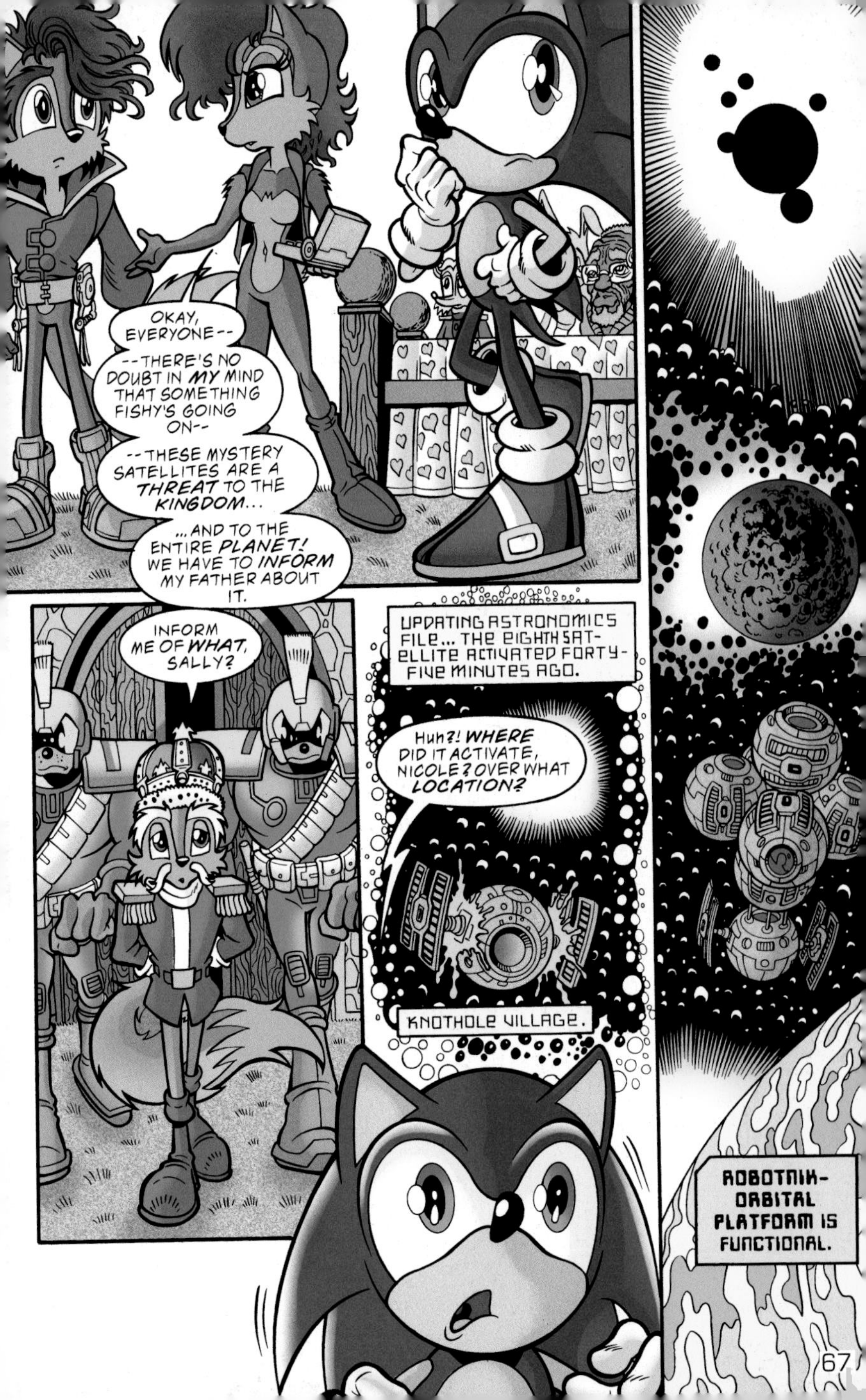
OKAY, EVERYONE--
--THERE'S NO DOUBT IN MY MIND THAT SOMETHING FISHY'S GOING ON--
--THESE MYSTERY SATELLITES ARE A THREAT TO THE KINGDOM...
...AND TO THE ENTIRE PLANET! WE HAVE TO INFORM MY FATHER ABOUT IT.
INFORM ME OF WHAT, SALLY?
UPDATING ASTRONOMICS FILE... THE EIGHTH SATELLITE ACTIVATED FORTY-FIVE MINUTES AGO.
Huh?! WHERE DID IT ACTIVATE, NICOLE? OVER WHAT LOCATION?
KNOTHOLE VILLAGE.
ROBOTNIK-ORBITAL PLATFORM IS FUNCTIONAL.

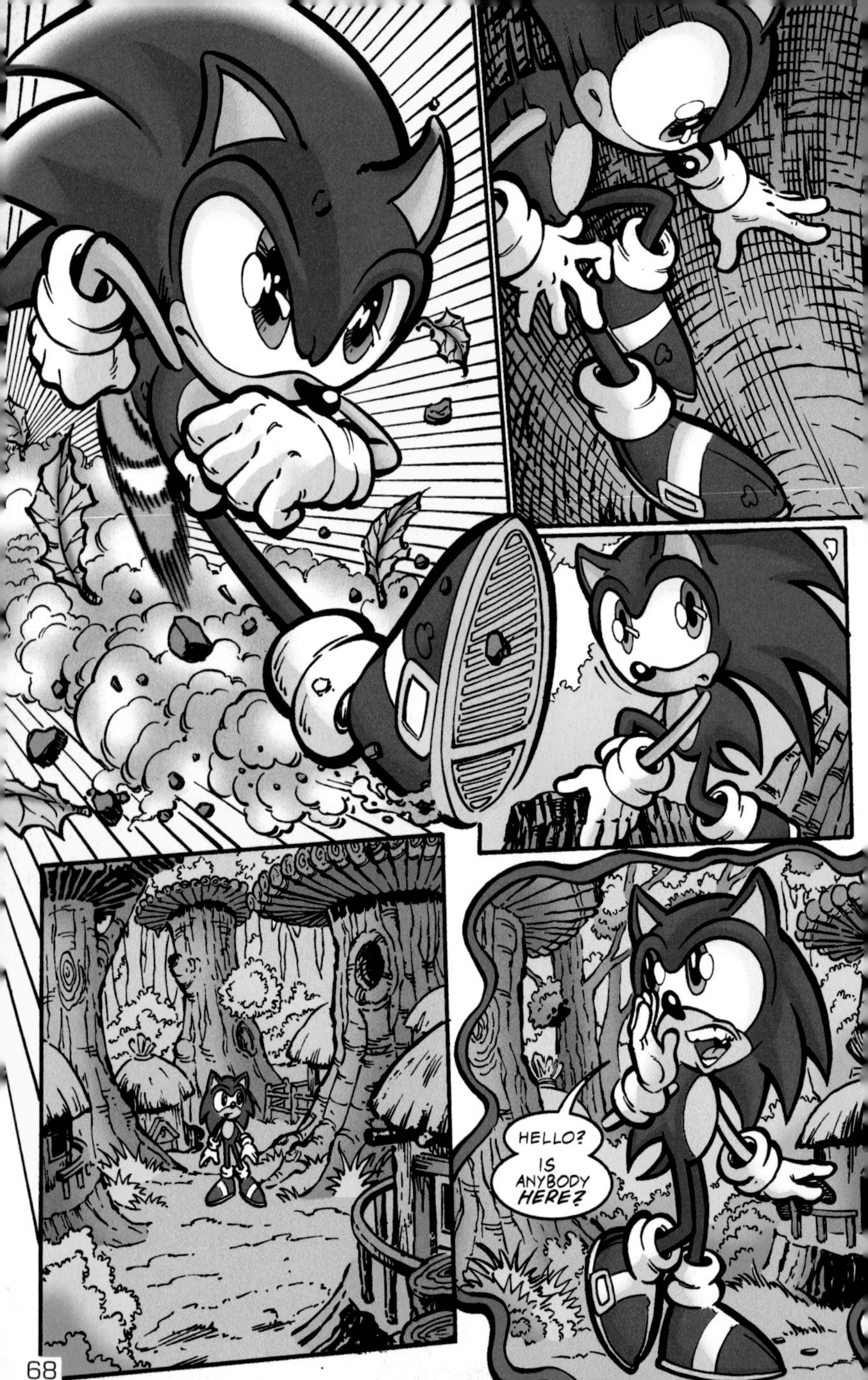
HELLO? IS ANYBODY HERE?

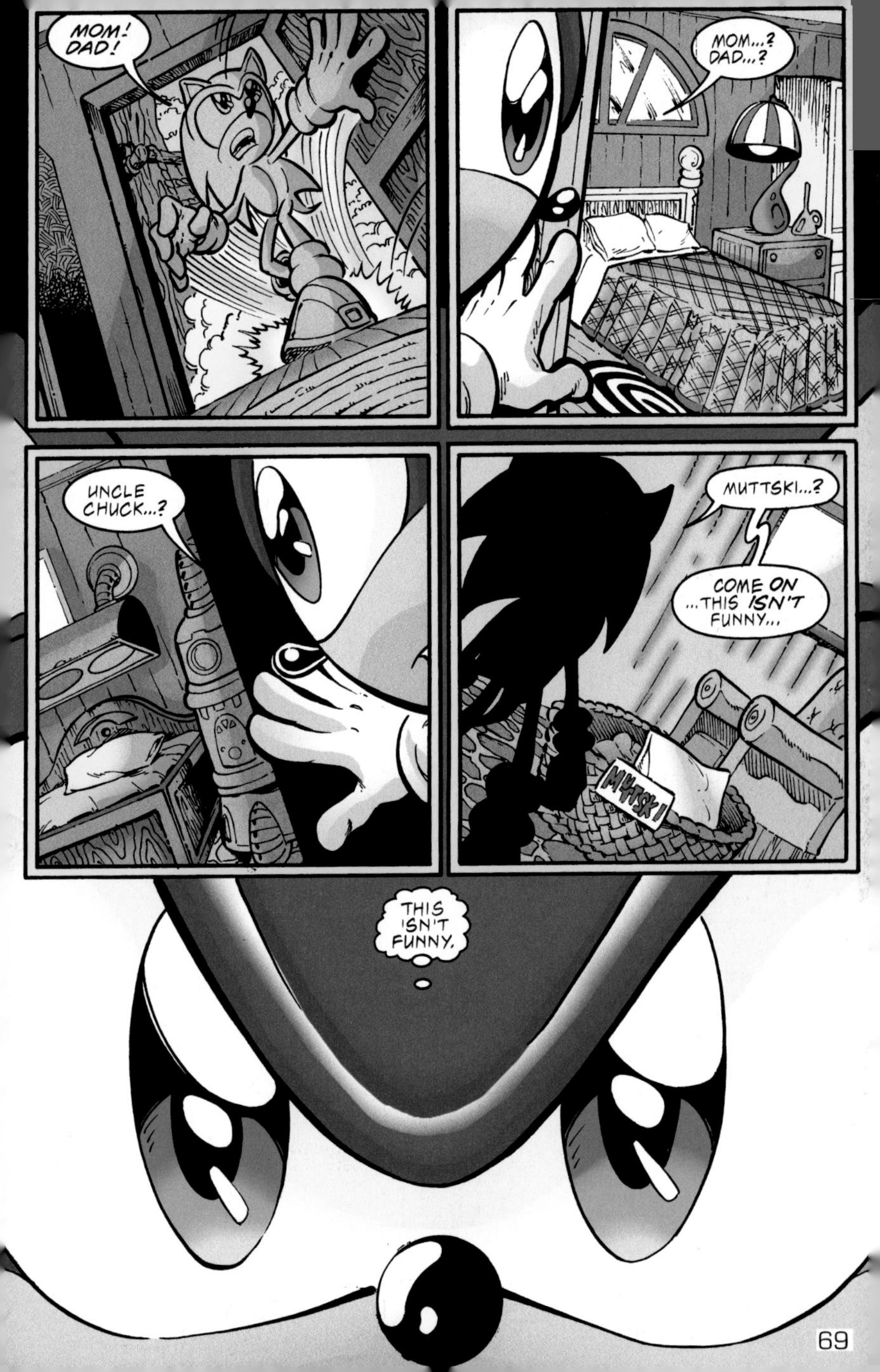
MOM! DAD!
MOM...? DAD...?
UNCLE CHUCK...?
MUTTSKI...?
COME ON ...THIS ISN'T FUNNY...
MUTTSKI
THIS ISN'T FUNNY.

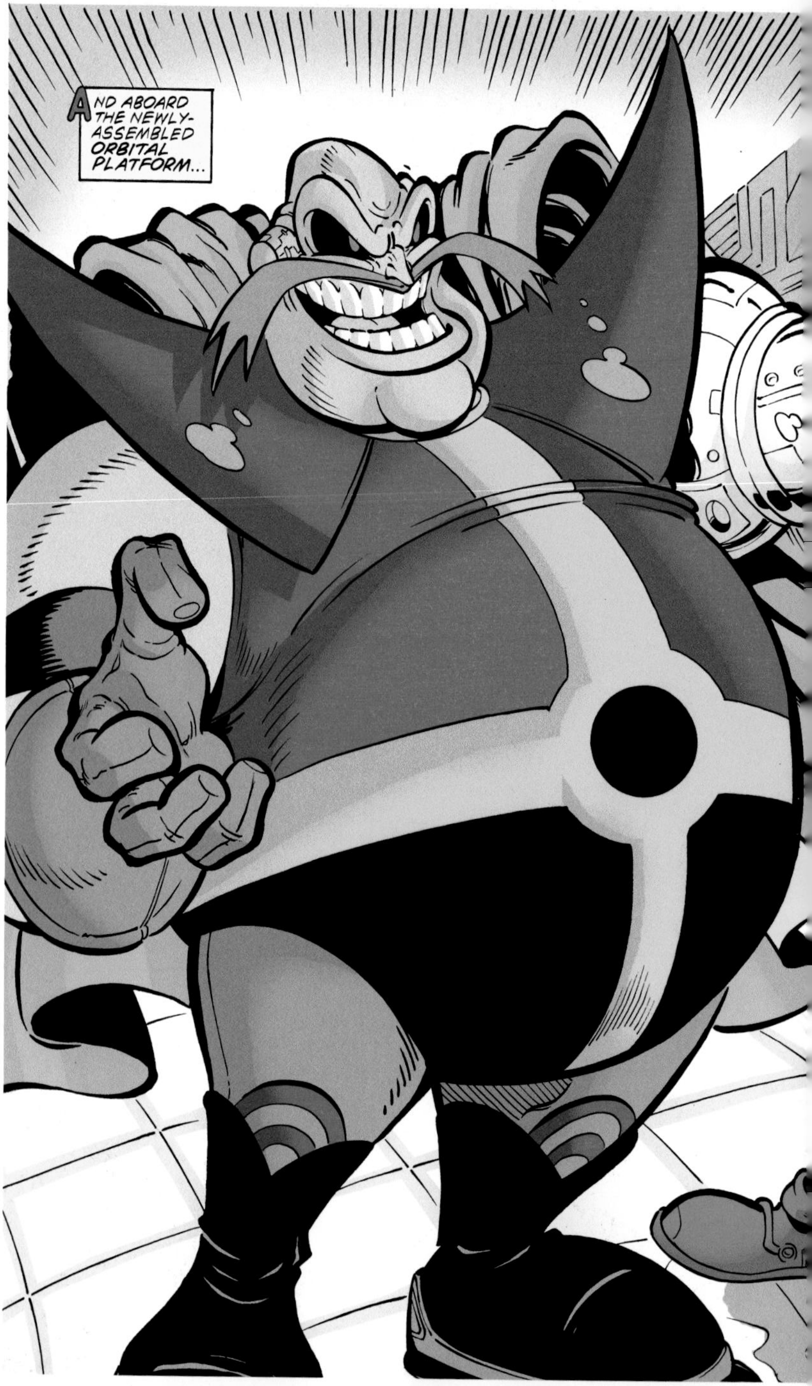
AND ABOARD THE NEWLY-ASSEMBLED ORBITAL PLATFORM...

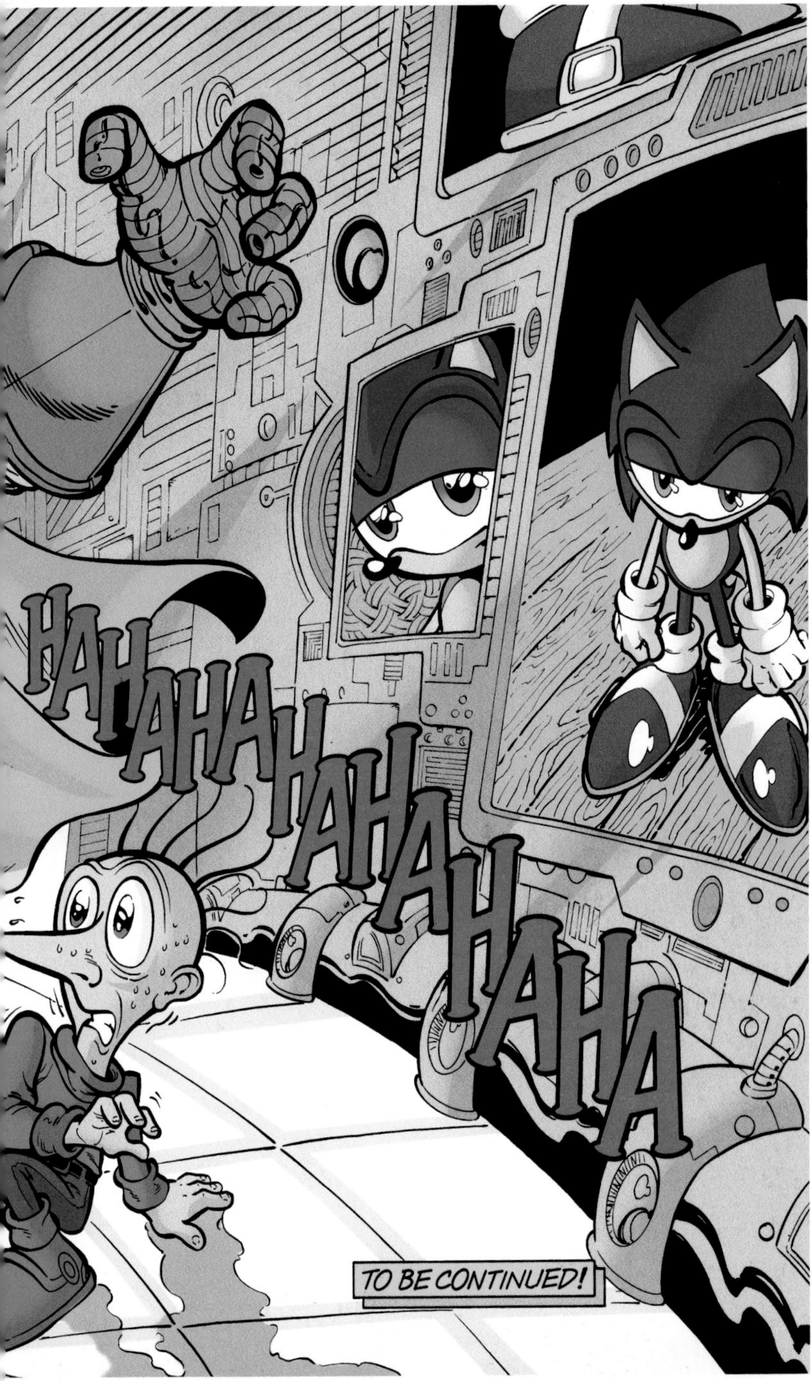
HAHAHAHAHAHAHAHAHAHA
TO BE CONTINUED!

NOTE: THE FOLLOWING HAPPENS BEFORE THE STORY YOU'VE JUST READ.

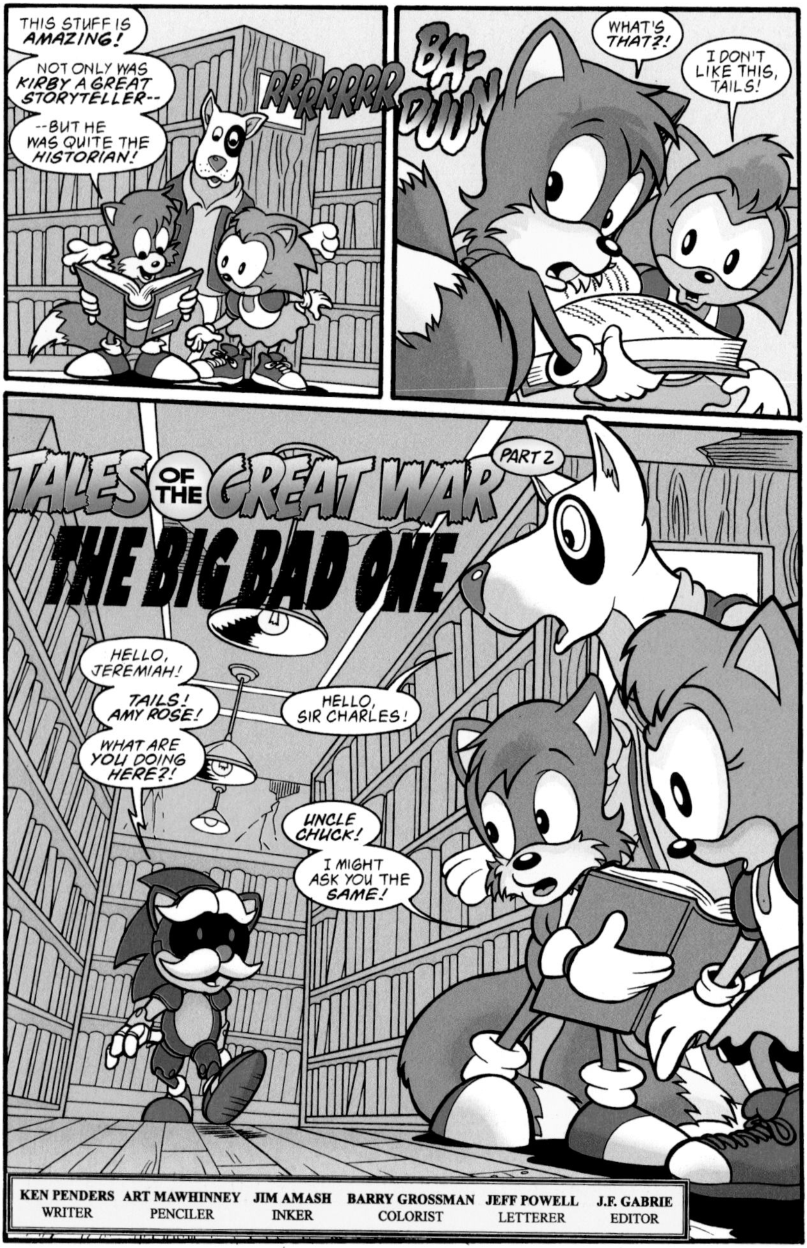
THIS STUFF IS AMAZING!
NOT ONLY WAS KIRBY A GREAT STORYTELLER--
--BUT HE WAS QUITE THE HISTORIAN!
RRRRRRR BA-DUUN
WHAT'S THAT?!
I DON'T LIKE THIS, TAILS!
TALES OF THE GREAT WAR PART 2
THE BIG BAD ONE
HELLO, JEREMIAH!
TAILS! AMY ROSE!
WHAT ARE YOU DOING HERE?!
HELLO, SIR CHARLES!
UNCLE CHUCK!
I MIGHT ASK YOU THE SAME!
KEN PENDERS WRITER
ART MAWHINNEY PENCILER
JIM AMASH INKER
BARRY GROSSMAN COLORIST
JEFF POWELL LETTERER
J.F. GABRIE EDITOR

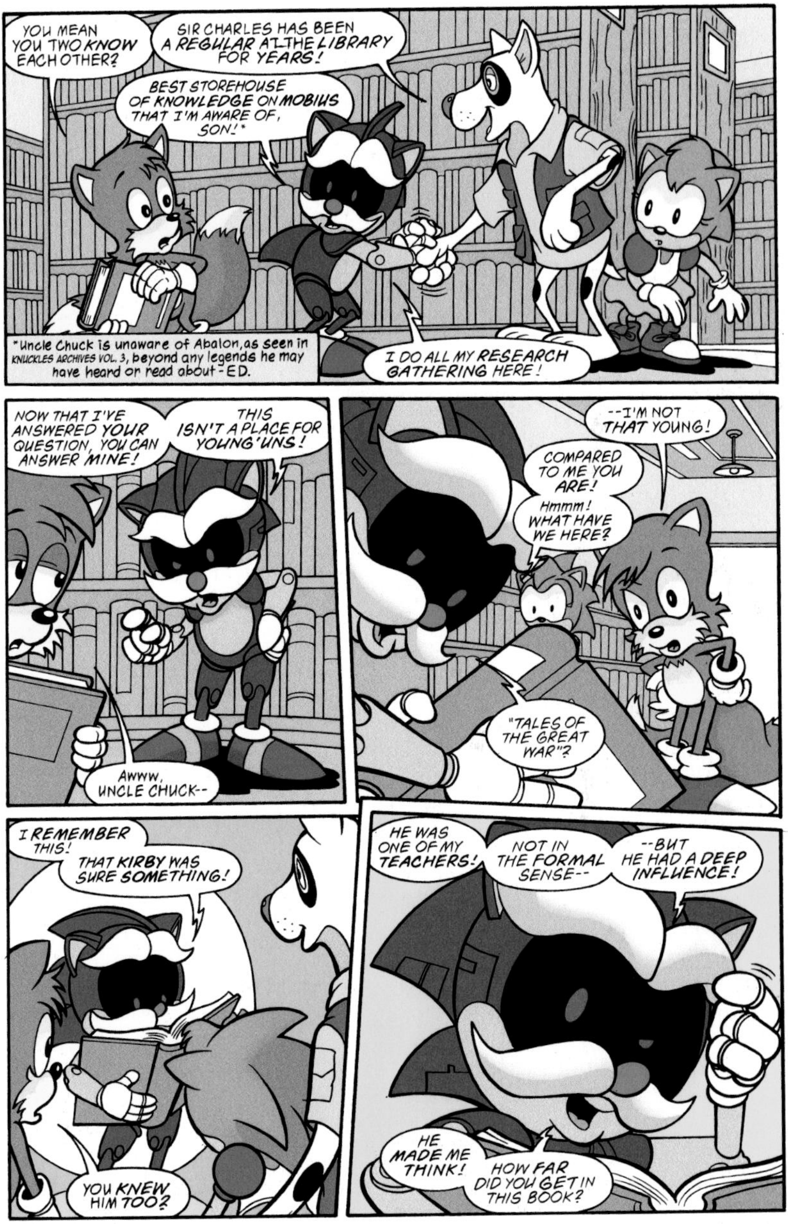

YOU MEAN YOU TWO KNOW EACH OTHER?
SIR CHARLES HAS BEEN A REGULAR AT THE LIBRARY FOR YEARS!
BEST STOREHOUSE OF KNOWLEDGE ON MOBIUS THAT I'M AWARE OF, SON!*
*Uncle Chuck is unaware of Abalon, as seen in KNUCKLES ARCHIVES VOL. 3, beyond any legends he may have heard or read about - ED.
I DO ALL MY RESEARCH GATHERING HERE!
NOW THAT I'VE ANSWERED YOUR QUESTION, YOU CAN ANSWER MINE!
THIS ISN'T A PLACE FOR YOUNG'UNS!
AWWW, UNCLE CHUCK--
--I'M NOT THAT YOUNG!
COMPARED TO ME YOU ARE!
Hmmm! WHAT HAVE WE HERE?
"TALES OF THE GREAT WAR"?
I REMEMBER THIS!
THAT KIRBY WAS SURE SOMETHING!
YOU KNEW HIM TOO?
HE WAS ONE OF MY TEACHERS!
NOT IN THE FORMAL SENSE--
--BUT HE HAD A DEEP INFLUENCE!
HE MADE ME THINK!
HOW FAR DID YOU GET IN THIS BOOK?

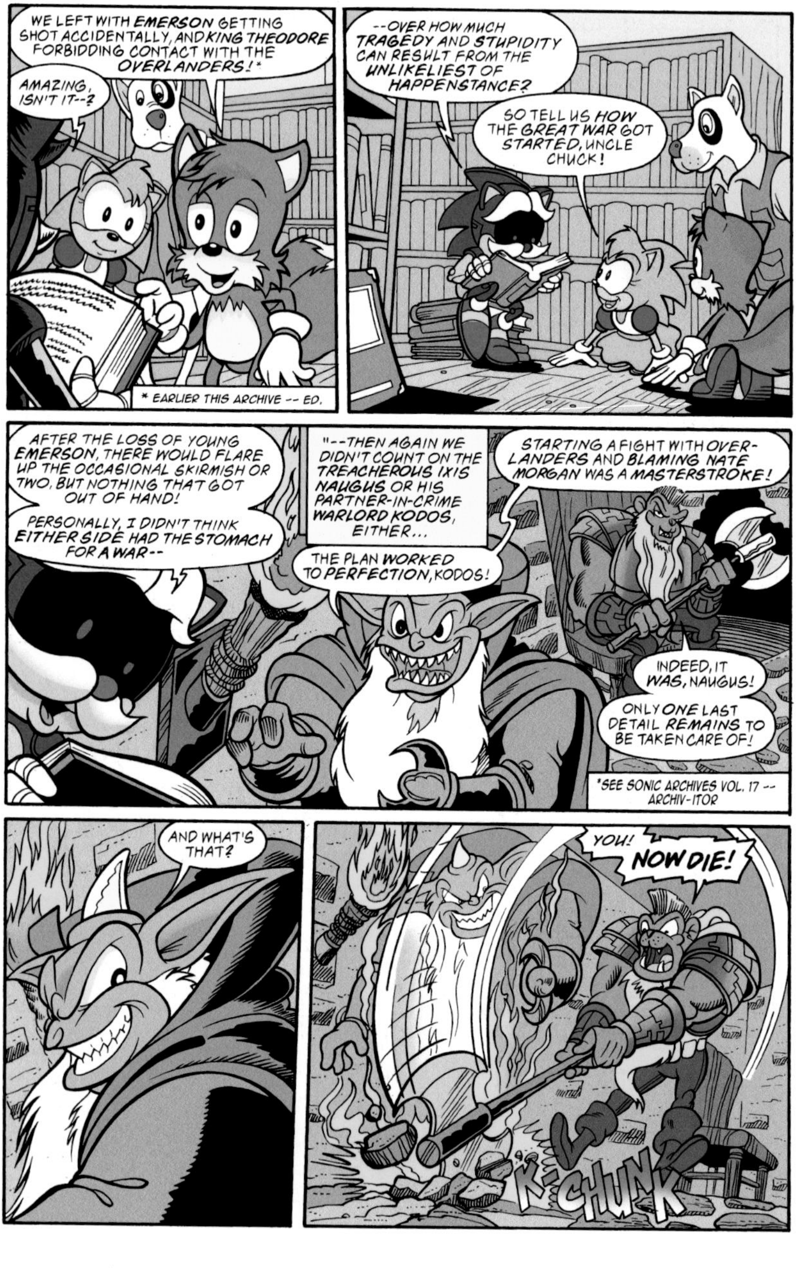

WE LEFT WITH EMERSON GETTING SHOT ACCIDENTALLY, AND KING THEODORE FORBIDDING CONTACT WITH THE OVERLANDERS!*
AMAZING, ISN'T IT--?
* EARLIER THIS ARCHIVE -- ED.
--OVER HOW MUCH TRAGEDY AND STUPIDITY CAN RESULT FROM THE UNLIKELIEST OF HAPPENSTANCE?
SO TELL US HOW THE GREAT WAR GOT STARTED, UNCLE CHUCK!
AFTER THE LOSS OF YOUNG EMERSON, THERE WOULD FLARE UP THE OCCASIONAL SKIRMISH OR TWO, BUT NOTHING THAT GOT OUT OF HAND!
PERSONALLY, I DIDN'T THINK EITHER SIDE HAD THE STOMACH FOR A WAR--
"--THEN AGAIN WE DIDN'T COUNT ON THE TREACHEROUS IXIS NAUGUS OR HIS PARTNER-IN-CRIME WARLORD KODOS, EITHER...
THE PLAN WORKED TO PERFECTION, KODOS!
STARTING A FIGHT WITH OVERLANDERS AND BLAMING NATE MORGAN WAS A MASTERSTROKE!
INDEED, IT WAS, NAUGUS!
ONLY ONE LAST DETAIL REMAINS TO BE TAKEN CARE OF!
*SEE SONIC ARCHIVES VOL. 17 -- ARCHIV-ITOR
AND WHAT'S THAT?
YOU!
NOW DIE!
K-CHUNK

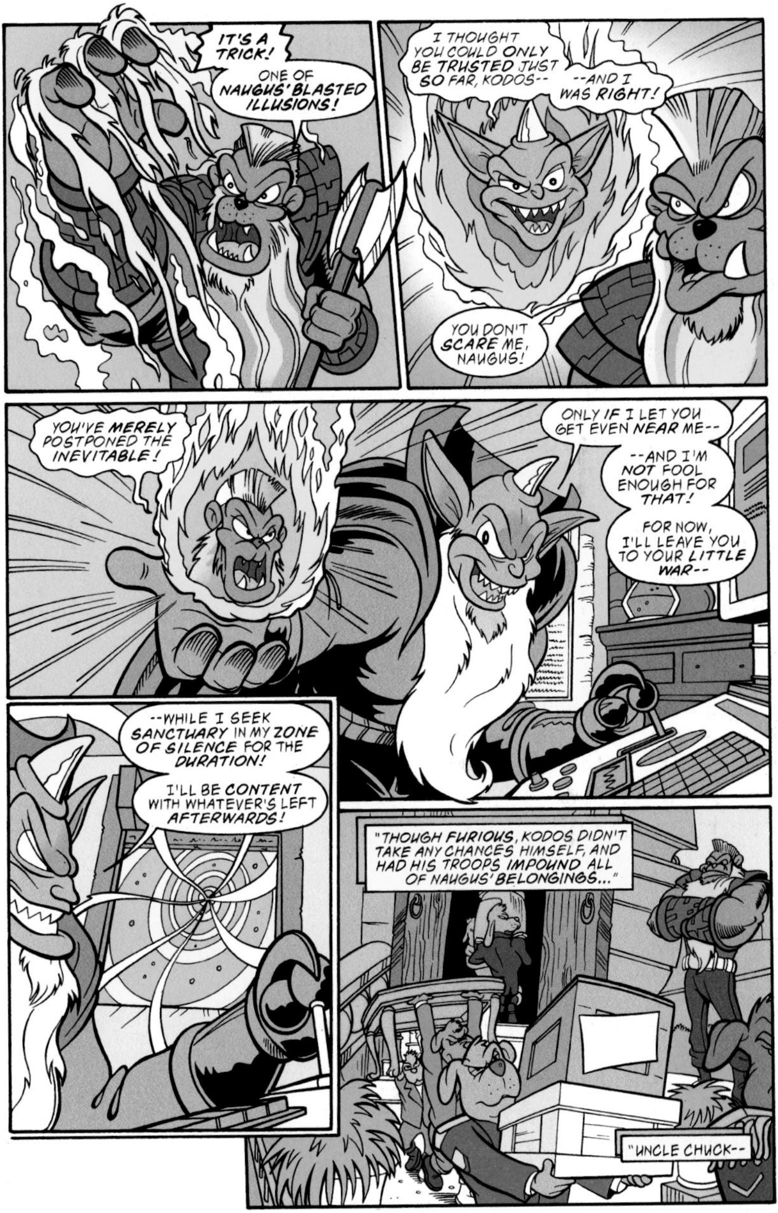
IT'S A TRICK!
ONE OF NAUGUS' BLASTED ILLUSIONS!
I THOUGHT YOU COULD ONLY BE TRUSTED JUST SO FAR, KODOS--
--AND I WAS RIGHT!
YOU DON'T SCARE ME, NAUGUS!
YOU'VE MERELY POSTPONED THE INEVITABLE!
ONLY IF I LET YOU GET EVEN NEAR ME--
--AND I'M NOT FOOL ENOUGH FOR THAT!
FOR NOW, I'LL LEAVE YOU TO YOUR LITTLE WAR--
--WHILE I SEEK SANCTUARY IN MY ZONE OF SILENCE FOR THE DURATION!
I'LL BE CONTENT WITH WHATEVER'S LEFT AFTERWARDS!
"THOUGH FURIOUS, KODOS DIDN'T TAKE ANY CHANCES HIMSELF, AND HAD HIS TROOPS IMPOUND ALL OF NAUGUS' BELONGINGS..."
"UNCLE CHUCK--

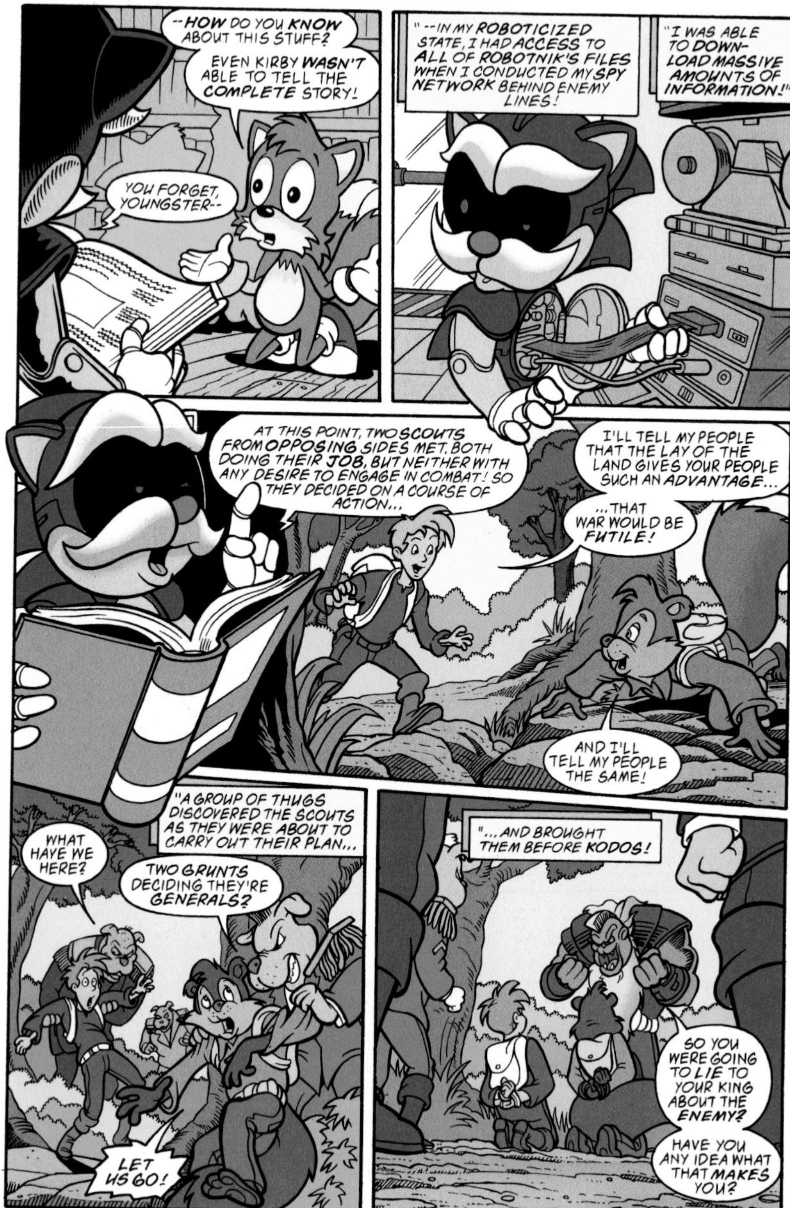
--HOW DO YOU KNOW ABOUT THIS STUFF?
EVEN KIRBY WASN'T ABLE TO TELL THE COMPLETE STORY!
YOU FORGET, YOUNGSTER--
"--IN MY ROBOTICIZED STATE, I HAD ACCESS TO ALL OF ROBOTNIK'S FILES WHEN I CONDUCTED MY SPY NETWORK BEHIND ENEMY LINES!
"I WAS ABLE TO DOWN-LOAD MASSIVE AMOUNTS OF INFORMATION!"
AT THIS POINT, TWO SCOUTS FROM OPPOSING SIDES MET. BOTH DOING THEIR JOB, BUT NEITHER WITH ANY DESIRE TO ENGAGE IN COMBAT! SO THEY DECIDED ON A COURSE OF ACTION...
I'LL TELL MY PEOPLE THAT THE LAY OF THE LAND GIVES YOUR PEOPLE SUCH AN ADVANTAGE...
...THAT WAR WOULD BE FUTILE!
AND I'LL TELL MY PEOPLE THE SAME!
"A GROUP OF THUGS DISCOVERED THE SCOUTS AS THEY WERE ABOUT TO CARRY OUT THEIR PLAN...
WHAT HAVE WE HERE?
TWO GRUNTS DECIDING THEY'RE GENERALS?
LET US GO!
"...AND BROUGHT THEM BEFORE KODOS!
SO YOU WERE GOING TO LIE TO YOUR KING ABOUT THE ENEMY?
HAVE YOU ANY IDEA WHAT THAT MAKES YOU?

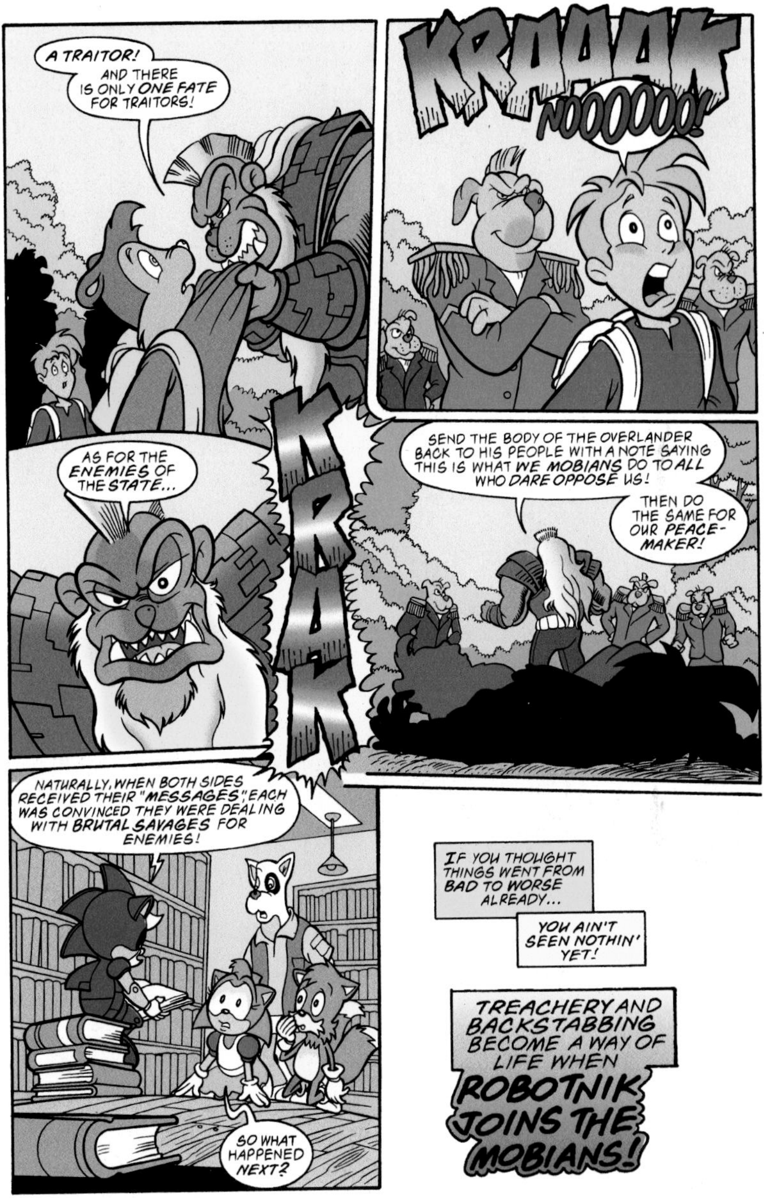
A TRAITOR!
AND THERE IS ONLY ONE FATE FOR TRAITORS!
KRAAAK
NOOOOOO!
AS FOR THE ENEMIES OF THE STATE...
KRAAK
SEND THE BODY OF THE OVERLANDER BACK TO HIS PEOPLE WITH A NOTE SAYING THIS IS WHAT WE MOBIANS DO TO ALL WHO DARE OPPOSE US!
THEN DO THE SAME FOR OUR PEACE-MAKER!
NATURALLY, WHEN BOTH SIDES RECEIVED THEIR "MESSAGES", EACH WAS CONVINCED THEY WERE DEALING WITH BRUTAL SAVAGES FOR ENEMIES!
SO WHAT HAPPENED NEXT?
IF YOU THOUGHT THINGS WENT FROM BAD TO WORSE ALREADY...
YOU AIN'T SEEN NOTHIN' YET!
TREACHERY AND BACKSTABBING BECOME A WAY OF LIFE WHEN
ROBOTNIK JOINS THE MOBIANS!

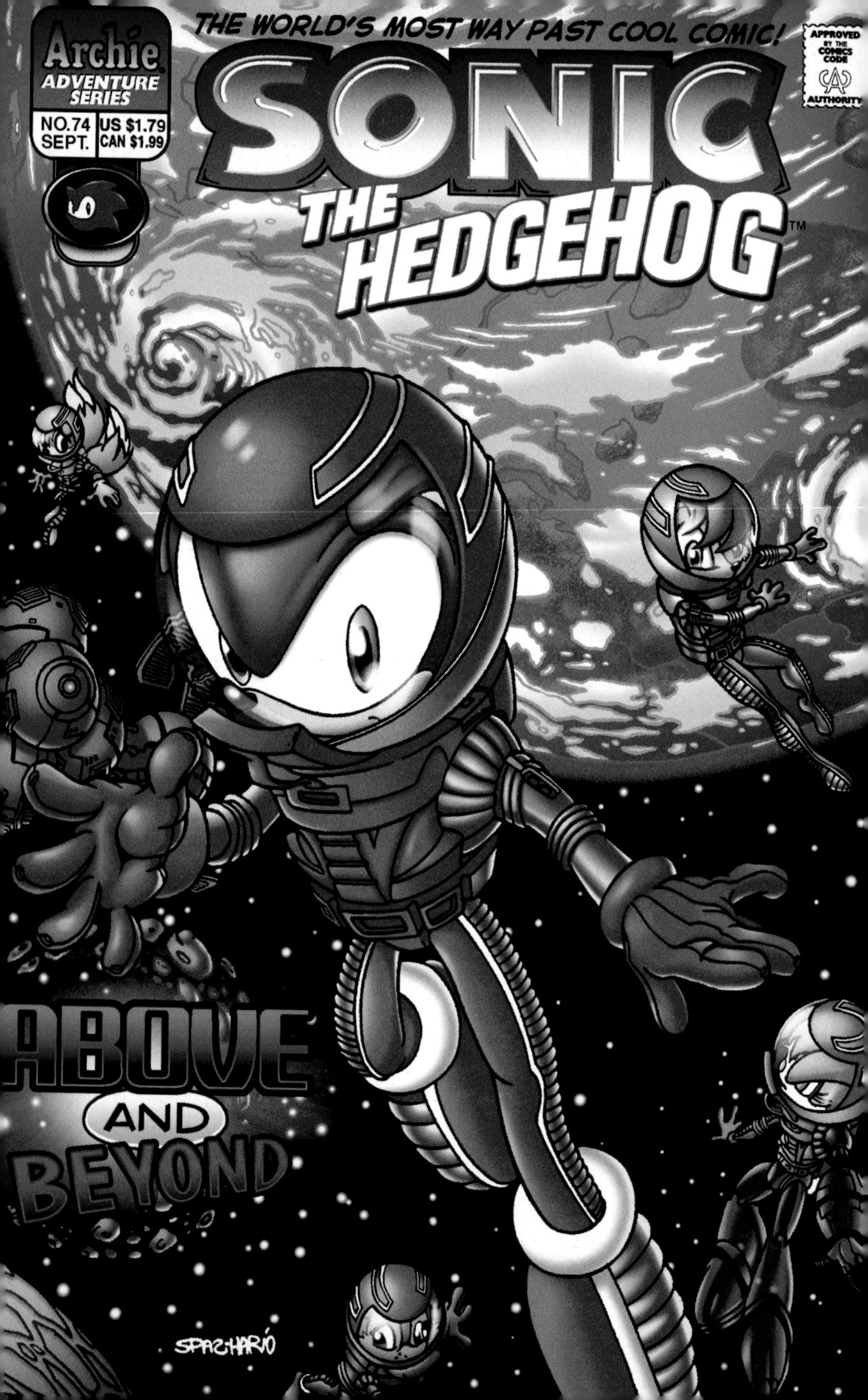
THE WORLD'S MOST WAY PAST COOL COMIC!
Archie ADVENTURE SERIES
NO.74 SEPT.
US $1.79 CAN $1.99
APPROVED BY THE COMICS CODE AUTHORITY
SONIC THE HEDGEHOG™
ABOVE AND BEYOND
SPAZIANTE

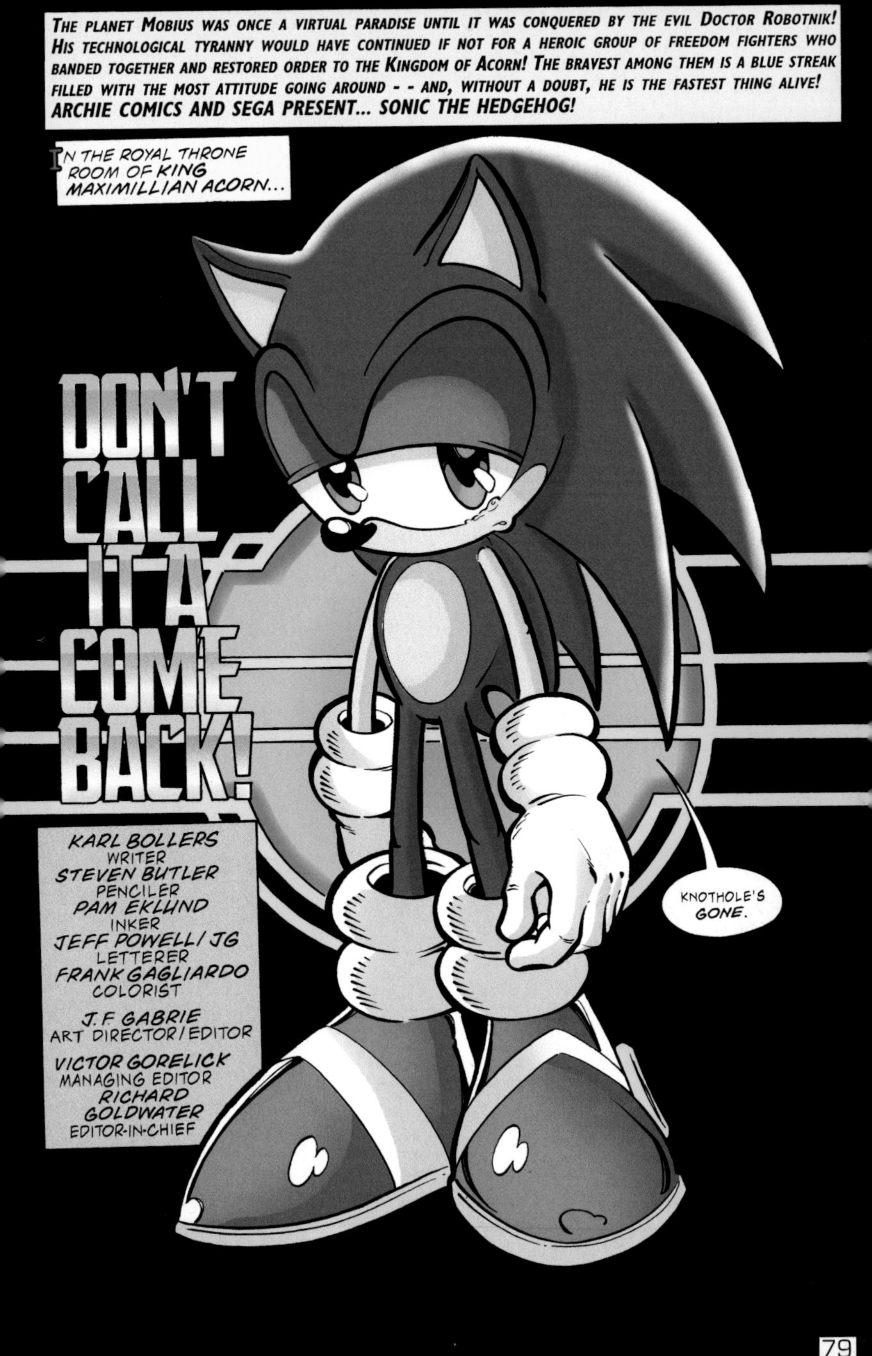
THE PLANET MOBIUS WAS ONCE A VIRTUAL PARADISE UNTIL IT WAS CONQUERED BY THE EVIL DOCTOR ROBOTNIK! HIS TECHNOLOGICAL TYRANNY WOULD HAVE CONTINUED IF NOT FOR A HEROIC GROUP OF FREEDOM FIGHTERS WHO BANDED TOGETHER AND RESTORED ORDER TO THE KINGDOM OF ACORN! THE BRAVEST AMONG THEM IS A BLUE STREAK FILLED WITH THE MOST ATTITUDE GOING AROUND - - AND, WITHOUT A DOUBT, HE IS THE FASTEST THING ALIVE! ARCHIE COMICS AND SEGA PRESENT... SONIC THE HEDGEHOG!
IN THE ROYAL THRONE ROOM OF KING MAXIMILLIAN ACORN...
DON'T CALL IT A COME BACK!
KARL BOLLERS WRITER
STEVEN BUTLER PENCILER
PAM EKLUND INKER
JEFF POWELL/ JG LETTERER
FRANK GAGLIARDO COLORIST
J.F. GABRIE ART DIRECTOR/EDITOR
VICTOR GORELICK MANAGING EDITOR
RICHARD GOLDWATER EDITOR-IN-CHIEF
KNOTHOLE'S GONE.

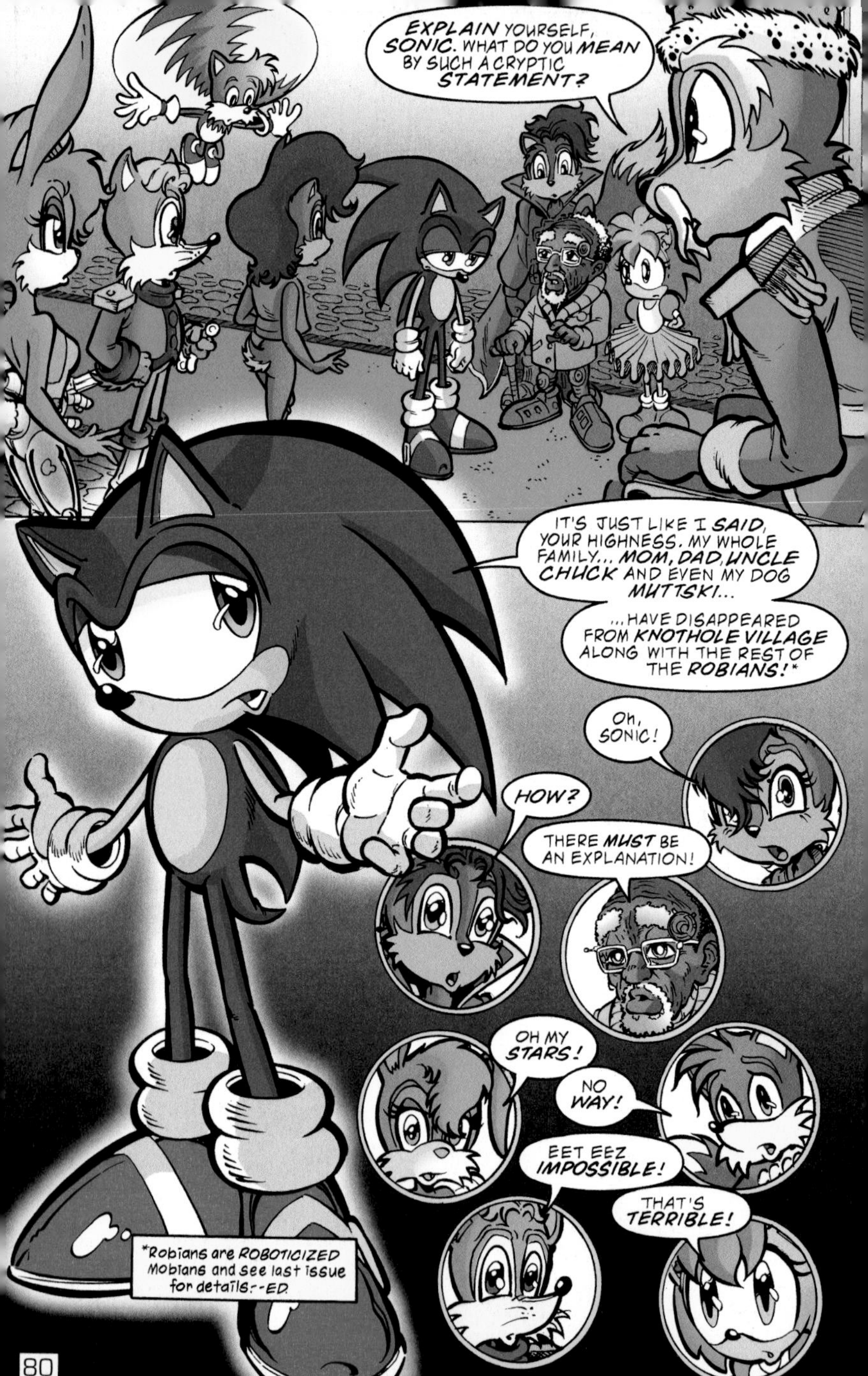
EXPLAIN YOURSELF, SONIC. WHAT DO YOU MEAN BY SUCH A CRYPTIC STATEMENT?
IT'S JUST LIKE I SAID, YOUR HIGHNESS. MY WHOLE FAMILY... MOM, DAD, UNCLE CHUCK AND EVEN MY DOG MUTTSKI...
...HAVE DISAPPEARED FROM KNOTHOLE VILLAGE ALONG WITH THE REST OF THE ROBIANS!*
Oh, SONIC!
HOW?
THERE MUST BE AN EXPLANATION!
OH MY STARS!
NO WAY!
EET EEZ IMPOSSIBLE!
THAT'S TERRIBLE!
*Robians are ROBOTICIZED Mobians and see last issue for details.--ED.

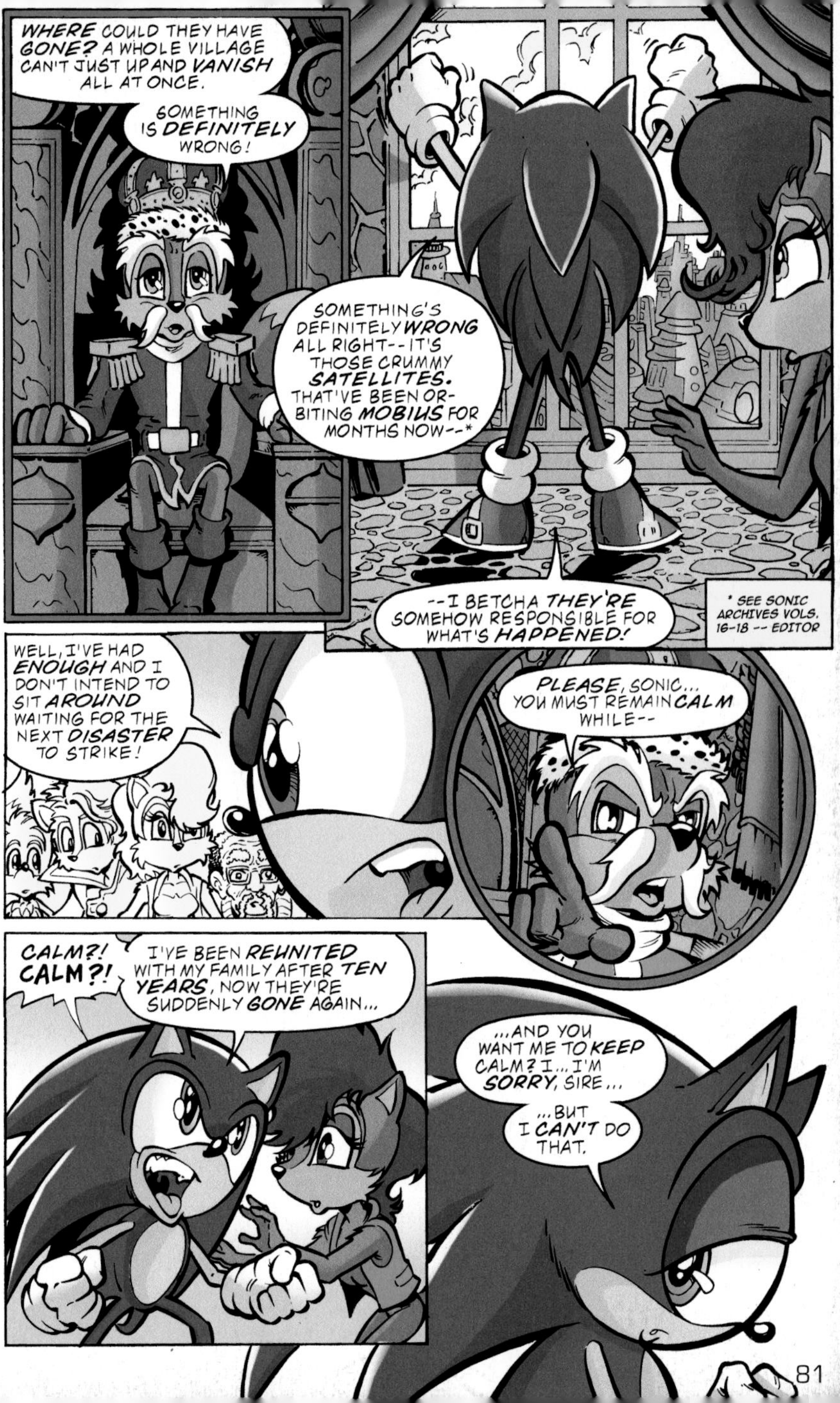
WHERE COULD THEY HAVE GONE? A WHOLE VILLAGE CAN'T JUST UP AND VANISH ALL AT ONCE.
SOMETHING IS DEFINITELY WRONG!
SOMETHING'S DEFINITELY WRONG ALL RIGHT--IT'S THOSE CRUMMY SATELLITES. THAT'VE BEEN OR-BITING MOBIUS FOR MONTHS NOW--*
--I BETCHA THEY'RE SOMEHOW RESPONSIBLE FOR WHAT'S HAPPENED!
* SEE SONIC ARCHIVES VOLS. 16-18 -- EDITOR
WELL, I'VE HAD ENOUGH AND I DON'T INTEND TO SIT AROUND WAITING FOR THE NEXT DISASTER TO STRIKE!
PLEASE, SONIC... YOU MUST REMAIN CALM WHILE--
CALM?! CALM?!
I'VE BEEN REUNITED WITH MY FAMILY AFTER TEN YEARS, NOW THEY'RE SUDDENLY GONE AGAIN...
...AND YOU WANT ME TO KEEP CALM? I...I'M SORRY, SIRE...
...BUT I CAN'T DO THAT.

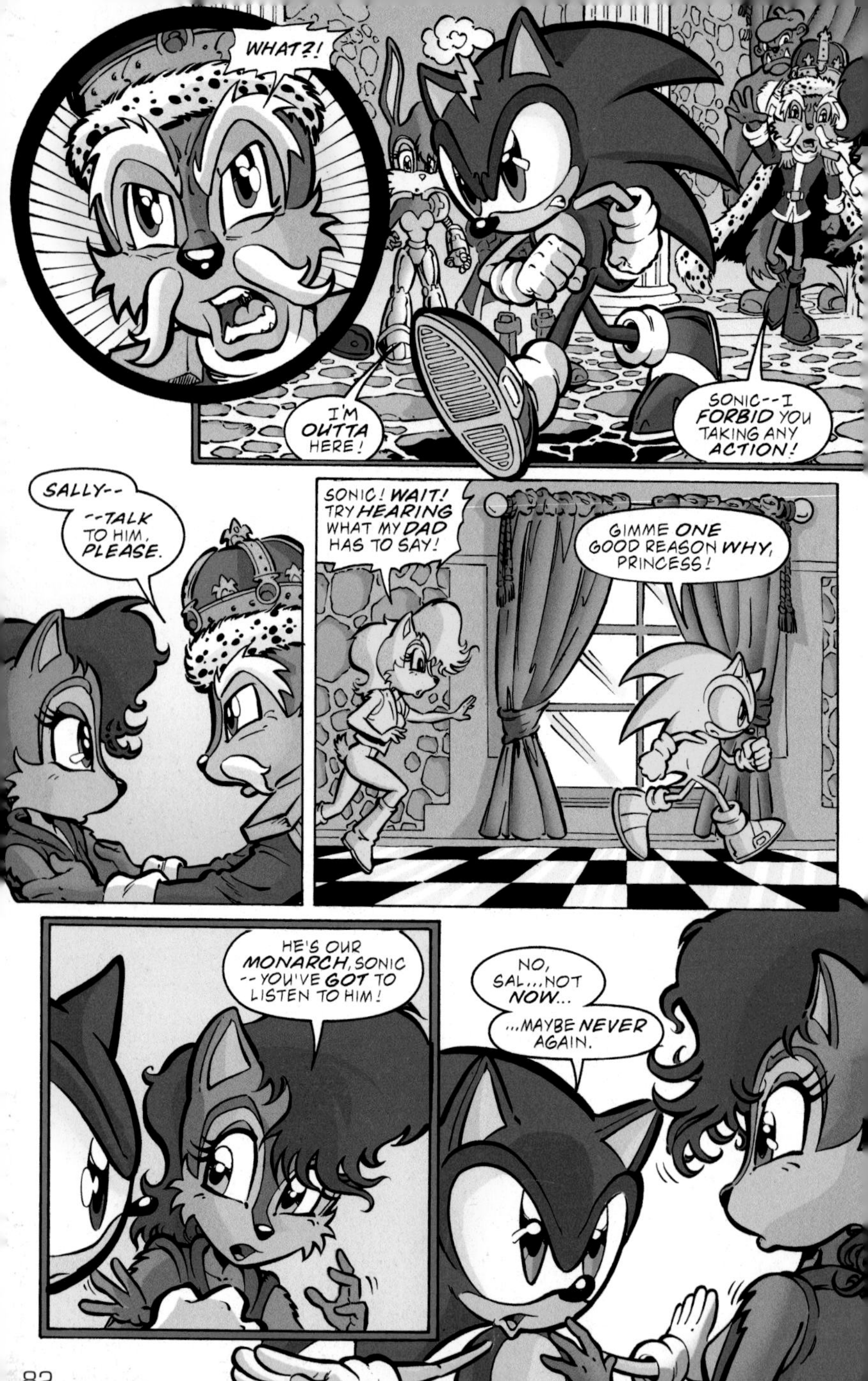

WHAT?!
I'M OUTTA HERE!
SONIC--I FORBID YOU TAKING ANY ACTION!
SALLY--
--TALK TO HIM, PLEASE.
SONIC! WAIT! TRY HEARING WHAT MY DAD HAS TO SAY!
GIMME ONE GOOD REASON WHY, PRINCESS!
HE'S OUR MONARCH, SONIC--YOU'VE GOT TO LISTEN TO HIM!
NO, SAL...NOT NOW...
...MAYBE NEVER AGAIN.

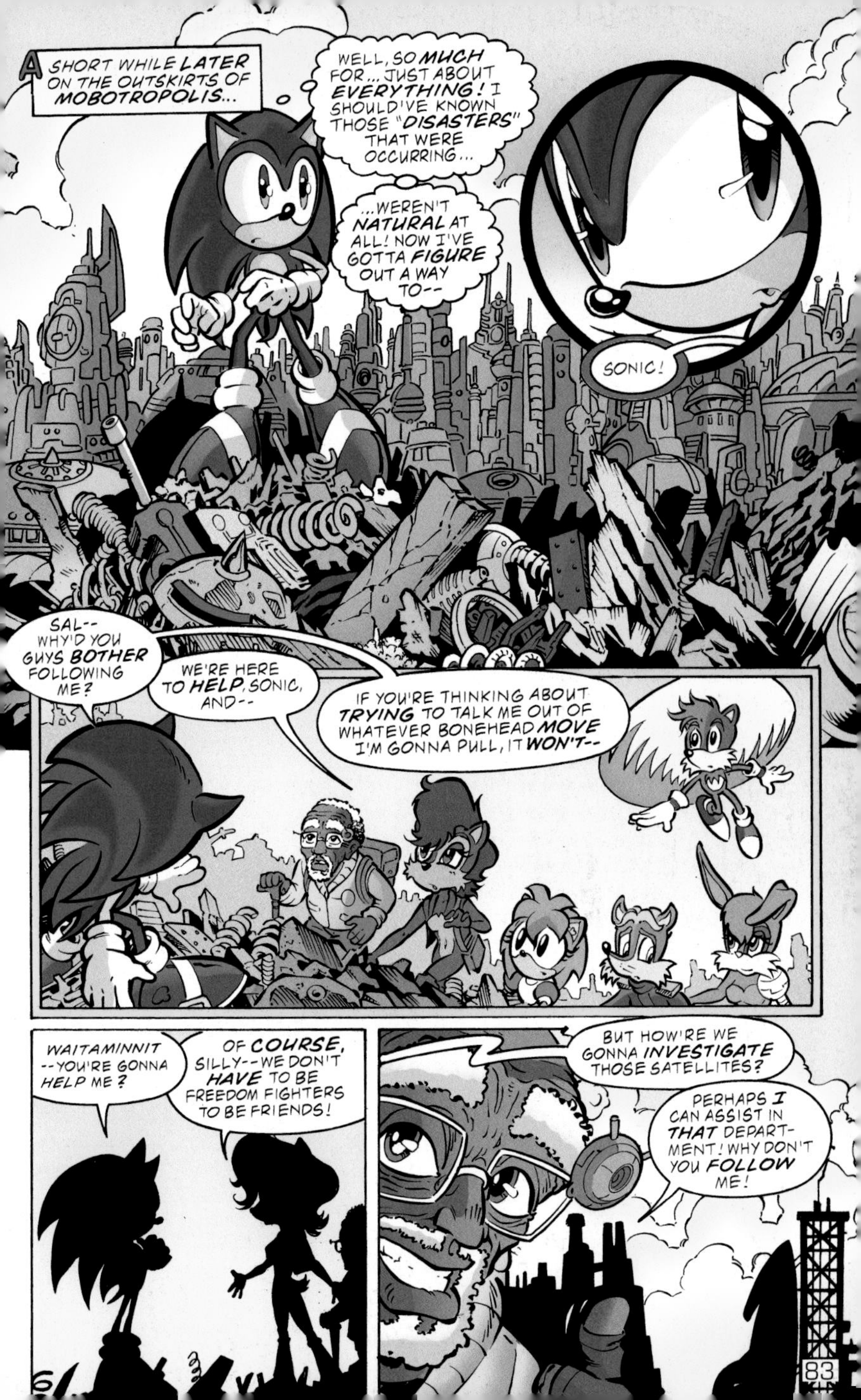
A SHORT WHILE LATER ON THE OUTSKIRTS OF MOBOTROPOLIS...
WELL, SO MUCH FOR... JUST ABOUT EVERYTHING! I SHOULD'VE KNOWN THOSE "DISASTERS" THAT WERE OCCURRING...
...WEREN'T NATURAL AT ALL! NOW I'VE GOTTA FIGURE OUT A WAY TO--
SONIC!
SAL--WHY'D YOU GUYS BOTHER FOLLOWING ME?
WE'RE HERE TO HELP, SONIC, AND--
IF YOU'RE THINKING ABOUT TRYING TO TALK ME OUT OF WHATEVER BONEHEAD MOVE I'M GONNA PULL, IT WON'T--
WAITAMINNIT--YOU'RE GONNA HELP ME?
OF COURSE, SILLY--WE DON'T HAVE TO BE FREEDOM FIGHTERS TO BE FRIENDS!
BUT HOW'RE WE GONNA INVESTIGATE THOSE SATELLITES?
PERHAPS I CAN ASSIST IN THAT DEPARTMENT! WHY DON'T YOU FOLLOW ME!

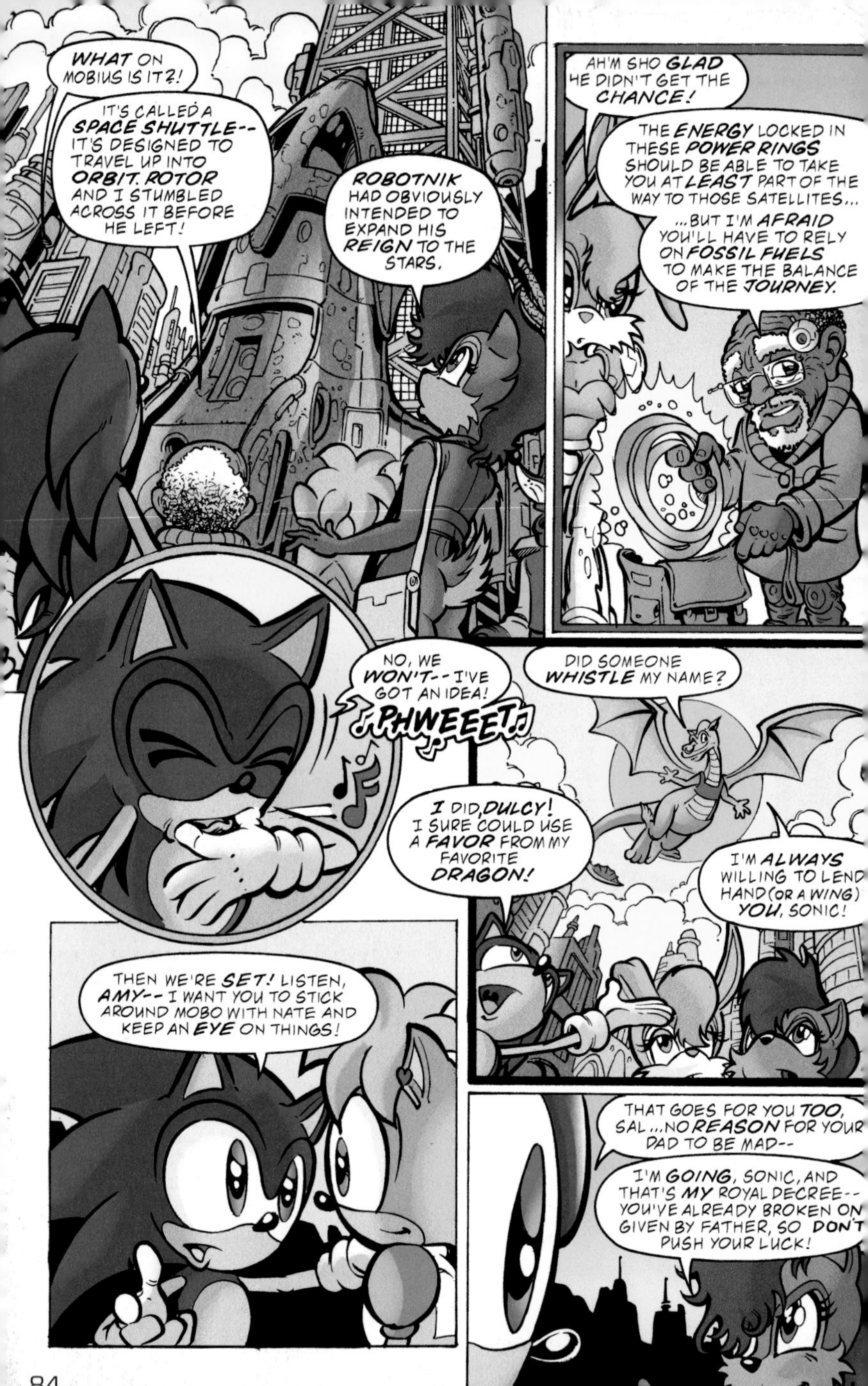
WHAT ON MOBIUS IS IT?!
IT'S CALLED A SPACE SHUTTLE-- IT'S DESIGNED TO TRAVEL UP INTO ORBIT. ROTOR AND I STUMBLED ACROSS IT BEFORE HE LEFT!
ROBOTNIK HAD OBVIOUSLY INTENDED TO EXPAND HIS REIGN TO THE STARS.
AH'M SHO GLAD HE DIDN'T GET THE CHANCE!
THE ENERGY LOCKED IN THESE POWER RINGS SHOULD BE ABLE TO TAKE YOU AT LEAST PART OF THE WAY TO THOSE SATELLITES...
...BUT I'M AFRAID YOU'LL HAVE TO RELY ON FOSSIL FUELS TO MAKE THE BALANCE OF THE JOURNEY.
NO, WE WON'T-- I'VE GOT AN IDEA!
PHWEEET!
DID SOMEONE WHISTLE MY NAME?
I DID, DULCY! I SURE COULD USE A FAVOR FROM MY FAVORITE DRAGON!
I'M ALWAYS WILLING TO LEND HAND (OR A WING) YOU, SONIC!
THEN WE'RE SET! LISTEN, AMY-- I WANT YOU TO STICK AROUND MOBO WITH NATE AND KEEP AN EYE ON THINGS!
THAT GOES FOR YOU TOO, SAL... NO REASON FOR YOUR DAD TO BE MAD--
I'M GOING, SONIC, AND THAT'S MY ROYAL DECREE-- YOU'VE ALREADY BROKEN ON GIVEN BY FATHER, SO DON'T PUSH YOUR LUCK!

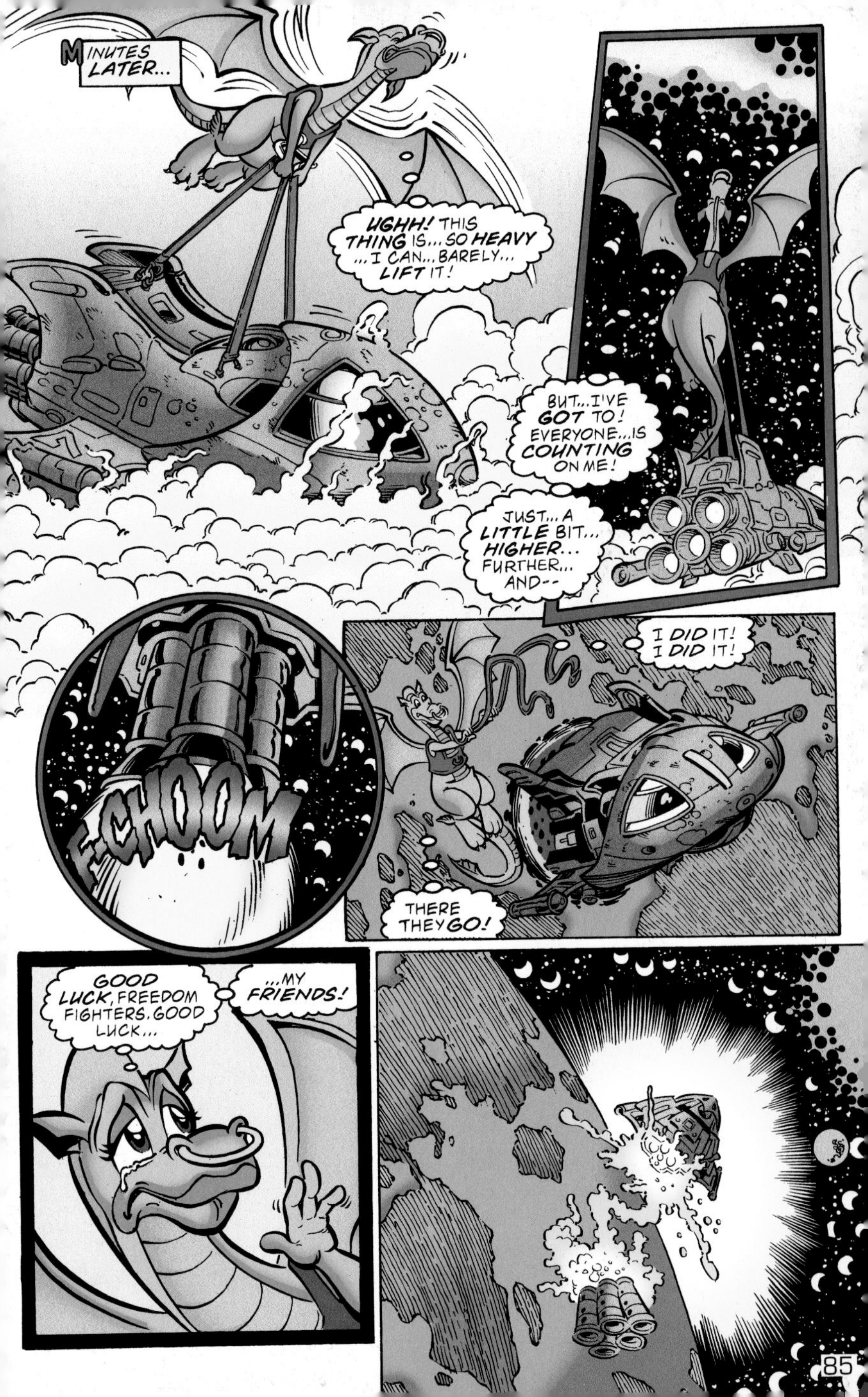
MINUTES LATER...
UGHH! THIS THING IS... SO HEAVY ...I CAN... BARELY... LIFT IT!
BUT... I'VE GOT TO! EVERYONE... IS COUNTING ON ME!
JUST... A LITTLE BIT... HIGHER... FURTHER... AND--
FCHOOM
I DID IT! I DID IT!
THERE THEY GO!
GOOD LUCK, FREEDOM FIGHTERS. GOOD LUCK...
...MY FRIENDS!

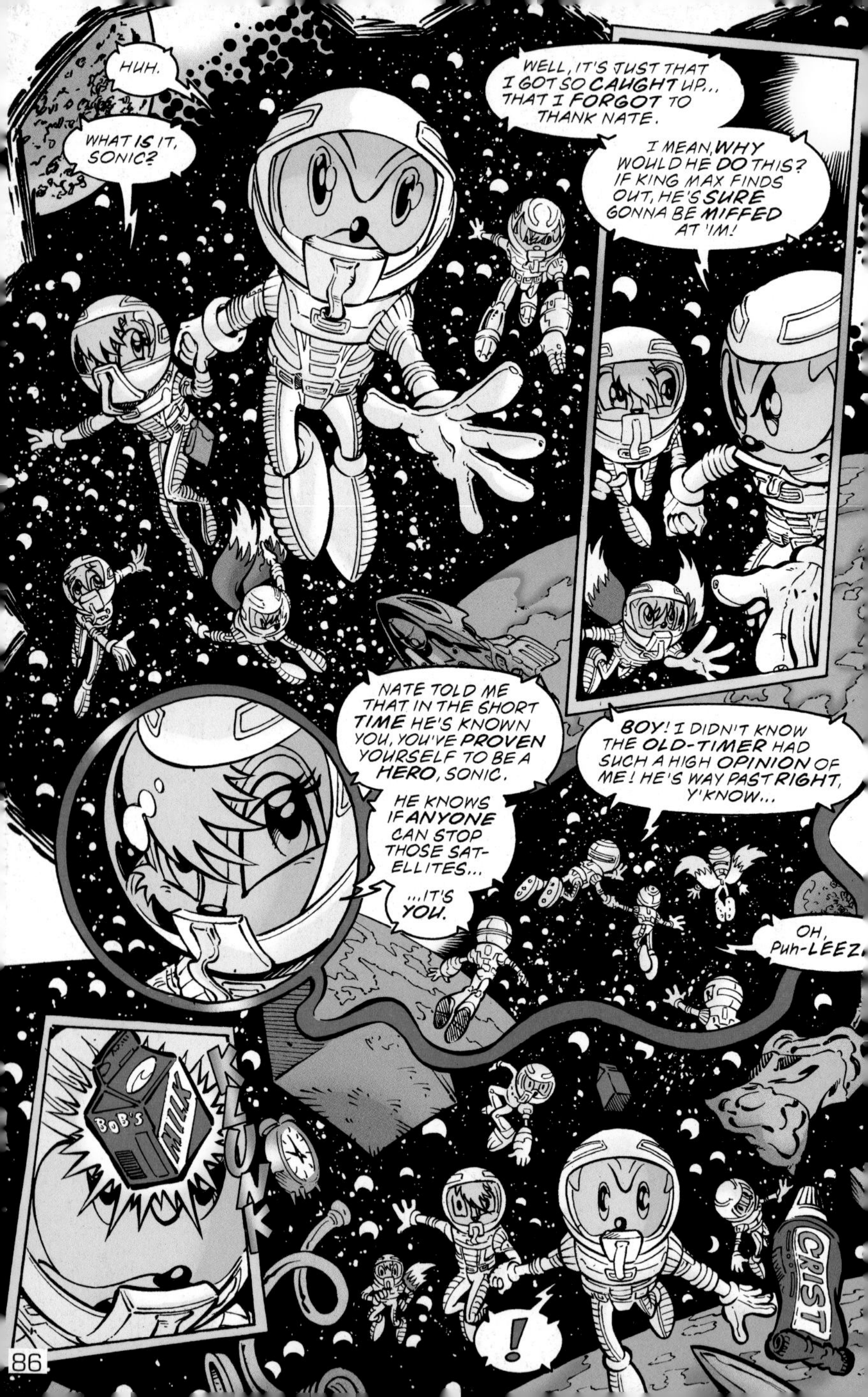
HUH.
WHAT IS IT, SONIC?
WELL, IT'S JUST THAT I GOT SO CAUGHT UP... THAT I FORGOT TO THANK NATE.
I MEAN, WHY WOULD HE DO THIS? IF KING MAX FINDS OUT, HE'S SURE GONNA BE MIFFED AT 'IM!
NATE TOLD ME THAT IN THE SHORT TIME HE'S KNOWN YOU, YOU'VE PROVEN YOURSELF TO BE A HERO, SONIC.
HE KNOWS IF ANYONE CAN STOP THOSE SAT-ELLITES...
...IT'S YOU.
BOY! I DIDN'T KNOW THE OLD-TIMER HAD SUCH A HIGH OPINION OF ME! HE'S WAY PAST RIGHT, Y'KNOW...
OH, Puh-LEEZ.
BOB'S MILK
KLUNK
CRIST
!

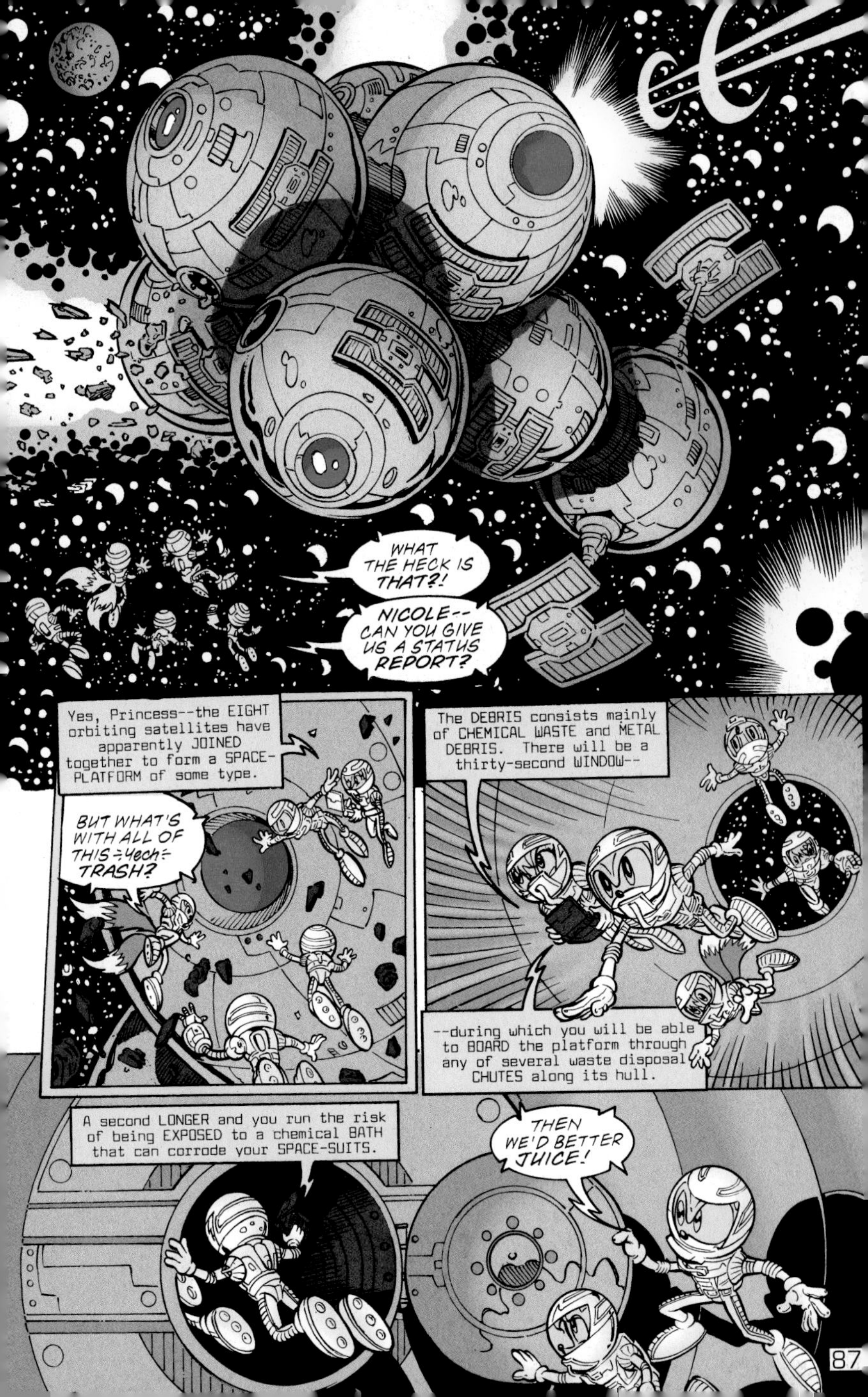
WHAT THE HECK IS THAT?!
NICOLE-- CAN YOU GIVE US A STATUS REPORT?
Yes, Princess--the EIGHT orbiting satellites have apparently JOINED together to form a SPACE-PLATFORM of some type.
BUT WHAT'S WITH ALL OF THIS =Yech= TRASH?
The DEBRIS consists mainly of CHEMICAL WASTE and METAL DEBRIS. There will be a thirty-second WINDOW--
--during which you will be able to BOARD the platform through any of several waste disposal CHUTES along its hull.
A second LONGER and you run the risk of being EXPOSED to a chemical BATH that can corrode your SPACE-SUITS.
THEN WE'D BETTER JUICE!

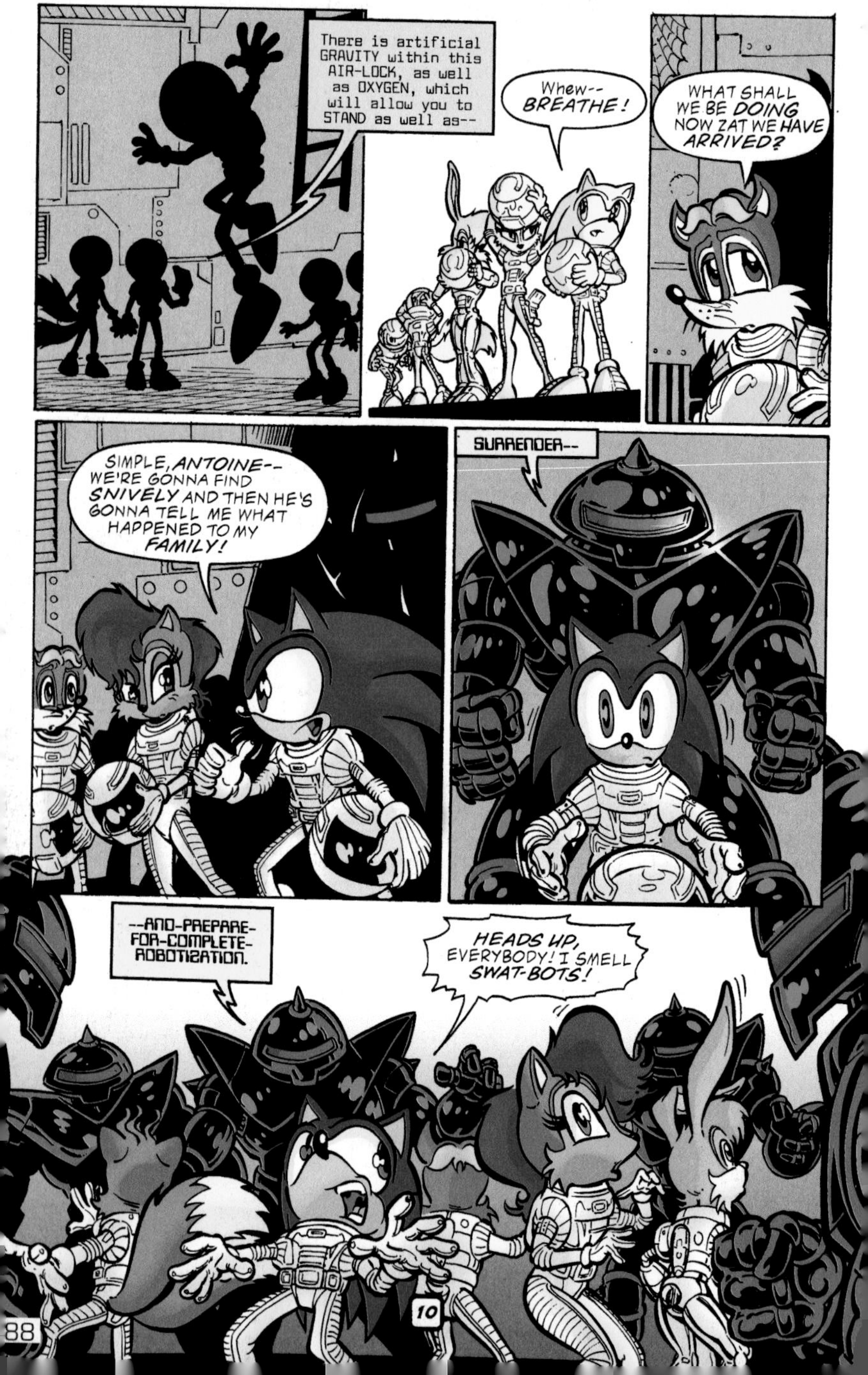

There is artificial GRAVITY within this AIR-LOCK, as well as OXYGEN, which will allow you to STAND as well as--
Whew-- BREATHE!
WHAT SHALL WE BE DOING NOW ZAT WE HAVE ARRIVED?
SIMPLE, ANTOINE-- WE'RE GONNA FIND SNIVELY AND THEN HE'S GONNA TELL ME WHAT HAPPENED TO MY FAMILY!
SURRENDER--
--AND-PREPARE-FOR-COMPLETE-ROBOTIZATION.
HEADS UP, EVERYBODY! I SMELL SWAT-BOTS!
10

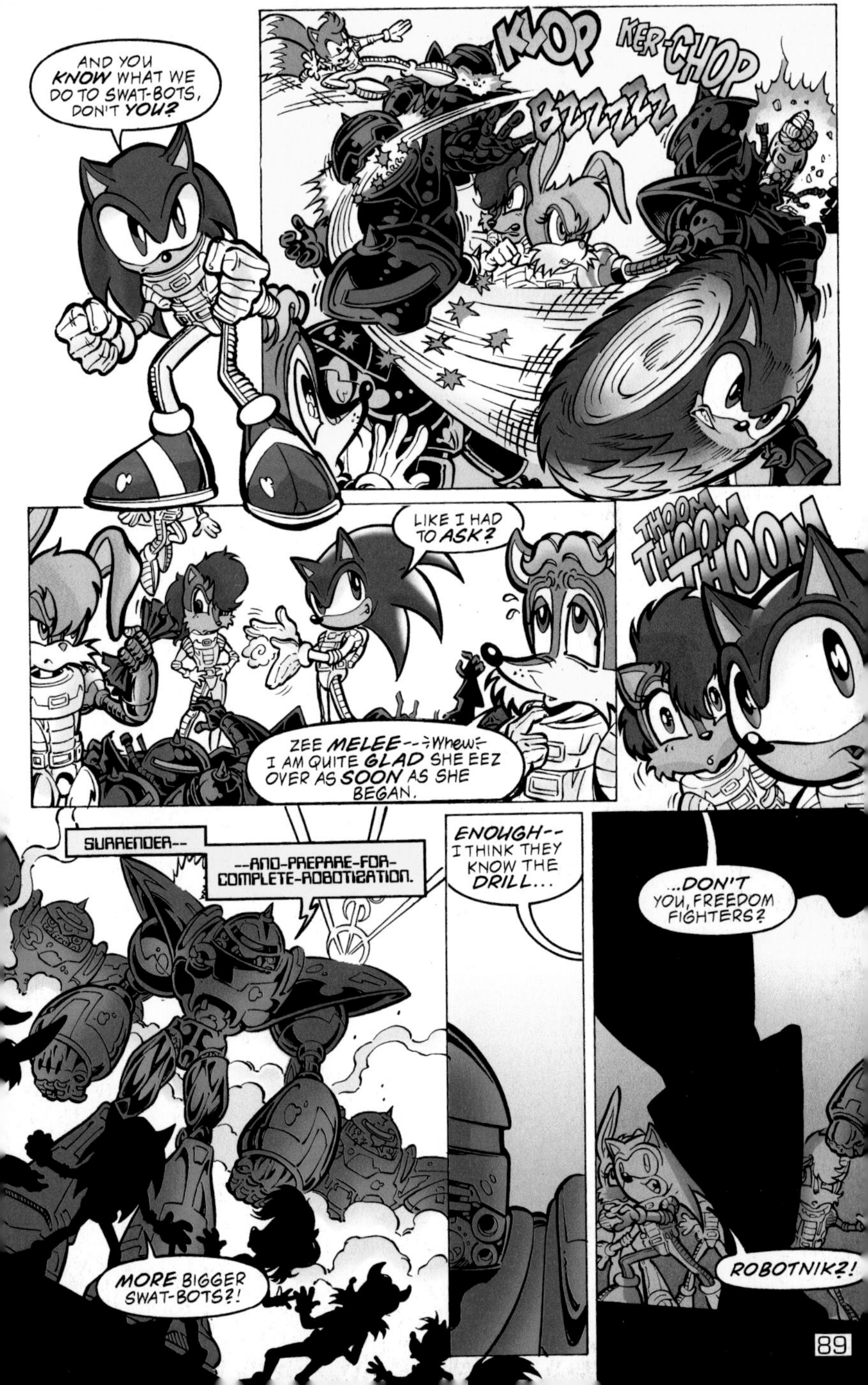

AND YOU KNOW WHAT WE DO TO SWAT-BOTS, DON'T YOU?
KLOP
KER-CHOP
BZZZZZ
LIKE I HAD TO ASK?
THOOM THOOM THOOM
ZEE MELEE-- whew I AM QUITE GLAD SHE EEZ OVER AS SOON AS SHE BEGAN.
SURRENDER--
--AND-PREPARE-FOR-COMPLETE-ROBOTIZATION.
ENOUGH-- I THINK THEY KNOW THE DRILL...
...DON'T YOU, FREEDOM FIGHTERS?
MORE BIGGER SWAT-BOTS?!
ROBOTNIK?!

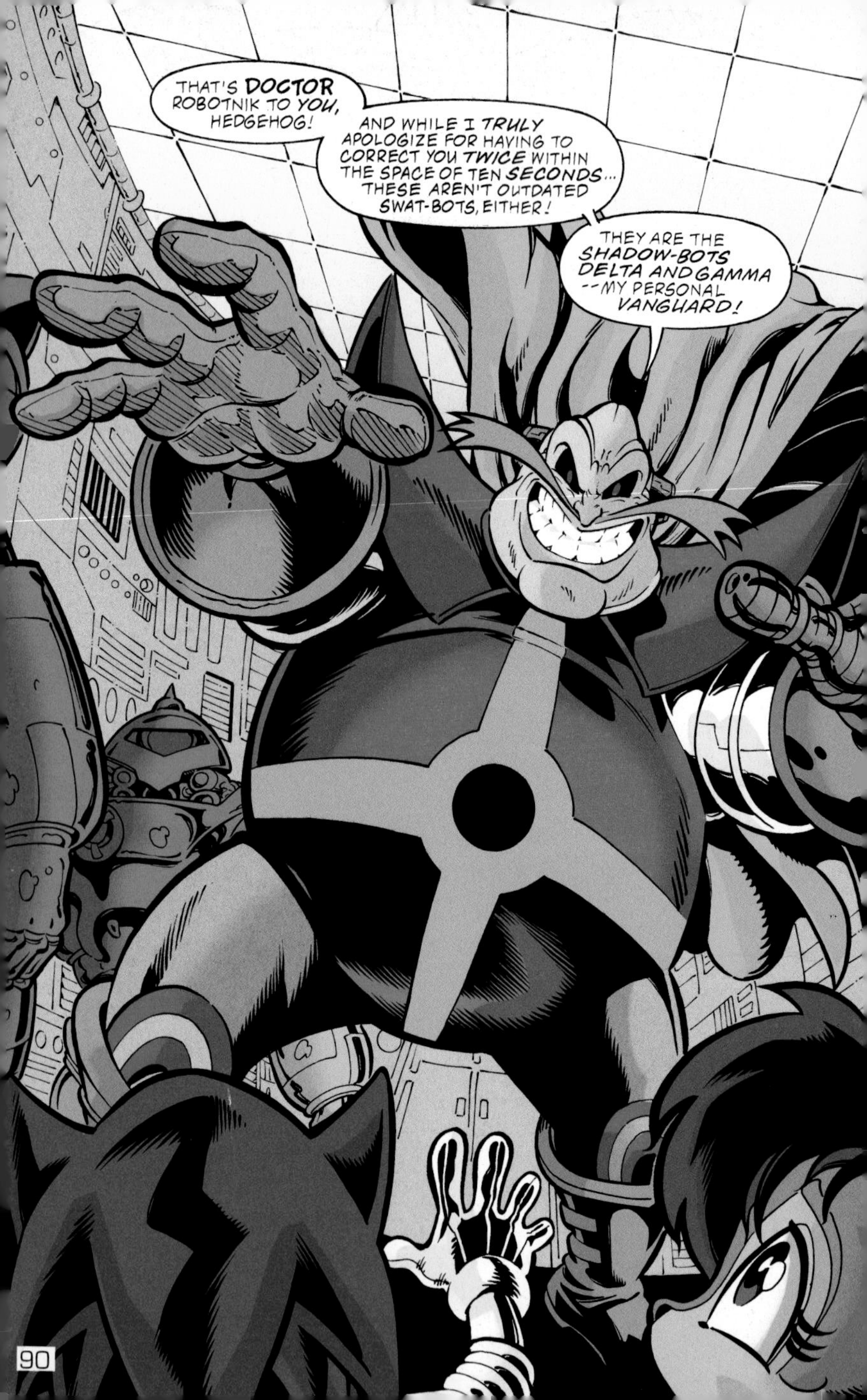
THAT'S **DOCTOR** ROBOTNIK TO *YOU*, HEDGEHOG!
AND WHILE I *TRULY* APOLOGIZE FOR HAVING TO CORRECT YOU *TWICE* WITHIN THE SPACE OF TEN *SECONDS*... THESE AREN'T OUTDATED SWAT-BOTS, EITHER!
THEY ARE THE *SHADOW-BOTS DELTA* AND *GAMMA* --MY PERSONAL *VANGUARD*!

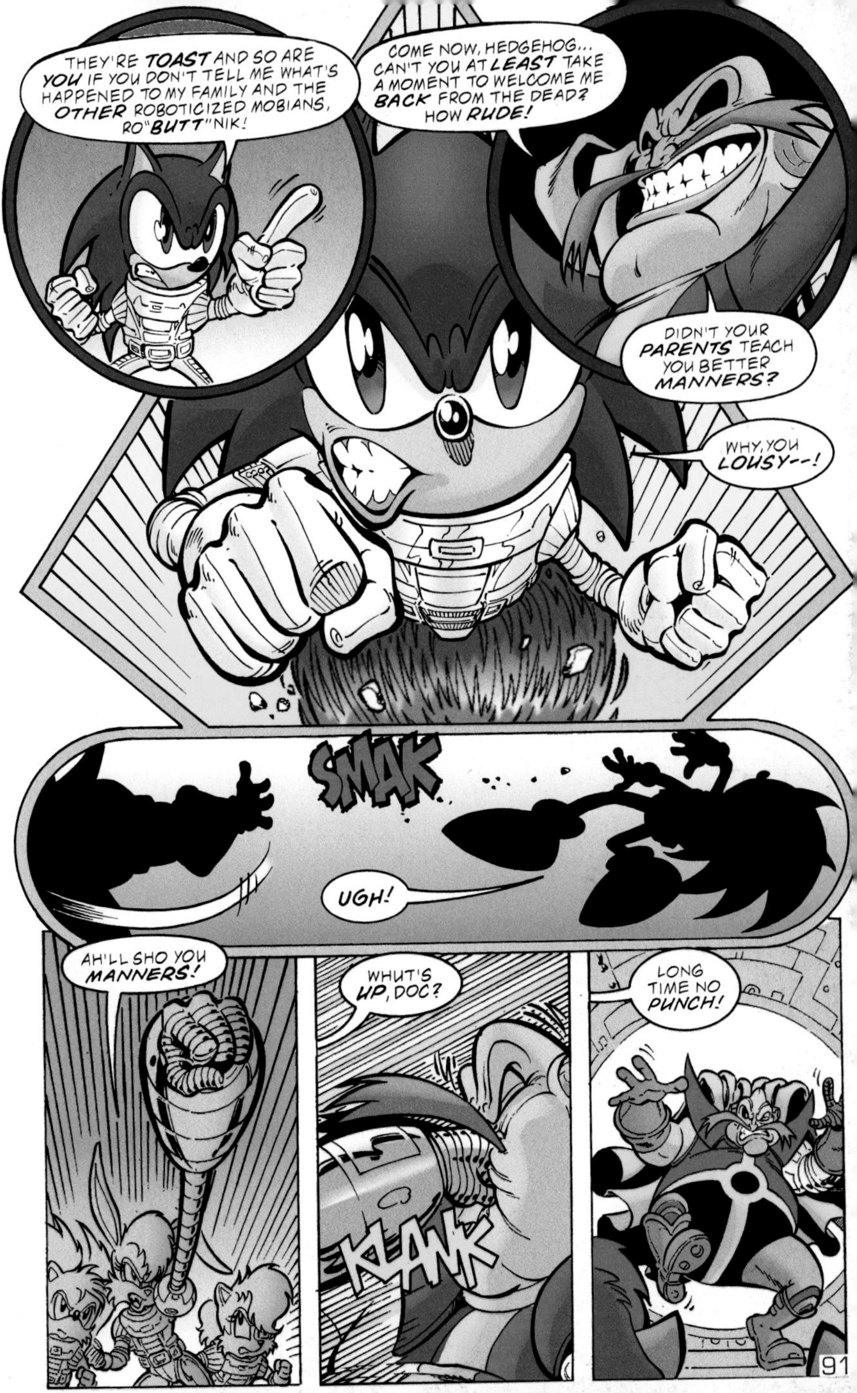
THEY'RE TOAST AND SO ARE YOU IF YOU DON'T TELL ME WHAT'S HAPPENED TO MY FAMILY AND THE OTHER ROBOTICIZED MOBIANS, RO"BUTT"NIK!
COME NOW, HEDGEHOG... CAN'T YOU AT LEAST TAKE A MOMENT TO WELCOME ME BACK FROM THE DEAD? HOW RUDE!
DIDN'T YOUR PARENTS TEACH YOU BETTER MANNERS?
WHY, YOU LOUSY--!
SMAK
UGH!
AH'LL SHO YOU MANNERS!
WHUT'S UP, DOC?
KLANK
LONG TIME NO PUNCH!

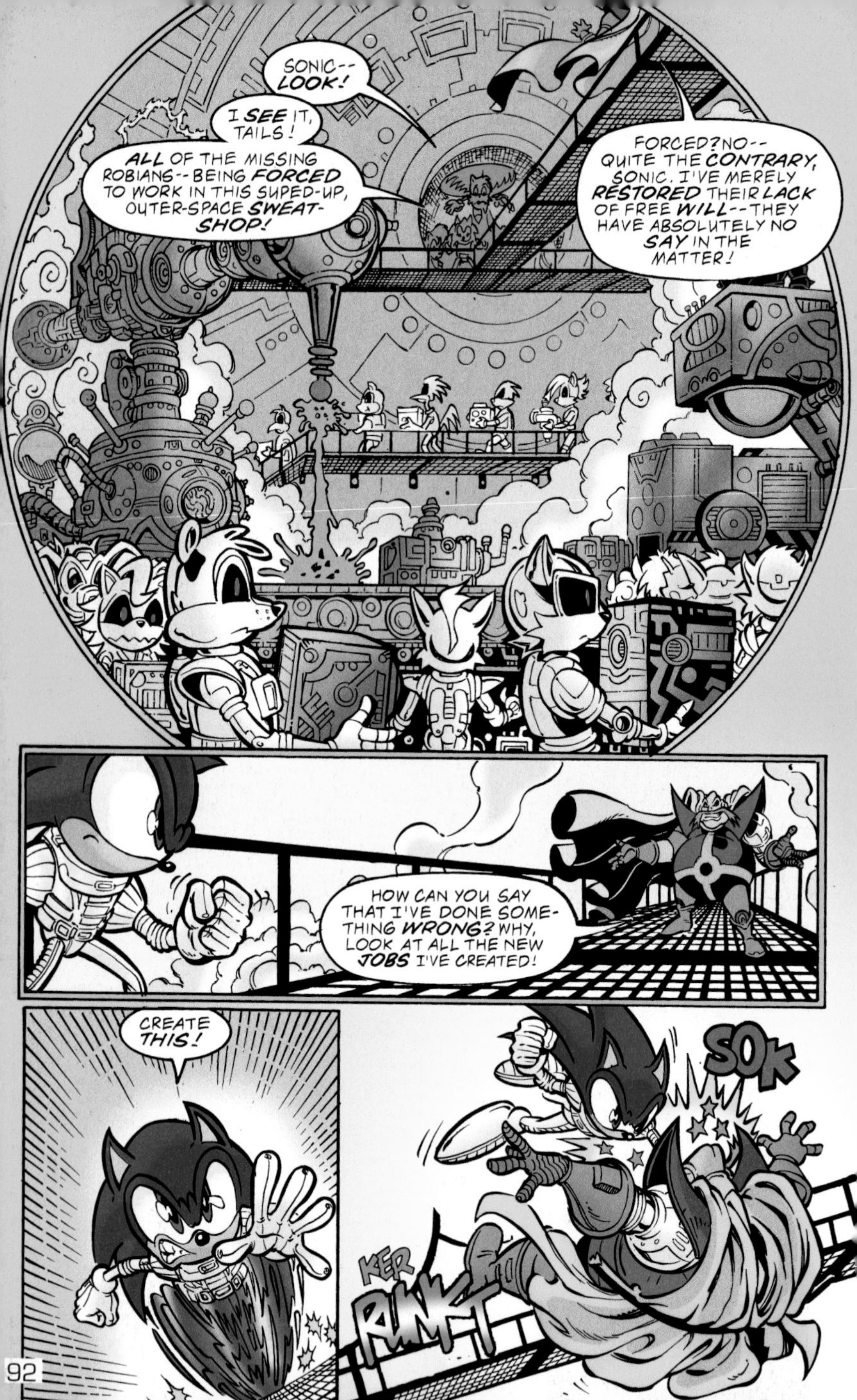

SONIC-- LOOK!
I SEE IT, TAILS!
ALL OF THE MISSING ROBIANS--BEING FORCED TO WORK IN THIS SUPED-UP, OUTER-SPACE SWEAT-SHOP!
FORCED? NO-- QUITE THE CONTRARY, SONIC. I'VE MERELY RESTORED THEIR LACK OF FREE WILL--THEY HAVE ABSOLUTELY NO SAY IN THE MATTER!
HOW CAN YOU SAY THAT I'VE DONE SOME-THING WRONG? WHY, LOOK AT ALL THE NEW JOBS I'VE CREATED!
CREATE THIS!
SOK
KER
PLUNK

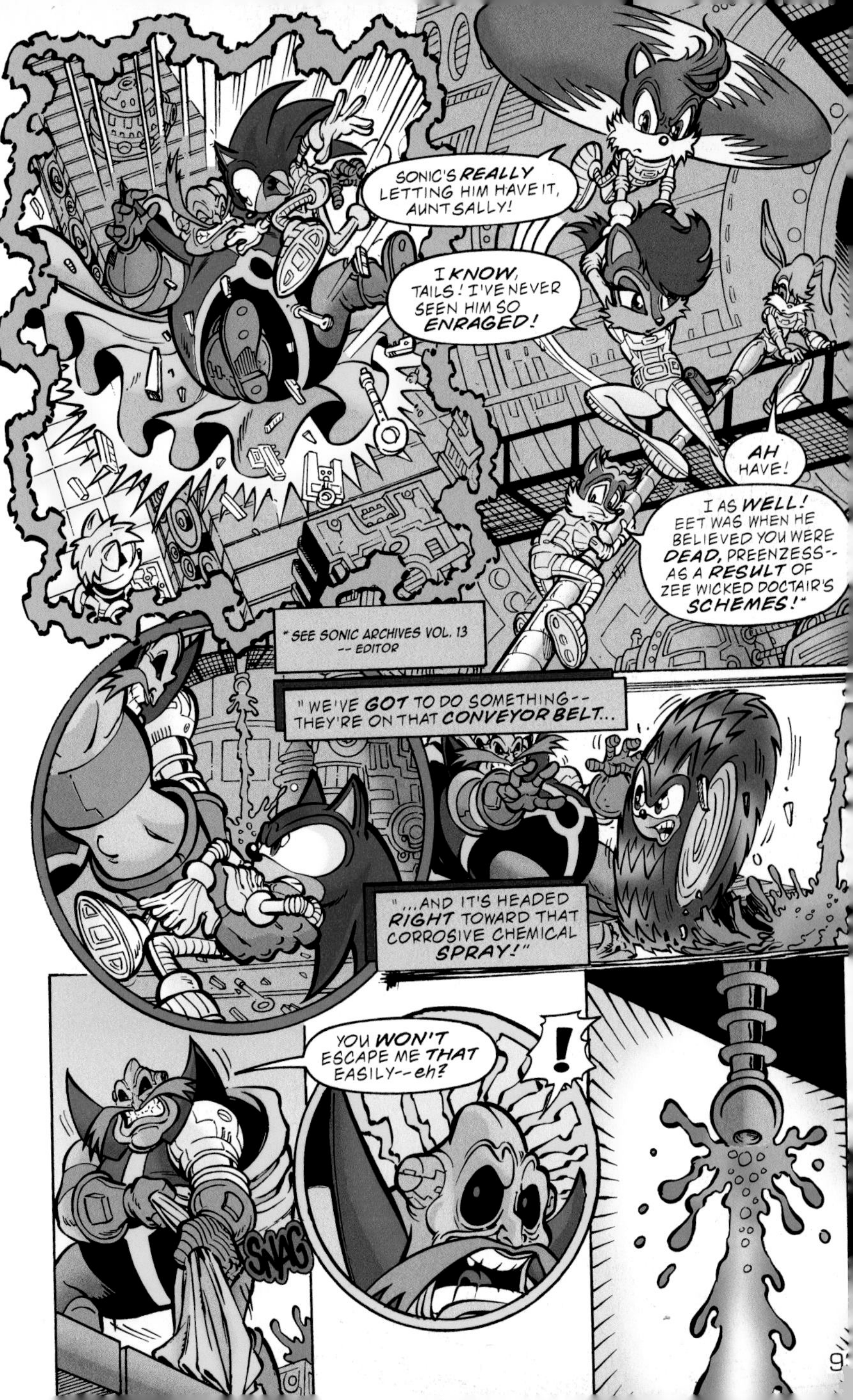
SONIC'S REALLY LETTING HIM HAVE IT, AUNT SALLY!
I KNOW, TAILS! I'VE NEVER SEEN HIM SO ENRAGED!
AH HAVE!
I AS WELL! EET WAS WHEN HE BELIEVED YOU WERE DEAD, PREENZESS-- AS A RESULT OF ZEE WICKED DOCTAIR'S SCHEMES!*
* SEE SONIC ARCHIVES VOL. 13 -- EDITOR
"WE'VE GOT TO DO SOMETHING-- THEY'RE ON THAT CONVEYOR BELT...
"...AND IT'S HEADED RIGHT TOWARD THAT CORROSIVE CHEMICAL SPRAY!"
YOU WON'T ESCAPE ME THAT EASILY--eh?
!
SNAG

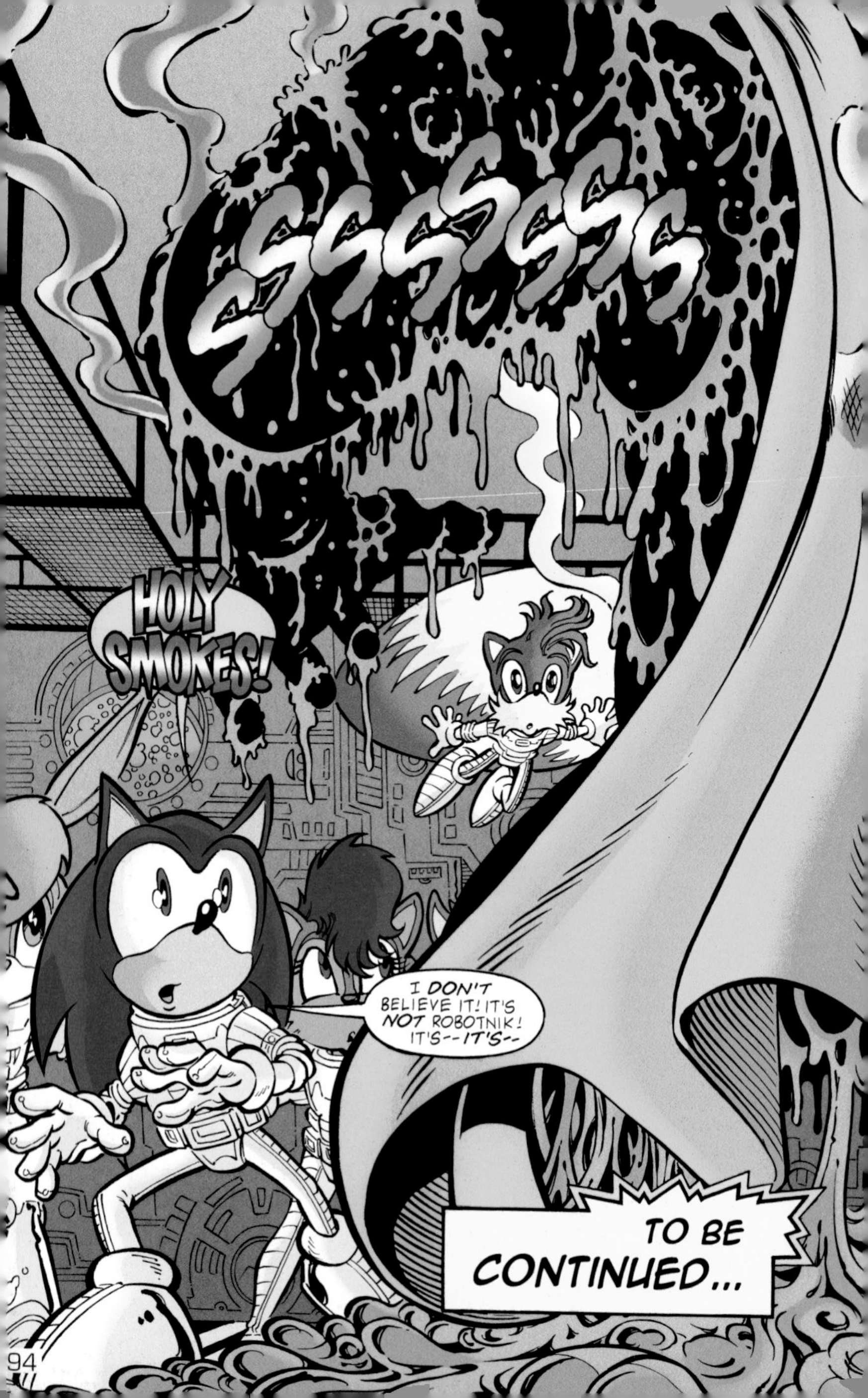
SSSSSS
HOLY SMOKES!
I DON'T BELIEVE IT! IT'S NOT ROBOTNIK! IT'S--IT'S--
TO BE CONTINUED...

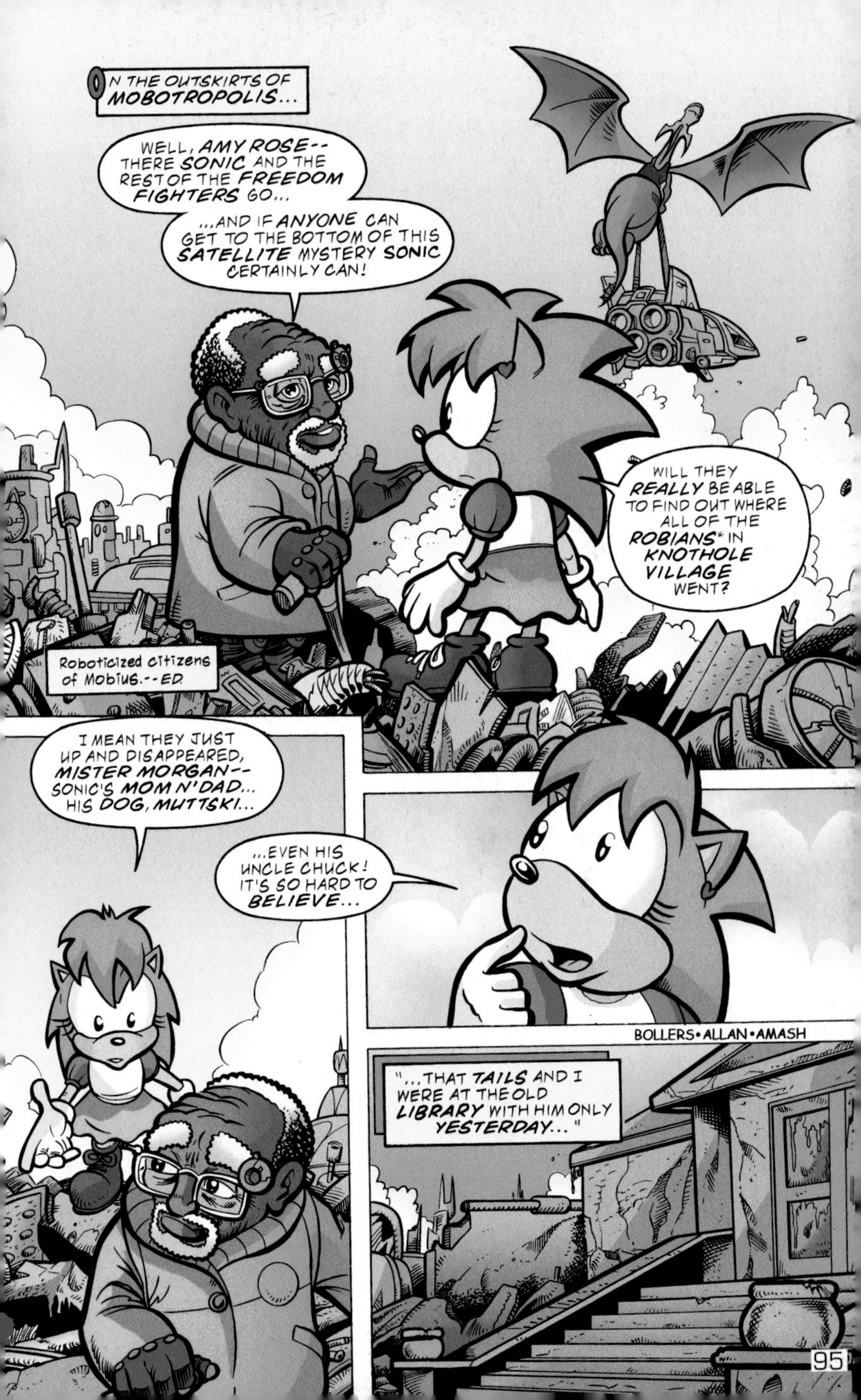
ON THE OUTSKIRTS OF MOBOTROPOLIS...
WELL, AMY ROSE-- THERE SONIC AND THE REST OF THE FREEDOM FIGHTERS GO...
...AND IF ANYONE CAN GET TO THE BOTTOM OF THIS SATELLITE MYSTERY SONIC CERTAINLY CAN!
WILL THEY REALLY BE ABLE TO FIND OUT WHERE ALL OF THE ROBIANS* IN KNOTHOLE VILLAGE WENT?
Roboticized citizens of Mobius.--ED.
I MEAN THEY JUST UP AND DISAPPEARED, MISTER MORGAN-- SONIC'S MOM N' DAD... HIS DOG, MUTTSKI...
...EVEN HIS UNCLE CHUCK! IT'S SO HARD TO BELIEVE...
BOLLERS•ALLAN•AMASH
"...THAT TAILS AND I WERE AT THE OLD LIBRARY WITH HIM ONLY YESTERDAY..."

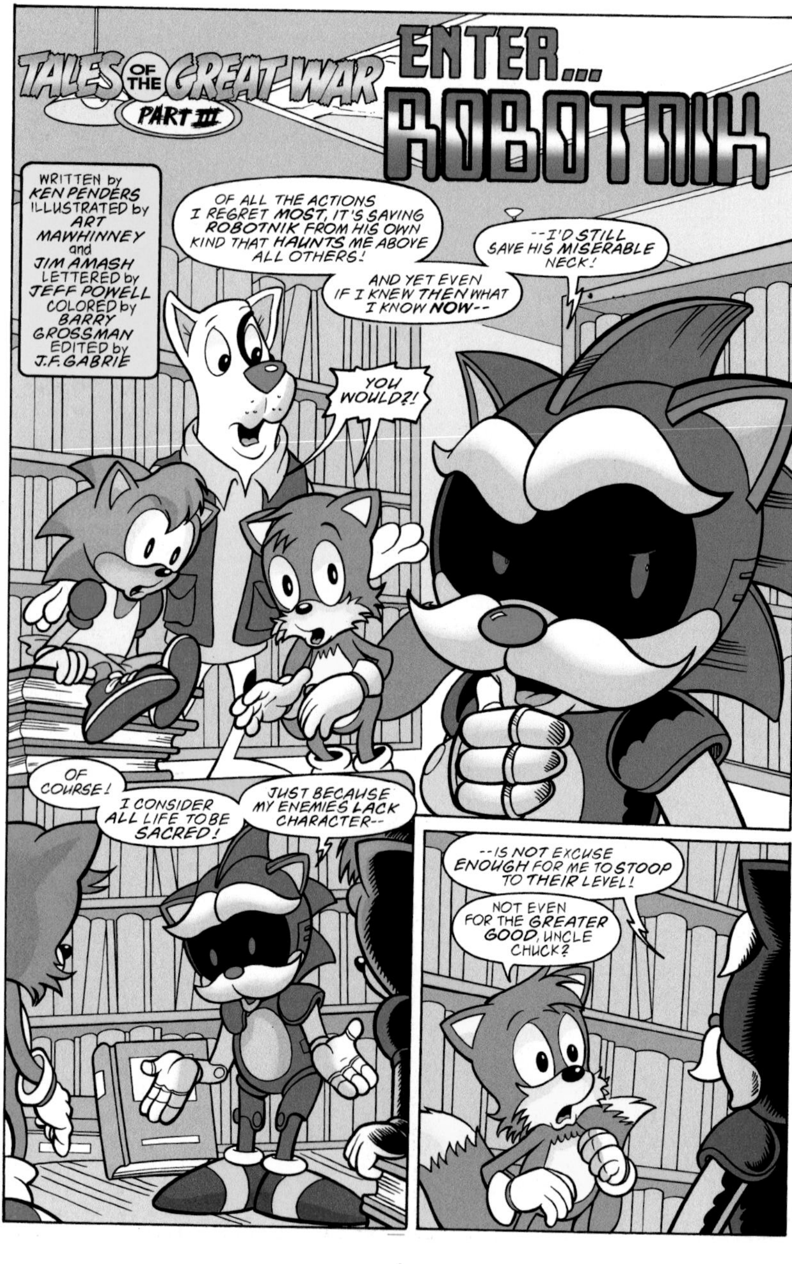
TALES OF THE GREAT WAR PART III
ENTER... ROBOTNIK
WRITTEN by KEN PENDERS ILLUSTRATED by ART MAWHINNEY and JIM AMASH LETTERED by JEFF POWELL COLORED by BARRY GROSSMAN EDITED by J.F. GABRIE
OF ALL THE ACTIONS I REGRET MOST, IT'S SAVING ROBOTNIK FROM HIS OWN KIND THAT HAUNTS ME ABOVE ALL OTHERS!
AND YET EVEN IF I KNEW THEN WHAT I KNOW NOW--
--I'D STILL SAVE HIS MISERABLE NECK!
YOU WOULD?!
OF COURSE!
I CONSIDER ALL LIFE TO BE SACRED!
JUST BECAUSE MY ENEMIES LACK CHARACTER--
--IS NOT EXCUSE ENOUGH FOR ME TO STOOP TO THEIR LEVEL!
NOT EVEN FOR THE GREATER GOOD, UNCLE CHUCK?

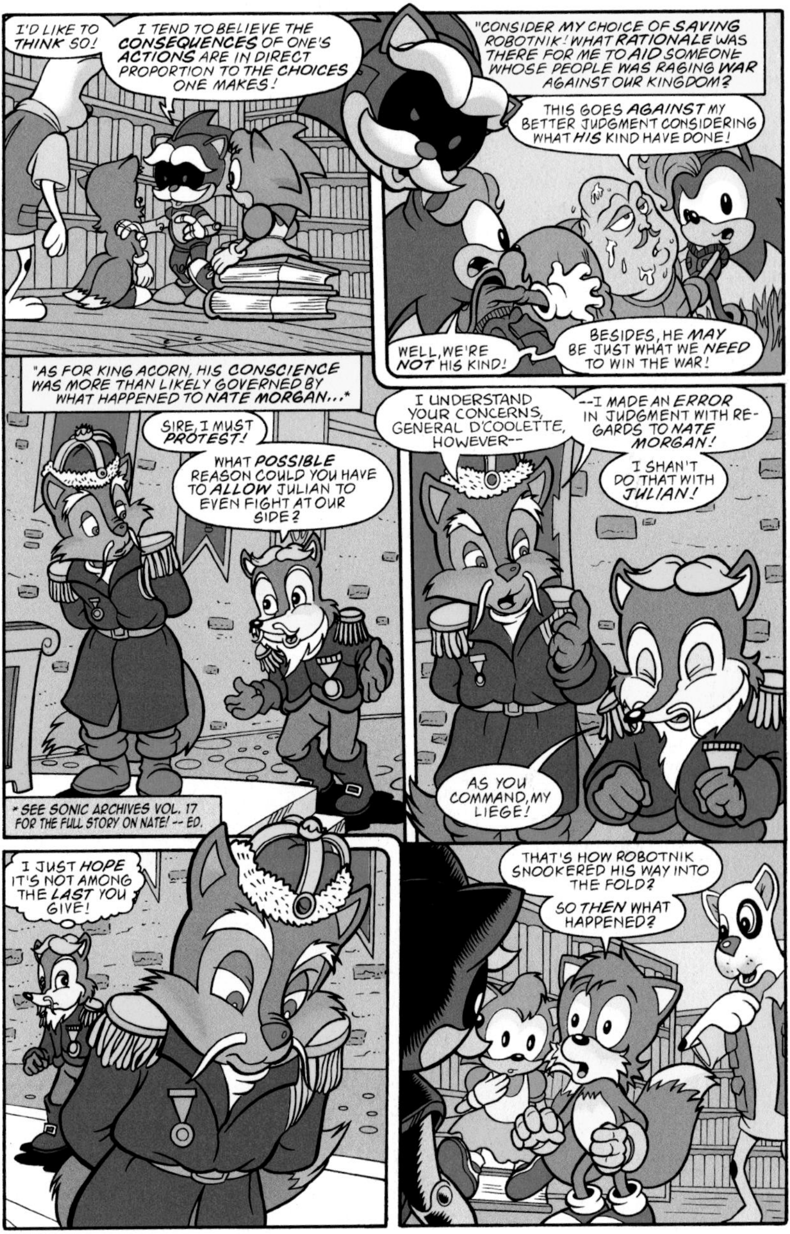
I'D LIKE TO THINK SO!
I TEND TO BELIEVE THE CONSEQUENCES OF ONE'S ACTIONS ARE IN DIRECT PROPORTION TO THE CHOICES ONE MAKES!
"CONSIDER MY CHOICE OF SAVING ROBOTNIK! WHAT RATIONALE WAS THERE FOR ME TO AID SOMEONE WHOSE PEOPLE WAS RAGING WAR AGAINST OUR KINGDOM?
THIS GOES AGAINST MY BETTER JUDGMENT CONSIDERING WHAT HIS KIND HAVE DONE!
WELL, WE'RE NOT HIS KIND!
BESIDES, HE MAY BE JUST WHAT WE NEED TO WIN THE WAR!
"AS FOR KING ACORN, HIS CONSCIENCE WAS MORE THAN LIKELY GOVERNED BY WHAT HAPPENED TO NATE MORGAN...*
SIRE, I MUST PROTEST!
WHAT POSSIBLE REASON COULD YOU HAVE TO ALLOW JULIAN TO EVEN FIGHT AT OUR SIDE?
* SEE SONIC ARCHIVES VOL. 17 FOR THE FULL STORY ON NATE! -- ED.
I UNDERSTAND YOUR CONCERNS, GENERAL D'COOLETTE, HOWEVER--
--I MADE AN ERROR IN JUDGMENT WITH REGARDS TO NATE MORGAN!
I SHAN'T DO THAT WITH JULIAN!
AS YOU COMMAND, MY LIEGE!
I JUST HOPE IT'S NOT AMONG THE LAST YOU GIVE!
THAT'S HOW ROBOTNIK SNOOKERED HIS WAY INTO THE FOLD?
SO THEN WHAT HAPPENED?

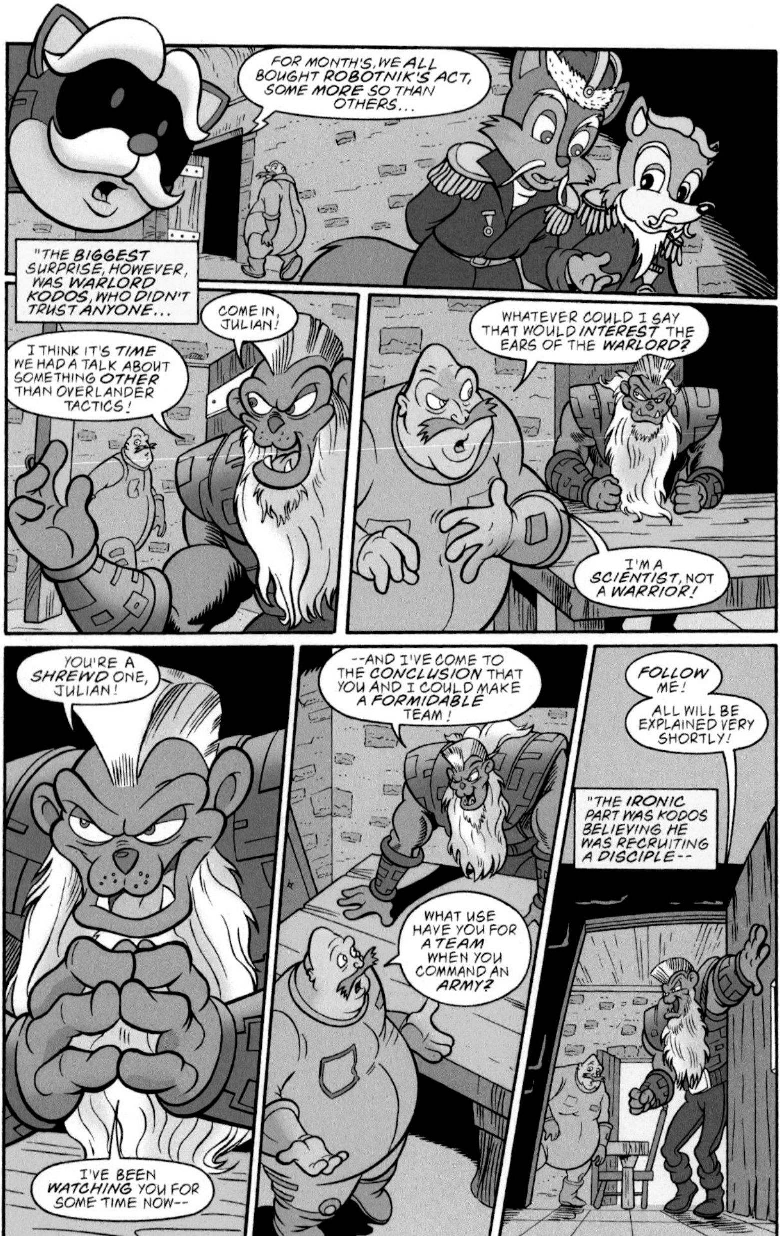
FOR MONTH'S, WE ALL BOUGHT ROBOTNIK'S ACT, SOME MORE SO THAN OTHERS...
"THE BIGGEST SURPRISE, HOWEVER, WAS WARLORD KODOS, WHO DIDN'T TRUST ANYONE...
COME IN, JULIAN!
I THINK IT'S TIME WE HAD A TALK ABOUT SOMETHING OTHER THAN OVERLANDER TACTICS!
WHATEVER COULD I SAY THAT WOULD INTEREST THE EARS OF THE WARLORD?
I'M A SCIENTIST, NOT A WARRIOR!
YOU'RE A SHREWD ONE, JULIAN!
I'VE BEEN WATCHING YOU FOR SOME TIME NOW--
--AND I'VE COME TO THE CONCLUSION THAT YOU AND I COULD MAKE A FORMIDABLE TEAM!
WHAT USE HAVE YOU FOR A TEAM WHEN YOU COMMAND AN ARMY?
FOLLOW ME!
ALL WILL BE EXPLAINED VERY SHORTLY!
"THE IRONIC PART WAS KODOS BELIEVING HE WAS RECRUITING A DISCIPLE--

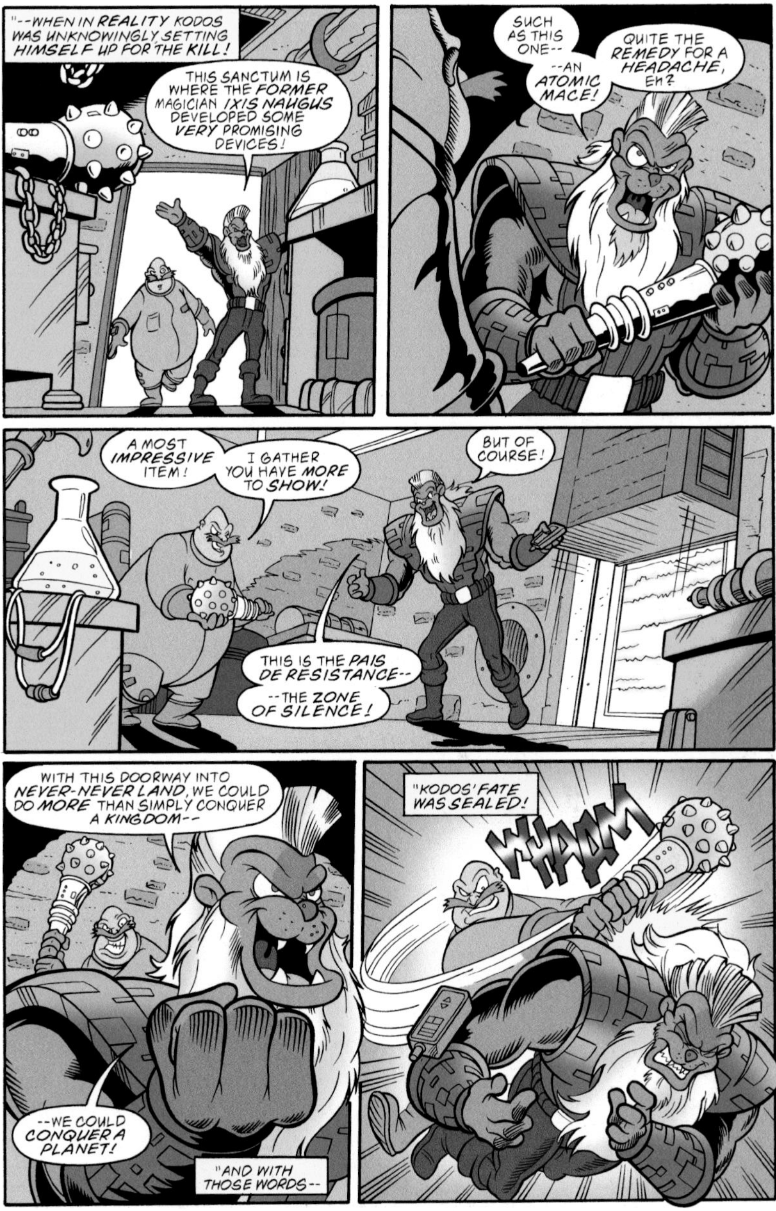
"--WHEN IN REALITY KODOS WAS UNKNOWINGLY SETTING HIMSELF UP FOR THE KILL!
THIS SANCTUM IS WHERE THE FORMER MAGICIAN IXIS NAUGUS DEVELOPED SOME VERY PROMISING DEVICES!
SUCH AS THIS ONE--
--AN ATOMIC MACE!
QUITE THE REMEDY FOR A HEADACHE, Eh?
A MOST IMPRESSIVE ITEM!
I GATHER YOU HAVE MORE TO SHOW!
BUT OF COURSE!
THIS IS THE PAIS DE RESISTANCE--
--THE ZONE OF SILENCE!
WITH THIS DOORWAY INTO NEVER-NEVER LAND, WE COULD DO MORE THAN SIMPLY CONQUER A KINGDOM--
--WE COULD CONQUER A PLANET!
"AND WITH THOSE WORDS--
"KODOS' FATE WAS SEALED!
WHAM

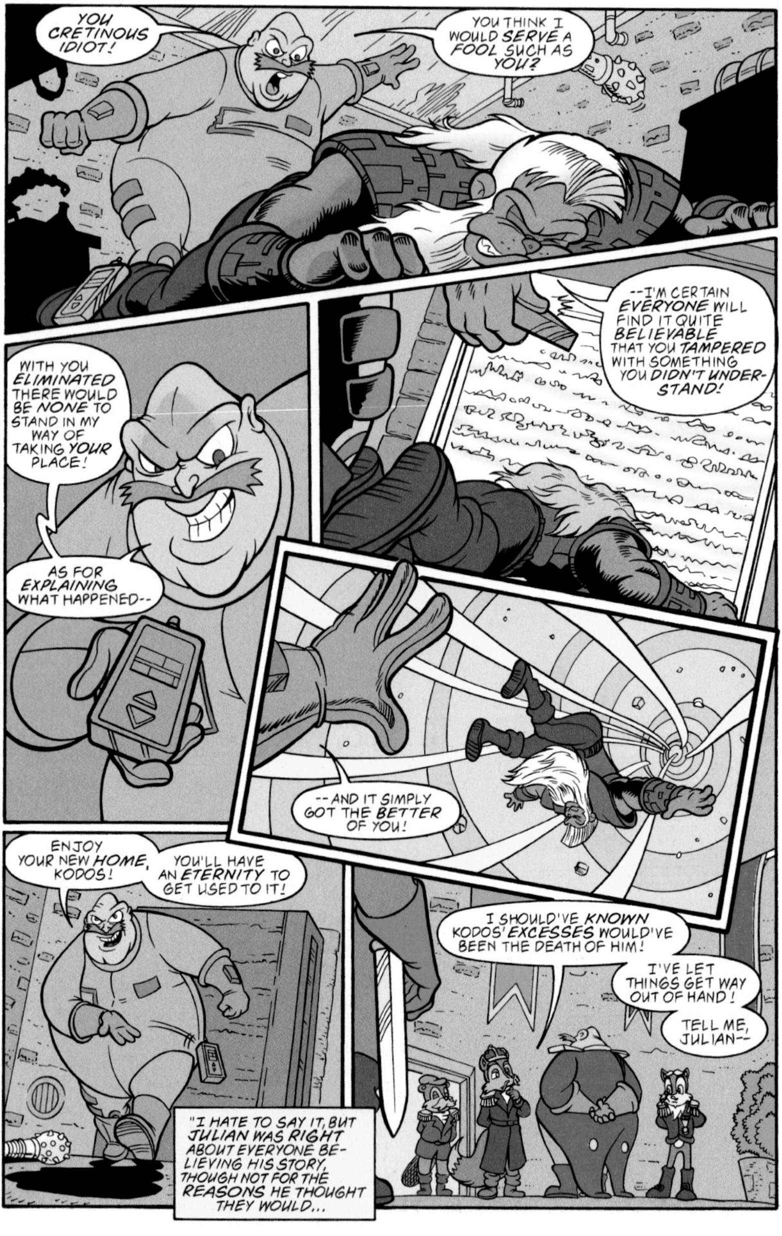
YOU CRETINOUS IDIOT!
YOU THINK I WOULD SERVE A FOOL SUCH AS YOU?
WITH YOU ELIMINATED THERE WOULD BE NONE TO STAND IN MY WAY OF TAKING YOUR PLACE!
AS FOR EXPLAINING WHAT HAPPENED--
--I'M CERTAIN EVERYONE WILL FIND IT QUITE BELIEVABLE THAT YOU TAMPERED WITH SOMETHING YOU DIDN'T UNDER-STAND!
--AND IT SIMPLY GOT THE BETTER OF YOU!
ENJOY YOUR NEW HOME, KODOS!
YOU'LL HAVE AN ETERNITY TO GET USED TO IT!
"I HATE TO SAY IT, BUT JULIAN WAS RIGHT ABOUT EVERYONE BE-LIEVING HIS STORY, THOUGH NOT FOR THE REASONS HE THOUGHT THEY WOULD...
I SHOULD'VE KNOWN KODOS' EXCESSES WOULD'VE BEEN THE DEATH OF HIM!
I'VE LET THINGS GET WAY OUT OF HAND!
TELL ME, JULIAN--!

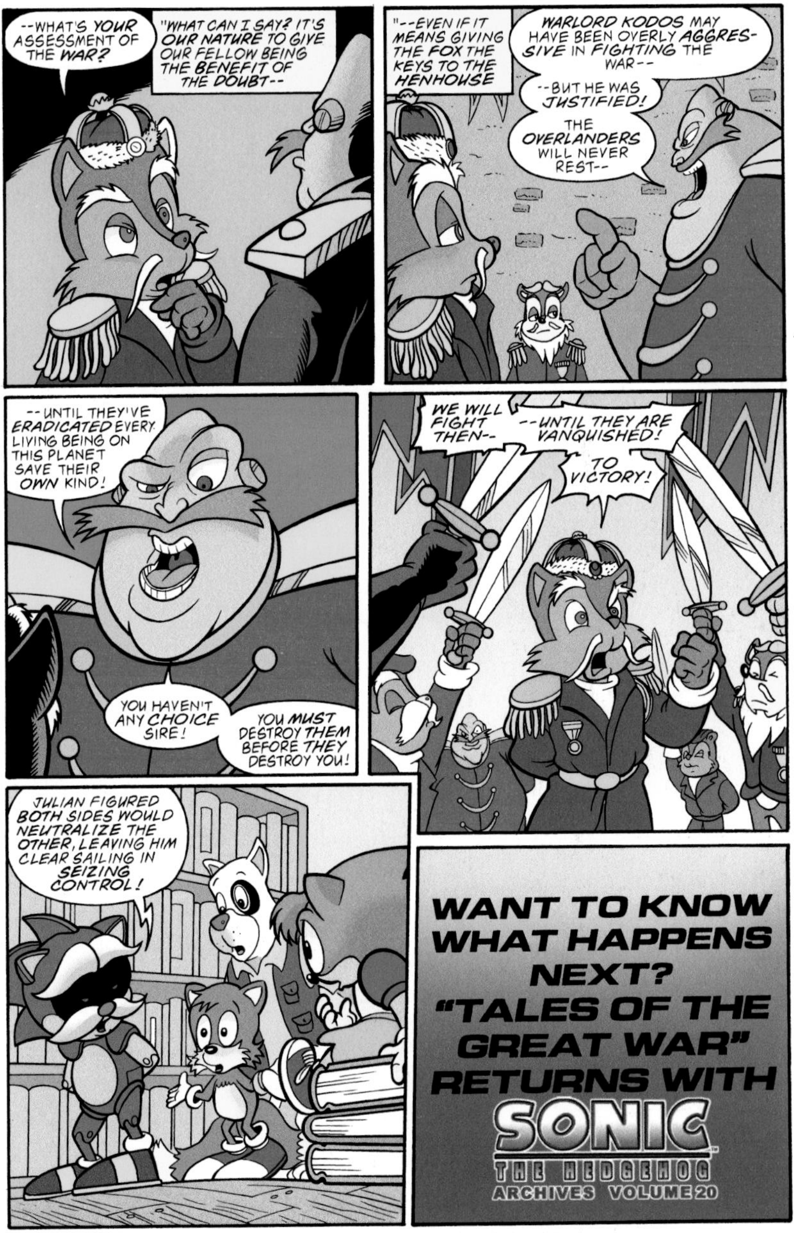
--WHAT'S YOUR ASSESSMENT OF THE WAR?
"WHAT CAN I SAY? IT'S OUR NATURE TO GIVE OUR FELLOW BEING THE BENEFIT OF THE DOUBT--
"--EVEN IF IT MEANS GIVING THE FOX THE KEYS TO THE HENHOUSE
WARLORD KODOS MAY HAVE BEEN OVERLY AGGRESSIVE IN FIGHTING THE WAR--
--BUT HE WAS JUSTIFIED!
THE OVERLANDERS WILL NEVER REST--
--UNTIL THEY'VE ERADICATED EVERY LIVING BEING ON THIS PLANET SAVE THEIR OWN KIND!
YOU HAVEN'T ANY CHOICE SIRE!
YOU MUST DESTROY THEM BEFORE THEY DESTROY YOU!
WE WILL FIGHT THEN--
--UNTIL THEY ARE VANQUISHED!
TO VICTORY!
JULIAN FIGURED BOTH SIDES WOULD NEUTRALIZE THE OTHER, LEAVING HIM CLEAR SAILING IN SEIZING CONTROL!
WANT TO KNOW WHAT HAPPENS NEXT? "TALES OF THE GREAT WAR" RETURNS WITH
SONIC THE HEDGEHOG
ARCHIVES VOLUME 20

SONIC THE HEDGEHOG ™

Welcome to a brief who's who
of the Sonic universe. You have
just read some of the earliest
and most loved stories from the
Sonic comic. We thought
you'd like to learn a little extra
about a few of our
favorite Sonic characters!

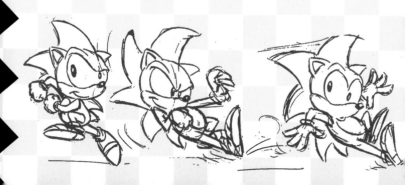

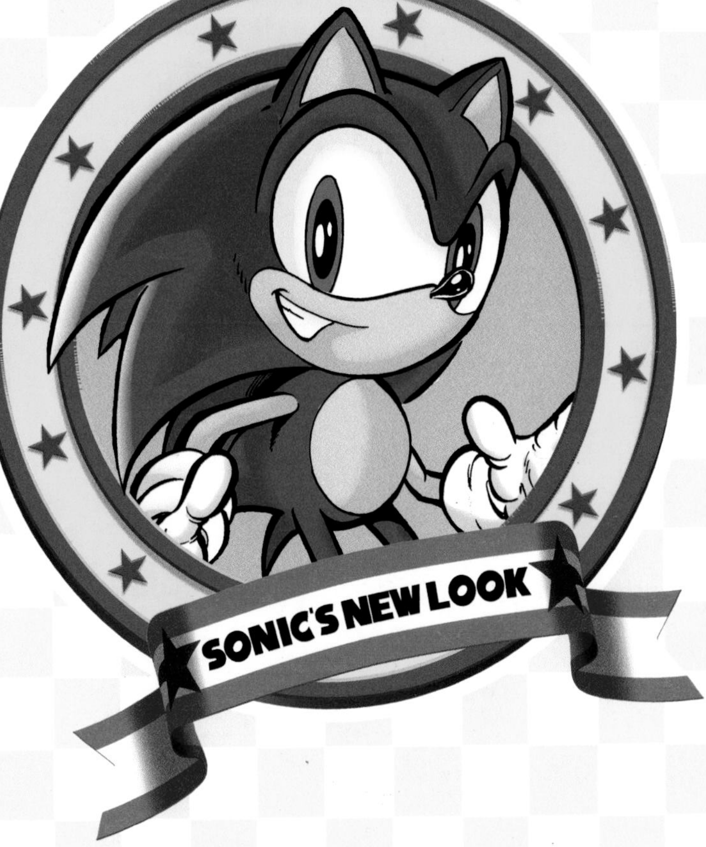
SONIC'S NEW LOOK

SONIC'S NEW LOOK

Goodbye brown eyes, short spines and pudge – a new, sleeker Sonic is here to stay! Thanks to a mixing of temporal and chaos energies, Sonic was physically warped to look the way he does today. What's gone unchanged is his cool, heroic nature!

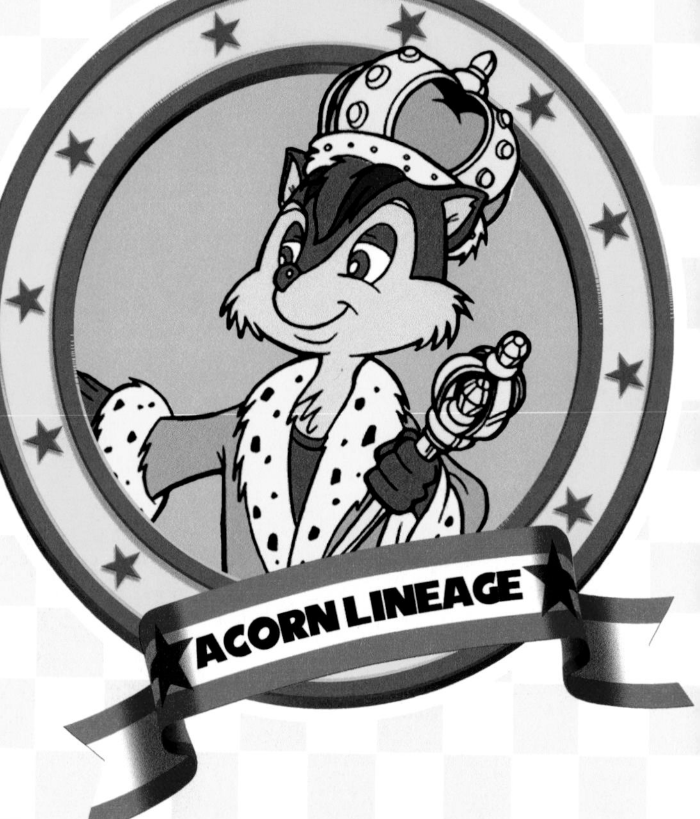
ACORN LINEAGE

ACORN LINEAGE

For hundreds of years, the Acorn Kings have watched over Mobotropolis. The lineage began with King Alexander Acorn who first brought the Mobians together and founded the city. He set a high standard for his ancestors.

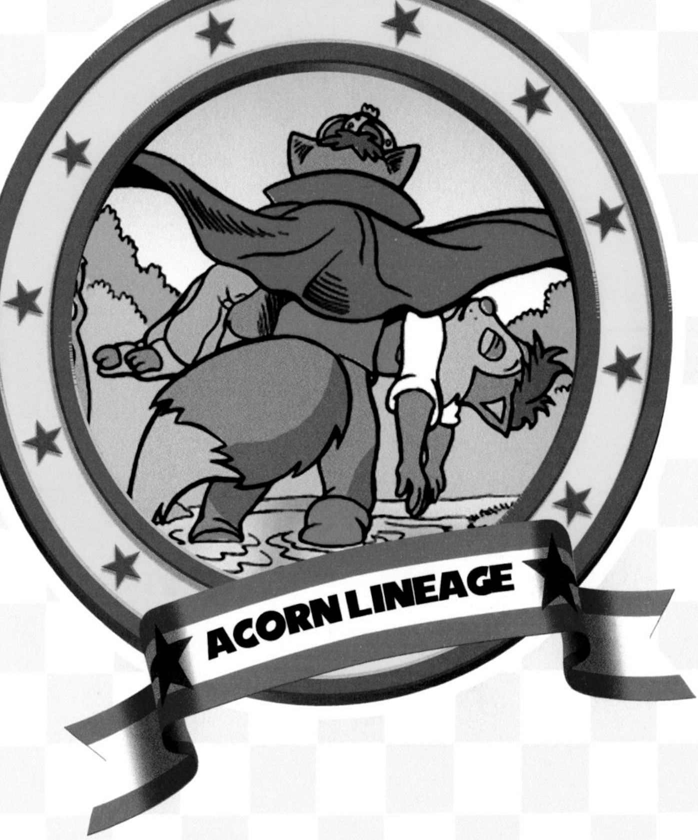
ACORN LINEAGE

ACORN LINEAGE

Thirteen generations of Acorns have ruled, each facing their own hardships and achieving their own triumphs. Looming over almost every single one of them was the neighboring Overland and the threat of the Great War.

PALADIN AND EMERSON

PALADIN AND EMERSON

Prince Emerson Acorn was the next in line for the Crown of Acorn until his fateful meeting with Paladin. What could've been the beginning of peace between two nations ended in tragedy and pushed everyone closer to war.

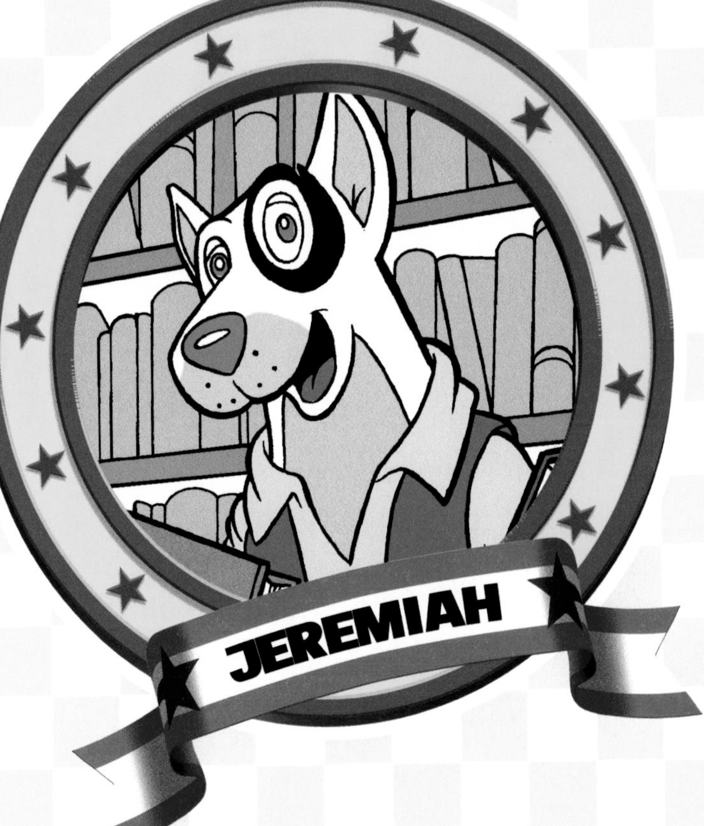
JEREMIAH

JEREMIAH

Grandson to a famous historian, Jeremiah continues the family tradition of maintaining the past for the present. He braved Dr. Robotnik's occupation to protect the old library. Now that's one great dane!

SONIC THE HEDGEHOG ™

Welcome to a brief what's what of the Sonic universe. You have just read some of the earliest and most loved stories from the Sonic comic. We thought you'd like to learn a little extra about a few of the items and places that make the Sonic universe so awesome!

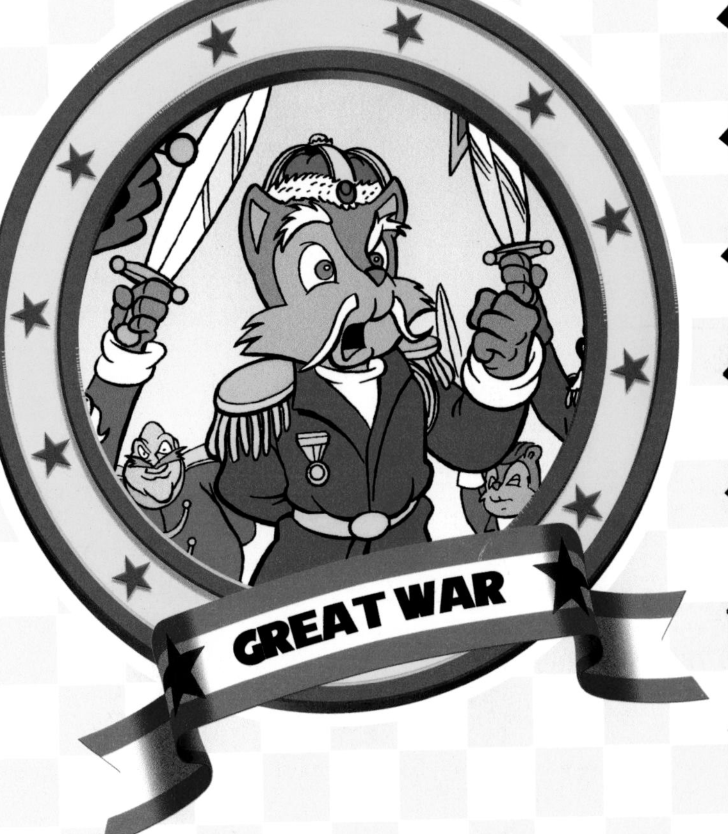
GREAT WAR

GREAT WAR

The biggest conflict ever to engulf the King of Acorn and Overland was the Great War. Both sides took heavy losses, and it ultimately set up Dr. Robotnik for his take-over of Mobius. It didn't matter who won the war – everyone lost in the end.

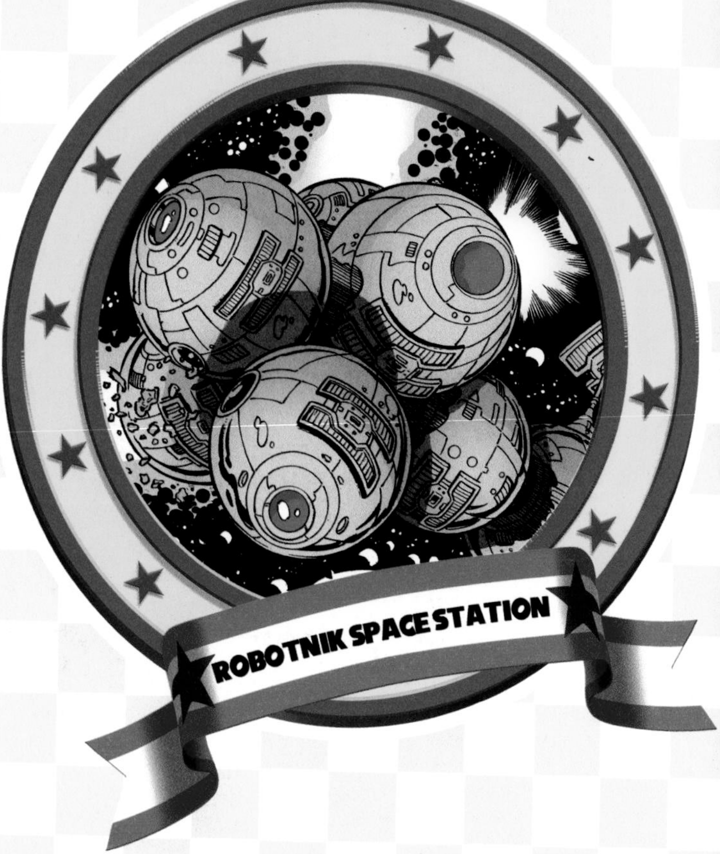
ROBOTNIK SPACE STATION

ROBOTNIK SPACE STATION

High above Mobius, a series of mysterious satellites harassed Sonic and his friends before coming together to create the Egg Station. Here, Dr. Robotnik staged his big return by kidnapping all the Robians!

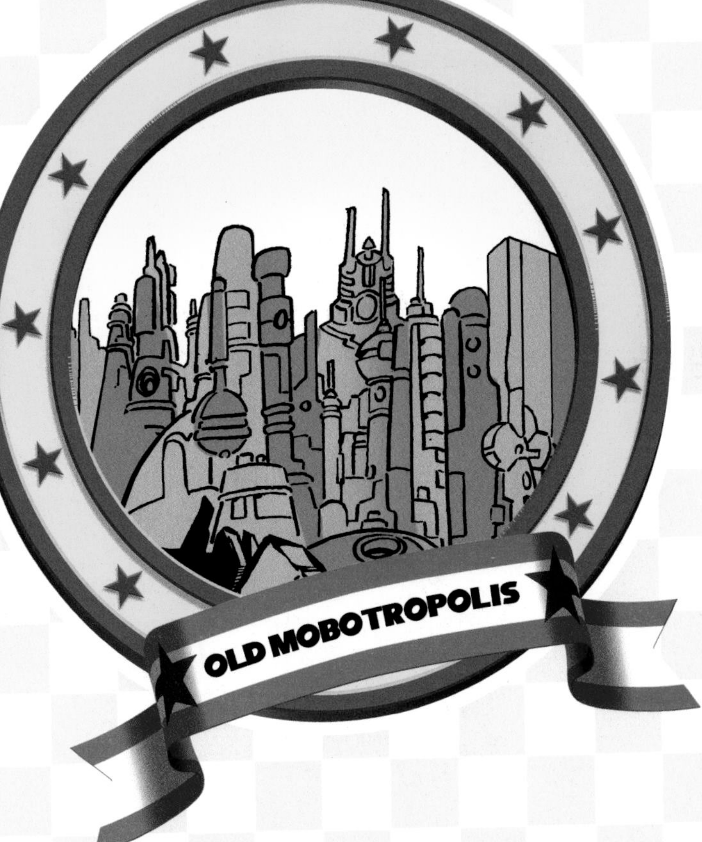
OLD MOBOTROPOLIS

OLD MOBOTROPOLIS

The original city of Mobotropolis was the first of its kind. Nowhere else would you find such a large gathering of different types of Mobians. The city was built to co-exist with the surrounding land. Too bad the Overlanders couldn't do the same.

NEXT TIME, IN THE SONIC ARCHIVES...

SONIC THE HEDGEHOG ARCHIVES VOLUME 20

THE EGGMAN COMETH

SONIC THE HEDGEHOG ARCHIVES VOLUME 20
SONIC THE HEDGEHOG ARCHIVES VOLUME 20
HEDGEHOG: PRIORITY ONE

IT'S A LIFE-OR-DEATH STRUGGLE ABOARD THE MADMAN'S SPACE STATION!

SONIC ARCHIVES VOLUME 20 collects SONIC THE HEDGEHOG #75-78 of the longest running video game-inspired hit comic ever! Get the complete series today!

ISBN: 978-1-936975-38-9

FOLLOW SONIC'S ADVENTURES FROM THE VERY BEGINNING WITH THE SONIC ARCHIVES GRAPHIC NOVEL LIBRARY!

ISBN: 978-1-879794-70-2 ISBN: 978-1-879794-78-5 ISBN: 978-1-879794-80-0 ISBN: 978-1-936975-07-5 ISBN: 978-1-936975-19-8

VOLUMES #0 - 19 AVAILABLE NOW AT ARCHIECOMICS.COM

CHECK OUT THESE TITLES ALSO COMING SOON:

SONIC LEGACY SERIES SONIC THE HEDGEHOG BOOK 2

SONIC LEGACY SERIES
SONIC THE HEDGEHOG
BOOK 2

ISBN: 978-1-936975-26-6

BEST OF SONIC THE HEDGEHOG PAPERBACK EDITION

BEST OF SONIC THE HEDGEHOG COMICS

ISBN: 978-1-936975-29-7

SONIC UNIVERSE JOURNEY TO THE EAST

SONIC UNIVERSE
JOURNEY TO THE EAST
FLYNN · YARDLEY · AMASH

ISBN: 978-1-936975-34-1

SONIC SELECT

SONIC SELECT

ISBN: 978-1-936975-36-5

SEARCH THE GRAPHIC NOVEL SECTION OF

www.ARCHIECOMICS.com

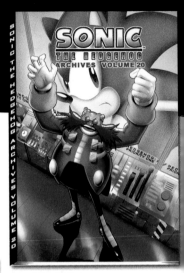